Marrying Mr. Darcy

Love Manor Romantic Comedy
Book 2

Kate O'Keeffe

Wild Lime Books

Marrying Mr. Darcy is a work of fiction. The characters and events portrayed in this book are fictitious.
Any similarity to real persons, living or dead, is purely coincidental and not intended by the author.
All rights reserved, including the right to reproduce, distribute, or transmit in any form or by any means.
ISBN: 979-8578067389

Edited by Wendi Baker
Cover design by Sue Traynor
Copyright © 2020 Kate O'Keeffe

Wild Lime
Books

About this book

Is it a truth universally acknowledged, that a girl can humiliate herself on reality TV and still get her fairy tale ending?

Emma Brady is in shock. She fell in love with Sebastian Huntington-Ross on national television, showing everyone that opposites can most definitely attract. Now, he's asked her to marry him and live happily ever after in his fancy English manor. It's a fairy tale ending.

Or is it?

The problem is the TV audience wanted Sebastian to marry someone else. And in choosing Emma to be his bride, Sebastian could lose everything his aristocratic family has held dear for generations. Not to mention Sebastian's granny, who goes out of her way to make Emma feel like she doesn't belong.

With enough hurdles to keep an Olympian jumping, can Emma and Sebastian find a way to stay together? Or will the pressures pulling them apart cancel their trip down the aisle?

Also by Kate O'Keeffe

It's Complicated Series:
Never Fall for Your Back-Up Guy
Never Fall for Your Enemy
Never Fall for Your Fake Fiancé
Never Fall for Your One that Got Away

Love Manor Romantic Comedy Series:
Dating Mr. Darcy
Marrying Mr. Darcy
Falling for Another Darcy
Falling for Mr. Bingley (spin-off novella)

Cozy Cottage Café Series:
One Last First Date
Two Last First Dates
Three Last First Dates
Four Last First Dates

High Tea Series:
No More Bad Dates
No More Terrible Dates
No More Horrible Dates

Wellywood Romantic Comedy Series:

Styling Wellywood
Miss Perfect Meets Her Match
Falling for Grace

Standalone title:
One Way Ticket

Writing as Lacey Sinclair:
Manhattan Cinderella
The Right Guy

Chapter One

You know when you've been humiliated on a reality TV show by a guy you're in love with, he chooses someone else, and now he tells you he made a big mistake and he's been in love with you the whole time?

No? Just me, then?

The thing is, that's our story. Sebastian's and mine. Well, it's the *start* of our story, anyway.

It's girl meets guy, girl and guy hate each other but secretly grow to like each other too, girl and guy overcome a bunch of obstacles, and then finally guy admits to being in love with girl on national TV and that he made mistake in not choosing her in the first place, girl forgives guy once he explains he will lose his house, and they live happily ever after.

It's a classic, straightforward tale, really.

Oh, I hear it. You don't have to tell me. It's complicated. *More* than complicated. It's a freaking soap opera, with a handsome lead, an evil rich bitch, and me, the girl who didn't win the show.

But I won something a whole lot better than that.

I won Sebastian's heart.

And I'm not giving it up for anything. Not when we've come so far.

"Seb, I cannot believe you've gone to all this effort." I lean my elbows on the tablecloth and smile across at my handsome boyfriend.

"I hadn't seen you for a while, Brady Bunch. I wanted to do something special for you. Timothy has stolen you away from me a little too often for my liking."

"A girl's gotta do what a girl's gotta do."

In case you're wondering, Timothy is the name of the activewear business I run with my bestie, Penny. It's *not* some other boyfriend. I'm a one-man woman, and I could not be happier.

Since getting exposure for the label on the reality TV show *Dating Mr. Darcy,* Timothy sales have gone through the roof, and with it my workload. I'm not complaining, though. Promoting Timothy was the reason I went on the show in the first place.

Without it, I'd never have met Sebastian.

I owe it a lot.

"I thought you might enjoy a simple candlelit dinner for two in the gazebo tonight. Now that it's late summer, we won't be able to do this much longer. Not without risking hypothermia, anyway," he says in his sexy, Henry Cavill accent.

I shake my head as my heart dances for him. Sebastian Huntington-Ross may be my boyfriend of the last three months, one week, and five days (yes, I'm counting—go ahead and judge me all you like), but he's still a little on the formal side of the equation. As I've been known to say, with being both English *and* an aristocrat, the guy never stood a chance on that front. But it's a part of who he is, and I love him for it.

"There's nothing simple about this meal, Seb." I eye the silverware lined up on the table in an order that still manages to mystify me, despite it being really quite logical when explained. There's a vase filled with a dozen red roses in the middle of the table, and I think I spied someone in a white shirt and waistcoat lurking in the bushes on our walk up to the gazebo from the house. But then I might be hallucinating. I did fly in from my hometown of Houston on the red-eye a mere handful of hours ago. A flight that long does things to your brain. Like scramble it and serve it on toast.

Sebastian reaches across the table and takes my hand in his. "I wanted to treat you, Brady Bunch." His gorgeous brown eyes with the gold chunks that so dazzled me when we first met turn soft, the skin around them crinkling into the smile that never fails to make me weak in the knees. Which can be a problem at times.

Like when I'm standing.

I return his smile, my heart full. "I can totally get on board with being treated."

"Good, because I've had a special meal prepared for you by this new caterer I've recently met."

"Oh, how awesome."

Inwardly, I groan. Sebastian's idea of a "special meal" usually involves something fancy. From pheasant to *escargot* (yup, you got it, snails) to this traditional English dish called tripe that put me off eating altogether for a full day it was that bad. Seriously, never try it.

He raises his hand, and someone dressed in a white shirt, black pants and waistcoat, and black bowtie materializes beside the table.

My eyes grow wide. "Zara?" I question, naming Sebastian's kid sister. My eyes land on her fake moustache.

"*Non non non.* I am ze Chef Henri Carron of ze renowned restaurant, Chez Henri," she replies in a fake French accent that sounds thoroughly convincing to me. "But 'ooh-ever this Zara is, she sounds extremely attrac*tive.*"

I let out a laugh. "Well, Chef Henri, it's great to meet you, and Zara is extremely attractive in that fake moustache kinda way."

Sebastian shakes his head and laughs. "My sister should be on the stage, don't you think?"

Zara—sorry, *Chef Henri*—takes my hand in hers and plants a kiss on it. Her moustache promptly drops to the table. She snatches it up and tries not to giggle as she replies, "Ah, *mademoiselle. Bien sur*, ze pleasure is all mine."

I begin to giggle myself, and it ends in an unladylike snort.

"Would you care for some-sing to drink, *mademoiselle*?"

"Sure. Whatcha got? Let me guess. A bottle of Châteauneuf-du-Pape?" I eye Sebastian as I name his favorite wine, the one we drank in his family library as we got to know one another away from the cameras on *Dating Mr. Darcy*.

It's also the place he delivered the then devastating news that he wasn't choosing me on the show, so I've got some seriously conflicting emotions about the room. I'm working through them, especially since I've moved over here on an extended working vacation. Yup, you heard it right—as of today, I'm going to be spending a lot of time here at Martinston, Sebastian's family home.

"Actually, I thought we'd forgo the wine and go with a Brady family tradition instead," Sebastian says. "Since you

Also by Kate O'Keeffe

It's Complicated Series:
Never Fall for Your Back-Up Guy
Never Fall for Your Enemy
Never Fall for Your Fake Fiancé
Never Fall for Your One that Got Away

Love Manor Romantic Comedy Series:
Dating Mr. Darcy
Marrying Mr. Darcy
Falling for Another Darcy
Falling for Mr. Bingley (spin-off novella)

Cozy Cottage Café Series:
One Last First Date
Two Last First Dates
Three Last First Dates
Four Last First Dates

High Tea Series:
No More Bad Dates
No More Terrible Dates
No More Horrible Dates

Wellywood Romantic Comedy Series:

Styling Wellywood
Miss Perfect Meets Her Match
Falling for Grace

Standalone title:
One Way Ticket

Writing as Lacey Sinclair:
Manhattan Cinderella
The Right Guy

Chapter One

You know when you've been humiliated on a reality TV show by a guy you're in love with, he chooses someone else, and now he tells you he made a big mistake and he's been in love with you the whole time?

No? Just me, then?

The thing is, that's our story. Sebastian's and mine. Well, it's the *start* of our story, anyway.

It's girl meets guy, girl and guy hate each other but secretly grow to like each other too, girl and guy overcome a bunch of obstacles, and then finally guy admits to being in love with girl on national TV and that he made mistake in not choosing her in the first place, girl forgives guy once he explains he will lose his house, and they live happily ever after.

It's a classic, straightforward tale, really.

Oh, I hear it. You don't have to tell me. It's complicated. *More* than complicated. It's a freaking soap opera, with a handsome lead, an evil rich bitch, and me, the girl who didn't win the show.

1

But I won something a whole lot better than that.

I won Sebastian's heart.

And I'm not giving it up for anything. Not when we've come so far.

"Seb, I cannot believe you've gone to all this effort." I lean my elbows on the tablecloth and smile across at my handsome boyfriend.

"I hadn't seen you for a while, Brady Bunch. I wanted to do something special for you. Timothy has stolen you away from me a little too often for my liking."

"A girl's gotta do what a girl's gotta do."

In case you're wondering, Timothy is the name of the activewear business I run with my bestie, Penny. It's *not* some other boyfriend. I'm a one-man woman, and I could not be happier.

Since getting exposure for the label on the reality TV show *Dating Mr. Darcy,* Timothy sales have gone through the roof, and with it my workload. I'm not complaining, though. Promoting Timothy was the reason I went on the show in the first place.

Without it, I'd never have met Sebastian.

I owe it a lot.

"I thought you might enjoy a simple candlelit dinner for two in the gazebo tonight. Now that it's late summer, we won't be able to do this much longer. Not without risking hypothermia, anyway," he says in his sexy, Henry Cavill accent.

I shake my head as my heart dances for him. Sebastian Huntington-Ross may be my boyfriend of the last three months, one week, and five days (yes, I'm counting—go ahead and judge me all you like), but he's still a little on the formal side of the equation. As I've been known to say, with being both English *and* an aristocrat, the guy never stood a chance on that front. But it's a part of who he is, and I love him for it.

"There's nothing simple about this meal, Seb." I eye the silverware lined up on the table in an order that still manages to mystify me, despite it being really quite logical when explained. There's a vase filled with a dozen red roses in the middle of the table, and I think I spied someone in a white shirt and waistcoat lurking in the bushes on our walk up to the gazebo from the house. But then I might be hallucinating. I did fly in from my hometown of Houston on the red-eye a mere handful of hours ago. A flight that long does things to your brain. Like scramble it and serve it on toast.

Sebastian reaches across the table and takes my hand in his. "I wanted to treat you, Brady Bunch." His gorgeous brown eyes with the gold chunks that so dazzled me when we first met turn soft, the skin around them crinkling into the smile that never fails to make me weak in the knees. Which can be a problem at times.

Like when I'm standing.

I return his smile, my heart full. "I can totally get on board with being treated."

"Good, because I've had a special meal prepared for you by this new caterer I've recently met."

"Oh, how awesome."

Inwardly, I groan. Sebastian's idea of a "special meal" usually involves something fancy. From pheasant to *escargot* (yup, you got it, snails) to this traditional English dish called tripe that put me off eating altogether for a full day it was that bad. Seriously, never try it.

He raises his hand, and someone dressed in a white shirt, black pants and waistcoat, and black bowtie materializes beside the table.

My eyes grow wide. "Zara?" I question, naming Sebastian's kid sister. My eyes land on her fake moustache.

"*Non non non*. I am ze Chef Henri Carron of ze renowned restaurant, Chez Henri," she replies in a fake French accent that sounds thoroughly convincing to me. "But 'ooh-ever this Zara is, she sounds extremely attrac*tive*."

I let out a laugh. "Well, Chef Henri, it's great to meet you, and Zara is extremely attractive in that fake moustache kinda way."

Sebastian shakes his head and laughs. "My sister should be on the stage, don't you think?"

Zara—sorry, *Chef Henri*—takes my hand in hers and plants a kiss on it. Her moustache promptly drops to the table. She snatches it up and tries not to giggle as she replies, "Ah, *mademoiselle*. *Bien sur*, ze pleasure is all mine."

I begin to giggle myself, and it ends in an unladylike snort.

"Would you care for some-sing to drink, *mademoiselle?*"

"Sure. Whatcha got? Let me guess. A bottle of Châteauneuf-du-Pape?" I eye Sebastian as I name his favorite wine, the one we drank in his family library as we got to know one another away from the cameras on *Dating Mr. Darcy*.

It's also the place he delivered the then devastating news that he wasn't choosing me on the show, so I've got some seriously conflicting emotions about the room. I'm working through them, especially since I've moved over here on an extended working vacation. Yup, you heard it right—as of today, I'm going to be spending a lot of time here at Martinston, Sebastian's family home.

"Actually, I thought we'd forgo the wine and go with a Brady family tradition instead," Sebastian says. "Since you

Marrying Mr. Darcy

and Frank have moved here for an extended period, I thought it only right."

I think of Frank, my prickly but lovable tabby cat, resting up in the house after his long journey today. I didn't want to leave him behind in Houston. A girl needs her cat, you know, even when that girl is currently dating a hot British aristocrat.

Zara places a bottle covered in beads of water on the table in front of each of us.

I look up at Sebastian in surprise. "You got Budweiser? Oh, I could totally kill for a beer right now."

Sebastian picks up his bottle, and we clink. "I thought it might go well with the special meal I have planned for us."

I lift the bottle to my lips and take a grateful swig. Although I love Sebastian's choice in wine, a girl can't go past a good old bottle of Bud every now and then, even if our surrounds at Sebastian's family's manor house are a lot more champagne and caviar than beer and chips. But then, that's the way we are. Opposites. And yes, we definitely attract.

Zara returns holding a plate covered in one of those silver bubbles that keeps the food warm (Sebastian tells me it's called a "cloche" but I prefer "silver bubble" because it sounds a lot cuter, plus I can pronounce it, which is a major plus). She places it in front of me and says, "No peeking, *mademoiselle*, or else you may lose ze fingers."

"Lose my fingers? Wow, Henri's a bit harsh," I say to Sebastian.

"You know Henri," he replies with a laugh.

Zara returns with another plate and places it in front of Sebastian. "And now, ze great unveiling of ze masterpiece."

She lifts both silver bubbles off with dramatic flair. I

fully expect to see some obscure dish that Sebastian's father's father's father once enjoyed after a jousting competition with the King of England or something, complete with enough saturated fat to clog everyone's arteries.

Instead, I'm met with a sight from my childhood.

I blink at my plate. "Mac and cheese?" I say in delight. "Seb, you know how much I love mac and cheese!"

"I do know. I also know you put on a brave face with all my family traditions, and I thought we could create a new one of our own."

I beam back at him. "Any tradition that involves mac and cheese is all right by me."

"Well, tuck in before it gets cold. We wouldn't want to upset Chef Henri. Fingers, remember?" He waggles his fingers at me.

I dig my fork into my meal and take a bite. It's creamy and cheesy and totally delicious. "Did one of you make this?" I ask with a mouthful as I look from sister to brother and back again.

"We had some help," Zara admits after a beat, her fake French accent dropped in favor of her everyday English one. "You know neither of us can cook. And Seb wanted it to be special. I'm not sure congealed, cheesy goop would have done the trick for you."

"Actually, I wouldn't have cared," I reply as I take another bite. "Bif iff bobally yubby."

"Didn't your mother tell you not to talk with your mouth full?" Sebastian teases. "But you're right, it is 'yubby.'"

My phone tells me a new message has arrived, and I swallow my mouthful. "Sorry, one sec. That'll be a message from Penny," I say as I pull it out of my purse.

Marrying Mr. Darcy

"Of course,' he replies graciously, because that's what Sebastian is, totally gracious. With Timothy taking off, I've got to work into the evenings sometimes when I'm here in England with him, and he never complains.

I read the screen, and my heart sinks. "Actually, it's from Jilly." I flip it over for Sebastian to see.

Sebastian takes my phone from me and knits his eyebrows together. "Why is Jilly sending you something like this?"

"She told me it was best to know what they're saying out there about me. I kinda agree. And anyway, she's not just your lawyer. You've known her since you were in diapers."

Jilly Fotherington has taken me under her wing since I began seeing Sebastian, and she's become a close friend. Without her here, I'm sure I'd feel like a fish out of water—or a Texan in the English countryside. Which fits, because that's exactly what I am.

"But it says 'When Emma sings, I be like...' with a picture of Macaulay Culkin screaming from that *Home Alone* movie. That's hardly something you need to know about, in my opinion."

I shrug. "At least it's not still carrying on about how they wanted you to marry Phoebe. That got real old, real fast."

Phoebe was the final contestant on the *Dating Mr. Darcy* show, and the public's hopes seemed to lie with her and Sebastian marrying. When she announced she was in fact in love with Johnathan, Sebastian's bestie, you'd think the world had imploded, so many people were upset by it all.

One headline stood out in my mind from the time Sebastian had told the world that he was head over heels in love with me—and yes, it was *the* most romantic experience of my life bar none. It was the famous British tabloid, *The Sun*, and it said succinctly, "Sod Off, Emma! Give Us Phoebe!" Don't get me wrong, I prefer it when people get straight to the point, but Phoebe had just proposed to Johnathan, so she was never going to end up with Sebastian in the first place.

Sadly, there were many, many more. None of them particularly nice about me and all questioning why such a hot, rich guy like Sebastian would choose someone like me.

Nice, huh?

Not that I've ever let it get to me.

Well, not that much.

Okay, it still gets to me. I mean, they say some pretty mean things, and I'm only human after all.

"One of those trashy magazines Zara likes to read had a supposedly exclusive interview with Phoebe, who said she'd made it all up and had been in love with you all along."

"It's utter tripe, Emma. Ignore it."

I slip my phone back into my purse. "You're right. And tripe is disgusting, by the way. Your granny made me eat it last time I was here."

"My point exactly."

Zara arrives at our table once more, her moustache and white chef's jacket now gone. Instead, she's dressed in a pair of skinny pants and a sparkly tube top.

"You look hot," I say to her.

"Thanks. I'm off to the pub."

"Not too many, okay? You know what happened last time," Sebastian scolds in his older brotherly way.

She rolls her eyes. "I told you, Seb, we had nothing to do with the fire alarm going off, and the bra the police found the next day hanging from the lamppost wasn't mine."

"Are you sure about that?"

"Absolutely," she replies, and it's totally clear to me she set the alarm off and the bra was undoubtedly hers. Zara's a bit of wild child to say the least. "The firemen made it all worthwhile, though," she adds as she fans herself.

Sebastian shakes his head at his sister. "Unbelievable."

"Now, you two love birds. There are some chocolate chip biscuits on the table over there. I'm going to leave you to it."

"Are they the chocolate chip *cookies* from that little café in the village?"

"We call them biscuits," Zara says, "and, yes, they're from Mia's."

My mouth begins to salivate as I think of Mia's to-die-for baked goods. They're almost as good as the ones I chow down on with Penny far too regularly back home. Almost.

"Yum."

"Well, I'm glad we cleared that up," Sebastian says. "Perhaps we could write an English-American dictionary."

"Already exists," I reply.

"Really? Why didn't I know about that?"

"Seb, there are websites, apps, you name it. We Americans have been trying to understand you Brits for*ever*."

Sebastian let out a low, rumbling laugh. "Is that so? You do know we invented the language, don't you?"

"And we perfected it."

"Is 'chillin' with my BAE' considered perfection, I wonder?" He's got a glint in his eye.

"Oh, definitely," I confirm.

Zara raises her hands. "I'm going to leave you two to your *extremely* romantic conversation."

"Thanks, little sister," Sebastian says. "For everything."

"Tell Chef Henri the mac and cheese is beyond amazing."

"Will do," she replies before she winks at us and turns to leave.

"Why did she wink?" I ask Sebastian.

"Who knows with Zara. She is a law unto herself."

"She's great, and you know it."

I've gotten to know Zara pretty well over the last few months, and I really like her. She's easy going, sweet, and always poking fun at her big brother. As amazing as Sebastian is, he can be a stick in the mud and super formal. The way I see it, Zara and I help to lighten him up a little.

We finish up our mac and cheese, and Sebastian collects the cookies from the table along with another couple of brewskies.

"Cheers," he says and we *clink* cookies.

I sink my teeth into mine. It's crispy on the outside and gooey on the inside, just the way it ought to be. "So good," I mumble as a couple of errant crumbs fall to the table.

Sebastian laughs. "And so ladylike."

I finish my cookie far too quickly and grin at him, "You know me. I am all about being a lady."

He stands up and takes me by the hand. "Come with me."

Together, we wander over to the edge of the gazebo. Lit by the glow of the setting sun, the gentle slope leads down a tree-lined stretch of lawn to an ornate fountain, with the beautiful, turreted Martinston in the middle distance. My belly twists at the sight of it. Not because it's beautiful, even though it's utterly breathtaking. Because by choosing me and not the wealthy Camille and her ready cash on *Dating Mr. Darcy*, Sebastian and his family risk losing their home.

He takes my hands in his and pulls me in for a kiss. "Speaking of being a lady," he leads.

"I promise I'm gonna keep trying my best to fit in as the English lady your granny expects me to be. It's just taking me some time to learn your ways."

Sebastian's granny hasn't exactly warmed to me, but I'm hoping to turn that around now that I'm here for an extended working vacay.

He shakes his head. "I'm not talking about Granny."

"What are you talking about?"

"You becoming a lady."

I'm still in the dark here. "R*iiii*ght?"

"Lady Martinston, to be precise."

"But that's your mom and your granny's title."

"It could also be yours—" he leads.

Finally, I catch his drift, and my heart rate instantly jumps up to OMG-is-this-really-happening levels. "Oh!"

"—if you'd agree to marry me," he finishes.

"What?!" I shriek, and I'm certain all the wildlife within a one-square-mile radius leaps into the air in shock.

"Did you…did you just ask…?" I ask breathlessly as my heart beats out of my chest. I give it another shot. "Did you just ask me to marry you?"

The edges of his beautiful eyes crease into a smile. "I did." He lowers onto one knee, and I swear my heart is in my mouth as he gazes up at me with love in his eyes.

"Emma Brady, you have my heart, now and forever. I cannot imagine my life without you."

My breath is ragged as I look down at him, his eyes soft, only the tightness of his jaw giving away his nerves.

Is this really happening?

"Emma, since we met, I've been captivated by your beauty, your quick wit, your intelligence, and your passion.

You have shown me what it is to love and to be loved in return. As you know, I was due to propose to someone at the end of filming *Dating Mr. Darcy*."

I nod rapidly like one of those bobbleheads you used to see in the rear windows of people's cars.

"Although I knew in my heart I wanted to spend the rest of my life with you, I wanted to give us time. My darling, I've had more than enough time."

I watch as though in a dream as he reaches into his pocket and pulls out a small, Tiffany blue box. Tiffany blue, people! As in the color, as in the store, as in…he presses the little silver button on the box and *wham!* I'm half blinded by the most beautiful solitaire diamond ring I've ever seen, nestled into its black cushion, glinting out at me.

Oh, my sweet Lord, he's proposing with my fantasy ring from my fantasy ring store.

I think I'm gonna faint.

"My love, will you do me the great honor of agreeing to be my wife?"

I drag my gaze from the ring to his hopeful eyes, my heart ready to burst, my legs threatening to give way at any moment. As tears leap into my eyes, I reply in a rush, "Yes, Seb. A thousand, million, *trillion* times yes! I will marry you!"

He straightens up, and I jump into his arms, and we kiss and kiss and kiss some more. We take a break long enough for him to take my left hand and, with shaking fingers I'd not noticed before, slip the ring onto my finger.

"I love you, Brady Bunch," he murmurs into my hair, using the nickname he gave me when we first met.

I look from the stunning ring on my finger and back into his eyes. I beam at him, profoundly content. Sebastian may be in fear of losing his family home, we may be from different worlds, and the media may have decided I'm the original she-devil of the British Isles. But I know in my heart that together we can leap over whatever hurdles are thrown our way—and man, are there some hurdles—and I know we'll do it together.

"Right back atcha, Mr. Darcy."

Chapter Two

"Tell me again how it happened," my best friend and business partner, Penny, asks through the phone from her house in Houston.

I glance at Sebastian sitting on a high-backed leather chair in Martinston's library. He's focusing hard on something on his laptop, and my heart fills to the brim with love for him as I watch the look of concentration on his handsome face, the way his brows are pulled in, the way he tightens and loosens his jaw.

Even when he's completely absorbed in reading some boring banking article (yawn), he's totally hot.

I move my phone to my other ear and wander over to one of the large windows overlooking the gardens. "Penn, it was beyond romantic. He got me my favorite meal—"

"Not mac and cheese."

"Mm-hm, and chocolate chip cookies."

"Oh, this guy is perfection, Em."

"I know, right?" I reply with a sigh. "He proposed in this gorgeous gazebo on top of a hill overlooking the house." I gaze out at it as I speak. "You'll have to see it when you come visit."

"You're gonna tell me it was at sunset, aren't you?"

"It was at sunset."

"I knew it!" she shrieks into my ear.

"Ouch," I complain.

"Sorry. I'm just super excited for you. I guess your working vacation has turned into a permanent move now, huh? You'll be a proper English lady."

"Can you seriously imagine me as a proper English lady?"

"Good point." She lets out a sigh.

I lift my left hand and admire the way the diamond catches the light. "I still can't quite believe we're getting married."

"Your proposal was so romantic. Remember Trey proposed to me at the Taco Bell drive-thru? Not quite as romantic as sunset in some gazebo on an English aristocrat's estate."

"I'm sure it was just as romantic."

"Well, he did order me those fries I like. So, yeah. Just as romantic."

I giggle. "You are a lucky girl."

"I know, right? But what Trey might lack in romance he makes up for in other ways, if you know what I mean."

"Penn, I do not want to know what those ways are."

"I meant he's an awesome griller. Get your mind out of the gutter, Ms. Engaged to be a Lady."

My tummy does a flip. "OMG, I'm actually going to be an official lady."

She laughs. "So fancy. My BFF is a *lad-ay*."

"I'll always be plain old Emma Brady."

"Are you going to take his name? Emma Huntington-

Ross does sound pretty good. Like out of a Jane Austen novel, which is totally apt, considering how y'all met."

"You know, he hasn't said anything about it, but I think it'd mean a lot to him if I did take his name. He's kinda old-fashioned in some ways."

"The women's movement means you get to choose, babe. As long as you don't do a Madonna on me and change your accent as well. I'm not sure I could cope with my bestie sounding like the Queen of England."

"No way," I reply with a laugh. "You can take the girl out of Texas..."

"Is your mom ecstatic?"

Sebastian and I had called Mom on speakerphone earlier in the day to share our news. She was being all polite and restrained at the time, but I knew what she really wanted to do was scream at the top of her lungs with excitement. She told me in private afterwards that she was so happy she could poop herself. She'd been watching *Downton Abbey* in preparation to know what to expect when she met the in-laws and knew she couldn't say that sort of thing in front of them. Which is the right call, really.

You don't want to put a foot wrong when it comes to Sebastian's formidable granny, that's for sure.

"Penn? There is one thing I wanted to ask you. Will you be my matron of honor?"

Her squeal is high-pitched and eardrum bursting. "Heck yes! I would love to be your matron of honor. Who else are you having in the bridal party?"

"I'm gonna ask Kennedy and Phoebe, because we're reality show soul sisters, and I thought I might ask Zara, too."

"That's such a nice idea, Em. Where and when?"

"No idea and June third. We're telling Seb's family real soon." My nerves spike at the prospect.

"They'll be over the moon, Em. Trust me."

"I wish I had your confidence."

"Why wouldn't you? I love you, so they've got to, as well."

I think of the looks Seb's granny shoots me, the way she asked about who "my people" were when we first started dating. She was shocked to learn my family tree gets seriously fuzzy past my grandparents. No long line of aristocratic landowners in the Brady clan, that's for sure. Well, not unless you include Mom owning a little house with its 80's pastels in every room and a kitchen with an oven that plays Russian roulette with the temperature gauge so you never know how your baking will turn out.

"And anyway, aren't those stuffy old English families all inbred? They're in major need of some new American blood, if you ask me."

"You cannot say that, Penn," I warn with a laugh, even if it's probably true for half the aristocracy. "And anyway, I'm not here just for Seb. I'm on a mission to bring Timothy to the British consumer."

"Gosh, I hope it works out. Imagine, our brand as an international activewear label. It's the dream, baby. It's the dream."

"I know, right?" My adrenaline amps up at the prospect. "I'm armed with my list of all the retailers that sell activewear in the UK. I'm going to start working on it first thing Monday."

"Hey, I don't want to burst your English love bubble."

"I can be in an English love bubble and still work, you know," I reply with a laugh.

Penny and I spend the next half an hour discussing our

strategy to get Timothy into Body Sports, one of the largest department stores in the UK. It would be huge if we could pull it off and really be the icing on the cake for our new venture. *Dating Mr. Darcy* has totally worked to launch Timothy into the US. Now, we need to keep that momentum going, and since I'm here in the UK, this is the logical next step for us.

The door to the library bursts open, and Jillian Fotherington, Lady of Some Manor House Down the Road (I can never remember its name because it's super long, although I know it starts with a B…or is it a Z?) unexpectedly comes waltzing into the room on a waft of perfume. As always, her waif-like figure drips in haute couture and pearls, and with her beautiful face, she fits in effortlessly in the elegant surrounds. Forget Kate and Meghan, Jilly Fotherington's style is all about the gorgeous and stylish 60's Princess Margaret. I know, I've watched *The Crown*.

Sebastian stands to greet her, and she air kisses him on both cheeks with a *m-wah, m-wah* sound. It's very English, and despite having spent lots of time here over the last three and a half months, I'm still not entirely used to it. What's wrong with a good old-fashioned hug?

"Sebastian, darling, how are you?" she coos, her perfect vowels rolling off her tongue like velvet. "Looking divine as always."

"I'm well, thanks Jilly. You?"

But Jilly's attention has already been diverted to me. "And here she is. The girl who stole your heart." She does the same kissing routine with me. I'm no good at the no touch air kiss thing and end up bumping my cheek against hers with a slap. "How perfectly lovely it is to see you back at Martinston, Emma. How was Texas? Your business? Family? All wonderful, I hope."

One thing I've learned about Jilly is that she's a whirlwind. A beautiful, well-meaning, extremely privileged whirlwind who happens to look like she could be on the cover of *Tatler*, but a whirlwind all the same.

Not that I feel insecure around her or anything.

"Everything's great. Thanks, Jilly," I reply with a bright smile.

"Marvelous, darling. So glad to hear it. You know I *adore* you." She sits down on one of the couches and lets out a pretty sigh. "I've just been with your mother," she says to Sebastian. "I cannot tell you both how trying this exhibition opening fundraiser has become. All the infighting and game playing. It's enough to make one want to poke one's eyes out with a blunt instrument. Perhaps a spoon or one of those things doctors use to check reflexes. What are those called?"

I shoot Sebastian a look. Jilly is nothing if not descriptive.

"Reflex checkers?" I offer. I've got no clue, and I've definitely never thought of poking my eyes out with them before.

"If it wasn't for the fact it's your father's foundation, Sebby, I'm not sure I'd dedicate my weekends quite so readily to the cause."

Whenever she calls him "Sebby" I've always got to work hard at not rolling my eyes. The guy's thirty-one, not a two-year-old in diapers and a playsuit (even though my heart melts at the thought of him as a cute toddler, all chubby-cheeked and unsure on his feet. Can I get an "Awwwww?").

"I tell you, your mother is a saint to have put up with these women for so long."

"Mother does have the patience of a nun," Sebastian replies with a smile.

19

"Well, I admire her immensely after working with Portia Fortescue-Seymour and Cecily Parker-Smithston. Beastly women! Not that I didn't admire your mother before, of course. Jemima's a real brick."

My questioning eyes find Sebastian's. "Is being a brick a good thing?"

"It is," he confirms as he takes a seat next to me on a couch, our thighs lightly touching.

"Oh, Emma, you still have so much to learn about we English. We have a lot of expressions and habits that you won't be at all acquainted with."

"Actually, we were just talking about the differences between American and British English over dinner last night, weren't we?" He gives my knee a squeeze and happiness bubbles up inside me.

"We were." I feel all goofy and in love as our gazes lock.

"You simply must come to the exhibition opening, Emma. It will be such fun!"

"You've not exactly sold it," I reply.

"Oh, I'm frustrated, that's all," she replies with a wave of her hand. "All the Huntington-Rosses will be there, of course, as well as my family and anyone who's anyone in the country set. It'll be good for you to get to know who's who around here, now that you're here for how long this time?"

I glance at Sebastian, and he smiles back at me. Happiness makes me tingle all over. "Penny and I decided to try to break into the British market, so I'm here for a while. I even brought Frank."

"Who the devil is Frank?"

"My tabby cat. He's somewhere around here."

"A cat? How lovely."

The door to the library opens once more and three generations of Huntington-Ross women walk into the room.

Zara, (aka Chef Henri), Geraldine, his granny, and Jemima, his mom.

Geraldine is protesting loudly about something, which is nothing new. Not exactly your warm and cuddly type, Sebastian's granny is more of a look-down-one's-nose-at-you-from-such-a-great-height-one-is-in-fear-of-vertigo type of person. I'm definitely one of the minions where she's concerned, despite my relationship with her grandson.

I'm hopeful our engagement announcement will help change all that.

"Darling, I don't understand why you're herding us in this fashion. The library is your least favorite room in the house," Geraldine complains. "In fact, I don't think you've opened a book since you were at boarding school, and even then, it was only under duress. I do love you, but you're so awfully intellectually benighted, Zara."

"Benighted?" I mouth to Sebastian, wondering if the word's got something to do with knights and maidens and the like. He simply pulls a face and shrugs.

Geraldine loves to use words I've never heard of, and I spend half my time when I'm with her saving them up to google them later—if I can remember them. She's either super smart or enjoys confusing people.

I haven't worked out which yet.

She looks to her daughter-in-law for support. "Isn't that right, Jemima?"

"That's so not true, Granny. I read all the time," Zara replies before her mom gets the chance.

"Zara, I'm not sure those romance things on your phone should be considered 'reading' per se," Sebastian's mother, Jemima, says in significantly better humor than Geraldine. Mainly because she's always in significantly better humor than Geraldine, so it figures. "Those things are mainly pictures."

Zara shakes her head. "They're called apps, Mum. Really, you need to pull yourself into this century before it's over."

"Thank you, Zara. I do know what an app is," Jemima sniffs. She turns her attention to Sebastian, me, and Jilly. "Oh, hello you three."

Zara waltzes over and plants a kiss on both my cheeks, but unlike Jilly's there's no additional *m-wah, m-wah* sound. "You'll like this, Emma. Mum thought an iPad was something you put over your eye."

"Well, to be fair, eye pads are used for your eyes, just not the electronic ones," I reply tactfully as I greet Jemima. I *am* the girl newly engaged to her only, beloved son, after all. Staying on her good side is vital, especially considering how Geraldine feels about me. I can do with whatever backup I can get.

The mere thought of sharing the news of our engagement with Geraldine and Jemima shoots adrenaline violently around my body. Don't get me wrong, Sebastian's mom has been very welcoming to me, possibly because, as she told me, she too was an outsider when she married Sebastian's dad. I know neither she nor Geraldine exactly approved of the fact we met on a reality TV show, but Sebastian has told them I was only on the show to promote my label, which Jemima seemed happy enough about.

Geraldine is a different story altogether. She decided any *Dating Mr. Darcy* contestant was a fame-hungry, gold-digging, manipulative piece of work not worthy of the title "Sebastian's Girlfriend." Of course, she threw in a few other adjectives, too, but I didn't know what they meant.

Did I mention Geraldine isn't my biggest fan?

I'm just thankful Sebastian makes it all worthwhile.

Sebastian greets his mom and grandmother, and we all take our seats, me sitting next to Sebastian again, trying to be subtle about the fact that I'm clutching onto his hand for dear life. What will they all think of me marrying him? Will they be happy for us? Supportive? Dead against it and determined to split us up?

The jangling of my nerves is almost deafening.

Sebastian shoots me an encouraging look, and I give him a nervous smile.

This is it.

"Granny, Mother. It wasn't Zara who wanted you all to come here today, actually. It was me," Sebastian says. "Well, Emma and me, to be precise. We have something we'd like to say to you."

"This sounds like a family matter," Jilly says, rising to her feet. "I knew I shouldn't pop in unannounced. Very bad form, Jilly."

That's the other thing Jilly does, talk about herself in the third person. It's just plain weird.

"I'll make myself scarce, shall I? I wouldn't want to intrude."

"No, Jilly, stay. Not only are you our lawyer, but you're a close family friend."

That's right, as the Huntington-Ross's lawyer, Jilly was the one who tried to talk Sebastian into choosing one of the other contestants on *Dating Mr. Darcy* for her money. I know, I know, saying that makes Sebastian sound like a truly horrible person, not to mention how it makes Jilly sound. Believe me, neither of them are horrible people. Very far from it, in fact. Sebastian only agreed to the plan because his family was at risk of losing Martinston, their home for centuries, and the girl in question, Camille, was the one who came up with the idea in the first place. Jilly and Sebastian were simply trying to do the right thing.

And anyway, in the end he rejected the idea because he was so very much in love with me.

See? Not horrible in the least. Quite the opposite, in fact.

Jilly sits back down slowly. "All right. I'll stay."

"Good." Sebastian slips his hand into mine, and our gazes lock before he looks back at the assembled women. "We have an announcement," he says.

"Are you doing another one of those ghastly television shows, my grandson?" Granny asks with an eyebrow arched in clear disapproval. Suffice it to say, Granny wasn't a fan of Sebastian posing as Mr. Darcy in the first place. I believe the words "ruinous" and "degrading" were bandied about a fair amount at the time. By her, that is. "Because really, I'm not sure our family can take such a preposterous experience twice in one lifetime. There are limits, you know."

"Oh, Geraldine," Jemima says with a smile. "It wasn't that bad, and Seb was only trying to help. I thought it was all rather fun. Other than that Camille person. She was quite frightening."

I've got to agree with Jemima on that. Camille made *Mean Girl*'s Regina George look like the best friend a girl could have.

"One shouldn't have to compromise one's morals for the sake of fortune," Granny sniffs. "I'm not sure my frail heart can take it again."

"There's nothing frail about you whatsoever, Geraldine," Jemima scolds gently.

"Mum? Granny? I've got to leave on the 11:30 train for London. Can you please let Sebastian speak?"

"Of course," Jemima replies as Granny grumps, "As

long as it's nothing to do with that awful television business." She shudders dramatically for effect, her three rows of pearls jiggling around her crêpe paper neck.

"It's nothing to do with reality television, Granny," Sebastian replies. "It's something much more important than that. It's about Emma and me. Emma has done me the great honor of agreeing to be my wife."

I grin at him. *I'm going to be Sebastian's wife.* Despite how wonderful the thought is, I'm definitely not used to it yet. But then, it has been less than twenty-four hours since he asked me.

"Oh, darlings!" Jemima leaps off her seat and collects first Sebastian and then me in a warm hug. "That's wonderful news. Truly, truly wonderful. You two are divine together. When did this happen?"

"Last night over dinner," I reply, my smile so broad it threatens to crack my face in two. "It was so romantic. He and Zara planned the whole thing."

"You knew?" Jemima asks Zara.

"There's not much that goes on in this family that I don't know about, Mum," she replies with a grin. "Isn't it fabulous?"

"Oh, it is," Jemima confirms. "Geraldine? Isn't it wonderful news? Sebastian and Emma are getting married!"

Geraldine remains in her seat, her mouth tight. "Yes. Wonderful," she replies, sounding as genuine as a used car salesman on a deadline.

"Well, I think it's marvelous," Jilly says as she gives me a squeeze. "Who knew Mr. Darcy would find his Miss Bennett on an American television show? Quite, quite thrilling."

"I certainly didn't," Sebastian replies, beaming down at me.

I gaze back at him. "Me neither."

"Have you set a date yet, guys?" Zara asks.

We share a look between ourselves. We'd talked about dates over breakfast this morning.

"We thought the first weekend in June next year," Sebastian says.

Jemima claps her hands together with glee. "A June wedding! How marvelous. We'll need to organize a marquee and find a planner and a caterer. Oh, and the cake! We must use Francois Chevret. He did Antonia's daughter's wedding cake last month, and it was spectacular, I tell you. It was five tiers high and—"

"Mother," Sebastian interrupts. "We haven't got to all the details yet. She only said yes last night."

"And doesn't the bride get to choose where she gets married?" Zara asks. "That's traditional, isn't it?"

"I guess," I reply. "Mom will want us to do it at her church, I know that for sure. But you know, there is this sweet little chapel near my apartment that I've always secretly thought I'd like to get married in one day. It's colonial and so picturesque. I've always had a feeling about it. It might be the place."

Sebastian kisses me on the forehead. "It might be."

"If you get married, it will be at Martinston," Granny announces gravely.

What does she mean "if"?

"Jemima was married here. I was married here. My mother was married here. It is the Huntington-Ross way."

"Granny, it's fine. Let them do what they want," Zara protests. "It's the twenty-first century after all."

"She has a point," Jemima says.

"Do you want to get married at your little chapel?" Zara

Marrying Mr. Darcy

asks, and all three generations of Huntington-Rosses turn to look at us both.

Sebastian slinks his arm around my shoulder. "We'll let you know as soon as we've had the chance to discuss it."

"You're right, you're right," Jemima replies as Geraldine's features harden. "Tell us all about the proposal, and don't leave anything out."

While we tell the story, I steal a glance at Geraldine. She's now smiling and nodding, uttering things like "oh, goodness" and "how perfectly lovely for you" while Sebastian explains what Budweiser and macaroni and cheese are to her. She's playing the part of an approving relation, the initial shock wiped skillfully from her face.

I can tell she doesn't approve. I can tell she thinks all of it—me, how we met on the dating show, everything—is beneath her and her family.

And I make a decision here and now. I'm going to do my best to prove to her that I am good enough for her grandson.

Even if it's the last thing I do.

Chapter Three

Despite Geraldine's obvious disapproval of "the match," as Jane Austen would have put it, the next couple of days with Sebastian are a blur of utter, unadulterated happiness. We spend as much time as we can together, basking in our newly engaged status, and enjoying some alone time. We wander around Martinston's beautiful grounds, we visit Mia's Café with its curved lead-light windows, brightly painted chairs, and quaint hanging baskets. And we perfect our bedroom skills behind firmly shut doors—and I will leave it to your imagination what I mean by that.

Hint: it's not using hospital corners to make the bed.

I'm leaning up against Sebastian, cupping a coffee in my hands, as we lounge on the terrace in the warm morning sun, when my phone beeps beside me.

"Don't answer it," Sebastian murmurs into my hair. "This feels too nice. Whoever it is can leave a message."

I nudge him on the arm. "It might be Penny. I've gone a bit AWOL on her lately, and I know she needs me."

He lets out a breath. "I suppose. Can I help it if I want you all to myself?"

Feeling relaxed and content with my life, I pick up my phone and see it's not from Penny. It's an alert on my name, something I set up when the show first began to air and I was paranoid about what people were saying about me in the media.

My heart sinks as I scan it.

"Everything okay?"

"It's about our engagement."

"Hand it to me."

I pass him my phone, and he reads the headline out. "*Dating Mr. Darcy star Sebastian Huntington-Ross has been spotted out with Emma Brady, the girl he left show favorite Phoebe Wilson for. They announced their engagement today. He looked as hot as ever in his polo shirt and shorts.* What's the problem with that? Other than the fact they're still banging on about Phoebe, of course, which they really do need to let go."

"Scroll down and look at the image."

He does so. "It's a photo of us from a day or two ago. We'd been to Mia's, if I remember correctly. You really do love their cookies."

I snatch the phone back. "Seb, it's a photo of you looking hot and me mid sneeze. It's horrible." I peer at the photo. My eyes are closed, my nose scrunched up, and my mouth is wide open as I sneeze all over my cookie.

"I think you look cute."

"There is absolutely nothing cute about this."

He pulls me down for a kiss. "Well, I think you're adorable, Brady."

"You're biased."

"I am biased, it's true, and I need you to know I love you before, during, and after all your sneezes."

I let out a giggle. "You like it when I sneeze? Is that some weird boarding school fetish thing you've got going on there, dude?"

His laugh rumbles through me. "Oh, yes. Although I think I prefer it when you fall out of limos and swear like a fishwife. That is so much sexier."

"Hey," I protest. He's referring to the moment we met when I fell backwards out of the limo and onto my butt. In my defense, I was wrangling with a sequined dress that had gotten stuck in my hair as I changed into my activewear line so I could promote it on reality TV.

A perfectly reasonable explanation, if you ask me.

"Granny cornered me this morning," Sebastian says, his voice sounding more serious.

At the mention of her name, my nerves kick up. "Did you have to stop her from going on about how amazing I am?"

"Granny takes a while to warm to people. She'll come around. Just give her time."

"I guess," I reply, totally unconvinced. I think for Sebastian's granny to "come around" to the idea of him marrying me, I'd have to morph into a member of the British landed gentry on her extremely short list of suitable partners for her grandson.

As Lady Catherine de Bourgh said of Lizzie Bennet in *Pride and Prejudice*, I'm a girl with no name, no family connections, and no fortune. That just ain't gonna cut it for Geraldine Huntington-Ross.

"Granny was talking about our wedding, actually."

"Well, that's a positive sign."

"She's adamant we marry here. I told her we hadn't made up our minds yet."

"It means a lot to her, doesn't it?"

"I think it's more about tradition than anything else, actually. Granny likes things done 'the right way,' you know."

"Oh, I know," I reply, thinking of the way I don't seem to be able to do anything right in her eyes. "Do you think she might 'come around' to me, as you put it, if we decided to have the wedding here?"

He kisses me on the forehead. "Don't try to force anything. As I said, she'll love you just as much as I do before too long."

I cock an eyebrow and shoot him a grin. "Just as much?"

"Okay, not quite, but you'll win her over just by being you."

"How big a wedding do you think she wants us to have if we have it here?"

"Well, if I think of Uncle Hector's last wedding, he had about four hundred guests, and I'm certain Granny won't want to be outdone by him. Wrong side of the family, in her opinion."

"*Four hundred?*" I repeat, trying to process how big a wedding that would actually be. *Freaking huge* is what I land on. "I was thinking small. Like way small."

"You were?"

"Yeah. I don't have a large family. I figured fifty to seventy-five, maybe? Nothing bigger because then all you do is spend your entire time making sure you talk to everyone and it becomes more about them than us."

He gives me a squeeze. "I think a small wedding sounds wonderful."

"What do you want?"

"I want whatever makes my beautiful bride happy."

I chew on my lip. I've loved the idea of that little chapel back home, committing myself to my husband in front of our closest friends and family. Rather that than the whole *My Big Fat American Gypsy Wedding* shebang. Not that I think Geraldine would countenance gypsies on the estate, considering how much of a snob she is.

But then, I do want Sebastian's family—and his granny in particular—to accept me, and something as small as where we get married could go a long to help with that.

I slip my arms around his neck and brush my lips softly against his. "Let's get married here."

"But your chapel?"

"It was a silly fantasy. I'll be living here afterwards, anyway. Holding the wedding here will kickstart my new life as Lady Martinston."

He kisses me back. "You're amazing, you know that, Brady?"

"Why, thank you, Mr. Darcy. Speaking of getting married, you promised me a run, and I'm an engaged woman." I wave my hands up and down my body. "I can't let all this go to wrack and ruin, you know."

"Let's just go for a gentle jog," he replies with a sigh. "I'm not up for much today."

Once we're up on our feet, I realize it's a ruse when he adds, "Race you to the woods," and takes off at breakneck speed.

"Hey!" I yell after him. I try in vain to catch up. "Not playing fair, dude!"

After chasing him for several minutes, he stops, and I finally catch him. We run the rest of the course together. When we reach the house, I'm pinker than a beet and am puffing hard.

"Who's that?" I ask as I spot a car I don't recognize pulling up outside the house.

"Ah, that'll be my surprise for you."

I take a large and much needed glug of water from my drink bottle. "What is it?"

"It's not a what, it's a who."

"Okay, now I'm completely confused."

The feeling doesn't last for long. Out of the car steps not only Sebastian's best friend, Johnathan, but my fellow *Dating Mr. Darcy* contestant Phoebe.

"Best surprise ever!" I grin at Sebastian before I rush over to greet them.

"OMG, guys! What are you doing here?" I give them both a warm hug. "Sorry I'm all sweaty. I didn't think I was going to get to see you until your wedding."

Although I got to know Phoebe while we were on the show together—and she was busy falling in love with Johnathan behind our backs while the cameras were focused elsewhere—I've only spent a small amount of time with Johnathan since the show. All I know about him is that he seems like a really nice guy, and he's got excellent taste in fiancées.

"Would you believe we were in the neighborhood?" Johnathan answers.

"I'm not sure Paris is considered 'the neighborhood,' Johnny," Phoebe says.

"You were in Paris?" I ask, and she gives an enthusiastic nod. "Is it as romantic as everyone says?"

Phoebe blushes, and I have my answer before she even opens her mouth to respond. "It is such a beautiful place, Emma. You've got to go there."

"I would love to."

Phoebe famously asked Johnathan to marry her on the

last episode of *Dating Mr. Darcy*—and he said yes. A lot of viewers were pretty upset because they wanted Phoebe to marry Sebastian, as the media loves to remind me.

"Well, come on in. Let's have some tea," Sebastian offers.

I hook my arm through Phoebe's as we walk into the house. "I'm still training him to drink coffee."

"Work in progress?"

"Some things are just too British, you know?"

"Oh, I hear you. Johnny still tells me my accent is endearing. Then I point out that *he's* the one with the accent. *I* sound normal."

I grin at her. "Totally."

Once we're settled in the living room—or the "reception room," as the Huntington-Rosses call it—Johnathan asks us what we've been up to.

"We have some news, actually," I say as I hold up my left hand to show off my engagement ring. Well, my engagement *rock*, to be more accurate. But I ain't complaining. For a Texan gal from the wrong side of the tracks, I sure have come a long way, baby.

"Emma!" Phoebe squeals as she leaps off her seat and collects me in a hug. "Why didn't you tell me the moment we arrived? This is huge news."

Johnathan shakes hands with Sebastian in that very formal, English way of theirs, and together, we share the story of the proposal.

Johnathan grins at us. "Two weddings from one reality TV show."

"Neither of which are going to be televised," Sebastian says.

"Well—" Johnathan darts a look at Phoebe.

Marrying Mr. Darcy

"We agreed to let them film ours," Phoebe finishes for him.

"Really?" I ask in amazement. "Remember on the show there were cameras everywhere, we had to wear those mics, and Mrs. Watson barked at us every five minutes?" I shudder as I think of the woman who bossed us contestants around every day, her Regency cap balanced on top of her head like a poufy shower cap. "Not that Mrs. Watson will be at your wedding, of course, because that would be plain weird," I add with a laugh.

"Actually, she will," Phoebe replies.

"Are you kidding me?"

"She's really great when you get to know her."

I scrunch up my nose. "Mrs. Watson is great?"

"Totally. In fact, she's got quite a good sense of humor."

I shake my head. "Phoebe, how you manage to see the best in everyone you meet is beyond me. You are too sweet for words."

Which is so true. Phoebe's never got a bad word to say about anyone, she's always happy, and she'd do anything for anyone anytime. Until I met Phoebe, I never knew people like her existed. Well, outside of Disney princesses, that is. And maybe Barbie.

"Which is why my fiancée is so perfect," Johnathan says as he slips his arm around Phoebe's waist.

"I'm not perfect," she coos.

Johnathan nuzzles her. "Sure you're not."

"Aw, you guys are the cutest," I say.

"Tell us how your wedding plans are coming along," Sebastian says.

"Can you believe we're getting married in only a matter of weeks?" Phoebe says excitedly. "It means so much to me that you're going to be here for it, Emma. I'm so excited you're going to be a bridesmaid."

"I wouldn't miss it for anything," I reply, although part of me wants to run and hide at the thought of being filmed again by the *Dating Mr. Darcy* production crew. I'll have to put my camouflage skills to good use and melt into the wallpaper. I don't want to do anything the media can pick up on and run with. Let's face it, the last thing I need is some new story about how *not* suitable I am for Sebastian.

#NinjaBridesmaid here I come.

Phoebe smiles at me. "Thank you, Emma. You're so kind."

"I will do my best," I reply. "I've only been a bridesmaid once before, and that was in a barn with haybales and a couple of goats out back. Not that I'm saying Penny and Trey's wedding wasn't all that, of course, but your wedding is gonna be quite something."

"Johnny's family's house is gorgeous. Not a patch on this place, though, of course. But I've always wanted an intimate wedding, and it's so wonderful to get married in England."

"And now you'll have TV cameras there to capture it all, too," Sebastian says with a sardonic twinkle in his eye that's not lost on me.

"They're paying us," Johnathan says. "Quite handsomely. You should consider it for your wedding."

Sebastian shakes his head vehemently. "There's no way I want our wedding to become public fodder."

"Are you sure? It could be very lucrative for you." Johnathan scoots forward to the edge of his seat. "In fact, when we met with Heather McCabe at the production company, she mentioned she'd discussed doing a show about saving the house."

"Martinston?" I ask in surprise.

The news doesn't come as quite a surprise to Sebastian, however. "I was going to mention it to you, Emma. I wasn't sure we'd want that level of intrusion in our lives, so I turned them down."

"Doing another reality show is not exactly top of my list right now," I reply.

"I imagine not," he says with a kind smile, and my heart squeezes. "They want to call it *Saving Pemberley*, can you believe."

"Of course they do. Pemberley was Mr. Darcy's house in *Pride and Prejudice*, and you *are* Mr. Darcy," Phoebe points out.

"Is the offer any good?" Johnathan asks.

"We haven't discussed figures. I didn't think we'd want to do it," Sebastian replies.

I chew on my lip. Sebastian has told me how much he was paid for doing *Dating Mr. Darcy*. Although it wasn't enough to save *his* Pemberley, it was definitely enough cash to make my eyes water, that's for sure. I might not exactly relish the idea of cameras on me once more—and the inevitable judgment that goes with it—but we're in this together. Maybe I need to put my concerns aside?

"Seb? Why don't you consider it? It wouldn't be like having cameras at our wedding or anything. As long as we could control it, we could have them document all the things we're doing to save the house."

"Are you considering this, Brady?" Sebastian asks in obvious surprise.

"Maybe?" I reply with a shrug. "If it's good money, we'd be fools to turn it down for fear of a few nasty memes."

"You know she's right, Seb," Johnathan says.

"But Brady, after all you went through," Sebastian protests.

"I'm still here, aren't I?" I reply with a sly grin.

Because I am. Despite all the crap they threw at me—at us—I'm still breathing. And what's more, I'm in love with the most incredible man, living in this amazing house, happy.

I'd say things have worked out pretty well for the contestant who didn't win the show.

Sebastian takes my hand in his. "You're wonderful. Did you know that?"

"Either that or a masochist," I reply with a grin.

Sebastian lets out a low laugh. "I'm going with 'wonderful.' But you know Granny would be apoplectic."

"Oh, she totally would." An image of a pink-faced Geraldine with steam coming out of her ears springs to mind, and I snort-giggle.

"Why don't you have a chat to Heather about it?" Johnathan suggests. "I'm sure she'd be keen."

"Who's Heather?" I ask.

"She produced *Dating Mr. Darcy*. We knew her from another life, which is why I thought of Sebastian for the show in the first place," Johnathan replies. "She'd been looking for Mr. Darcy for months, and when she met Sebastian, she sent me a bottle of my favorite scotch, gushing about how perfect he was for the show."

I shoot Sebastian a teasing smile. "Bit of a fan, is she?"

"What can I say," he replies with a shrug. "I can't help it if women adore me, Brady. It's a gift." His grin tells me he's totally pulling my leg.

I giggle. "That's what I love about my future husband—he's so modest."

"Oh, I like that, Emma. Your future husband," Phoebe says, her eyes bright.

"He's also talking out of a hole in his head. Heather has been happily married to my good friend Jeremy for years now. Lives in the suburbs, got a Labrador, three sprogs, the works," Johnathan replies with a laugh. "There's no harm in exploring the idea."

"You're right," Sebastian concedes. "As long as we have control, it could work."

I curve my lips into a smile. Although the idea of another reality show would never appear in a *Sound of Music* list of my favorite things, it could go a long way to saving the house. And that's *got* to be a very good thing.

Chapter Four

That evening, I'm lounging on the couch in front of the empty fireplace in our bedroom, waiting for him to get dressed for dinner while I catch up on work emails. That's one of the weirder things that happens here at Martinston, we all "dress" for dinner. As in change out of whatever you were wearing during the day. It doesn't matter if you were wearing a fancy ballgown all day—not that I ever am, of course, because that would be plain weird—but you still need to change into "suitable attire" for dinner. Which seems to mean cocktail dresses for the women and a jacket and tie for the men.

Believe me, it's a whole other world from the hastily microwaved dinner-for-one on my lap in front of Netflix with Frank my cat for company.

On my first visit to Martinston, I didn't realize that it was expected of me every night, so I turned up with a suitcase full of jeans and Timothy activewear and one, solitary dress—which I ended up wearing every single night, until I eventually made it into the local village to buy a couple more.

This time I came prepared with a suitcase full of evening clothes, even if they're not Geraldine's preferred label, Chanel. My budget isn't exactly in that ballpark these days.

Or *ever*.

Frank slinks into the room and announces his presence with a meow.

"Hey, Frank," I say as he hops up onto the couch and rubs up against me to tell me now would be the perfect time to pet him. Not one to argue, I scratch him under his chin and am rewarded with a loud purr. "How do you like your new place, huh? A little roomier than the old one, by like a hundred rooms, right?"

He purrs in response, shifting his head so I can tickle him under his chin.

Even though I'm only here on a working vacation, I couldn't bear to leave my beautiful boy at home again. So, I got him all the requisite shots, a cat passport (who knew such a thing existed?), and *voila*, he's now the Cat of the Manor, a position I personally think he was born to.

"Let's go out for dinner tomorrow night, just you and me," Sebastian says as he looks in the mirror and fixes his tie. "It's great that you're getting to know my family so much better now, but I'm selfish and want you all to myself at least some of the time."

I grin at him. "Sounds great. You look hot, by the way. A little Mr. Darcy, only less haughty."

He arches an eyebrow and shoots me a disapproving look. "Better?"

I snap my laptop shut, get to my feet, and pad over to him. I stand on my tippy-toes and pull him down for a kiss. "Mmm, much better. I feel judged and left wanting, just like Lizzie Bennet."

In one fluid movement, he wraps his arms around me, lifts me off my feet, and I let out a squeal of delight before he kisses me long and hard, making my head spin.

"What was that for?" I ask, breathless.

"Because I love my future wife."

"Wow. Future wife."

"Sound strange to you?"

I run my fingers through his hair and reply, "It sounds wonderful." I kiss him once more, and then he puts me back on my feet.

"I suppose we'd better get down to dinner."

"Yup. I'm starving. Now, where did I plunk my shoes?" I search for them. Nowhere to be seen, I drop to the floor and peer under the bed.

"I called Heather McCabe this afternoon while you were working."

"From the TV company?"

"The producer of *Dating Mr. Darcy* herself. She wants to meet to talk about *Saving Pemberley*."

"I'm glad you decided to go for it." I pat my hand around under the bed until my hand lands on one shoe and then another. "Aha!" I pull them out and slip them on, leaning down to buckle the straps. "How do you think your family will feel about it, by which I mean your granny?"

"As long as it's not invasive, I think I can talk them 'round. Granny will be a hard sell, that's for sure."

"Won't she like it if she knows it'll make money?"

"Perhaps. I think we need to have a serious family talk tonight about the future of the house, and I want you included in that conversation."

"You do?" Although we have talked about it before, I've never been to any of the family discussions or meetings with

Jilly in her capacity as the family lawyer. To be included now feels...nice.

Like I belong.

"Brady, you're the future Lady Martinston. You need to be involved."

"Lady Martinston." I make a face. "Gawd. That's so grand and *old* sounding. I'm not sure I'll ever get used to that."

He places his hands on my shoulders and plants a kiss on my forehead. "You're going to rock it."

"Rock it? Did the pompous English aristocrat really just say that?"

He shrugs. "I'm trying to evolve, you know. And thank you for calling me 'pompous,' by the way."

"You can always rely on me to call it how I see it."

"Oh, that I do know."

"Actually, I've been doing lots of reading, and I've got some ideas for the house."

"You have?"

"I'm not just a pretty face, you know. I've got the smarts."

He loops his arm around my shoulders as we make our way out of the room and down the sweeping staircase. "That's why I love you, Brady. Beauty and brains. So, what have you been reading about?"

"Well, a bunch of different manor houses have been saved by their owners. Most are open to the public and allow visitors to walk through the house and gardens for a fee. One place I read about has cafés and restaurants on site, some do high tea, some even hire themselves out for TV productions."

"I know a little about that last one."

"I know you do, honey."

I made a reluctant Sebastian watch *Downton Abbey* with me on his first visit to Houston after he'd declared his love for me on my doorstep. As in the entire boxset of the first series. I loved it, even though I knew everything that was going to happen. He, on the other hand, told me that although it felt a little too close to home, he was glad he'd shared it with me and then promptly asked to never have to watch it again.

I guess some things aren't made to be shared with English aristocratic fiancés.

"Did you know one manor house has a safari park in the grounds?" I shake my head at how insane that seems to me. "As in real African animals live there in cold, damp England where it rains more than in the Amazon."

"I don't think it rains here more than the world's largest rain forest."

"It sure feels like it at times. There's another one that has a theme park in the grounds, and another one that has a water park."

"Well, at least the last one would be aided by the rain," he says with a wry smile. "But can you imagine living with something like that here?" He shudders, and I take a mental note—no safari park, no theme park, and no water park allowed. Not that I was exactly considering them anyway. "I have been thinking we should open the house up to the public in spring. It seems like the obvious way forward to me."

"Exactly. We can close off the private living areas of the house and charge entry. People will love it."

He pauses by the double doors that lead into one of the reception rooms. "I ran some numbers with my accountant before I did *Dating Mr. Darcy*. It's not going to make us rich, but it will certainly help. The only problem is, Granny wasn't overly enamored of the idea."

What is Geraldine ever "enamored" with?

Not me, that's for sure.

"We're not exactly in a position to be picky anymore, though," he continues.

"Are we going in?" I ask.

He pulls me in for a kiss. "I want to say that I'm incredibly happy to have you by my side in this, Emma. You're quite something."

My grin stretches from ear to ear as love fills my heart for him. "Well, you're totally worth it."

Sebastian pushes the door to the reception room open, and out of nowhere, Frank darts past us and into the room, coming to a sudden stop to survey his surroundings.

We follow him in to see Geraldine, Jemima, and Zara already sitting in front of the grand fireplace, which crackles as it warms the room, lending it a warm, golden glow. Zara, who's come back from her flat in London for the weekend, is regaling them with a story.

"Who knows how she got down from there. That tree was three stories high! Not the best position for a girl in nothing but a pair of Manolos and a flimsy Stella McCartney dress. Oh, hello you two, and hello Frank." Zara rubs her fingers together and Frank, terrible flirt that he is, rushes over to her for some love.

Traitor.

"Hello, everyone," I say as I take a seat. "Who was up where in a Stella McCartney dress?"

"Zara was telling us a delightful story about one of her inebriated friends," Granny says in a tone that tells me she thinks the story is anything but delightful. "I see your cat is here, too." She purses her lips as she regards him with suspicion.

"It's Frank," I say to remind her of his name. "He's real friendly."

"Yes. I can see that."

"She wasn't inebriated, as you put it, Granny," Zara protests as Frank nestles on her lap. See? Total traitor. "Well, no more than she usually is on a Tuesday."

"We're talking about Tabitha, aren't we?" Sebastian hands me a glass of red wine. Although he knows I prefer a beer, I think Granny would implode from class-induced shock if she saw me suck on a bottle in Martinston's grand reception room with its ornate high ceilings, antique furniture, and gilded paintings.

Trying hard to win her over here, remember?

"How did you know I'm talking about Tabitha?" Zara asks him.

He shrugs. "Just a wild hunch."

"Did I see Johnathan here earlier?" Jemima asks.

"He popped by with Phoebe, which was such a nice surprise. I didn't think we'd get to see them before their wedding," I reply.

"You're a bridesmaid, aren't you?" Jemima says.

"I am." I think of the tasteful blush-colored, three-quarter length dress with the off-the-shoulder detailing and pretty bow. I sent my measurements to Phoebe, and she's had it made by a wedding store in a village near Johnathan's family's home. It's not very me, but it's *very* Phoebe—feminine, sweet, beautiful, and refined. Apparently, the other bridesmaids and the maid of honor are all Phoebe's sisters and cousins, so I'm honored she asked me. And also deeply thankful she didn't ask the more horrible contestants from the show, Hayley and Camille. Although I hear they're invited to the wedding.

I bet they're super excited to see me, the girl who got sent home before the top four contestants and then ended up with the guy anyway.

I take a sip of my wine. "Their wedding is only a few weeks away, can you believe? They're having it filmed for TV."

"Really?" Jemima exclaims as Zara says, "How cool!" and Geraldine pulls a face that needs no words.

"I for one don't understand it," Sebastian says as he sits down next to me. "Why would you want something as personal as your wedding made into a TV show?"

"This from the man who allowed the search for his bride to be made into a public game show," Granny scoffs. "Really, Sebastian. You can be quite paradoxical at times."

"That's not fair, Granny, and you know it," Zara protests. "Seb was only trying to help save our home. Without him we'd all have been turned out onto the street a long time ago. The fact he fell in love with the lovely Emma on the show was simply an added bonus."

I grin at her and mouth the words "thank you" discretely. Did I mention how much I like Sebastian's kid sister?

"If only it were enough," Sebastian says.

"We'd hardly be on the street," Jemima protests. "Would we?"

Granny scoffs. "The idea is preposterous. Huntington-Rosses have held a position of power and influence in this country for hundreds of years. We're not going to become street urchins, selling posies and sweeping chimneys for a living."

Geraldine clearly thinks we all live in a Charles Dickens novel.

"Of course not, Granny. Emma and I have been talking about how we can make some more money," Sebastian begins. "We've got some ideas."

"Ooh, I know! Emma could pose topless for the tabloids," Zara suggests, although I know she cannot be serious.

Can she?

I open my mouth to tell her I won't be doing anything of the sort when Jemima protests with, "Zara! Please. No one associated with this family is going topless."

Geraldine looks aghast.

Zara shrugs. "It's a big thing here. Emma might not know about that."

I glance down at my meagre cleavage. There's nothing "big" about it.

Zara clears her throat. "I meant a lot of reality TV stars do that sort of thing," she clarifies. "Tabitha has a friend whose friend did it, and she made a mint."

"Yup. Got it. Not gonna happen." I shake my head fervently.

Geraldine is gawking at me with an appalled expression on her face, like this whole posing topless thing was my idea.

Zara shrugs. "I thought I'd check all the same. Desperate times and all that."

"We're not that desperate," Geraldine quips.

I raise my hands in the stop sign. "As I said, it's not gonna happen, so you can all chill."

"What were your ideas, you two?" Jemima asks, deflecting the conversation in a far less embarrassing direction.

Marrying Mr. Darcy

Sebastian nods encouragingly at me.

"Well, as an absolute minimum, I think you need to open the house and gardens up to the paying public. A lot of houses do it, as I'm sure you know, and it works. People love to see how the other half live, you know. I know I was super impressed when I first saw Martinston."

To me it's a total no-brainer. They've literally got this major asset under their noses, and they're doing nothing with it. I might not have been able to afford to go to anything but a community college, but even I know that's Business 101, make your assets work for you. If I had a freaking huge palace-like house with gardens that look like Marie Antoinette herself sat and ate cake in them, I'd be shouting from the rooftops about it. Not that I think Marie Antoinette actually did eat cake here, but you get the idea. Fancy gardens. Old.

"It's a great idea," Zara says as she takes a sip of her wine. "Lulu's parents have been doing that for years, and they've got cafés in the house, too. They make a lot of bread out of it."

"Don't use that expression, Zara," Geraldine scolds. "It's awfully common."

"Granny doesn't like it because it's Cockney rhyming slang," Zara explains to me. "Bread and honey, money. See? I think it's cute."

"Got it." I smile at her, grateful for her support.

"You're always banging on about how Emma needs to learn the 'British way,' Granny," Zara says, using air quotes. "What's more British than Cockney?"

I know Zara's teasing her granny at best and trying to annoy her at worst. I change the subject back to the house. *Much* safer territory. "I know about that place, Zara. Their cafés are super popular, right?"

"Oh, yes. Lulu's trust fund is huge because of it."

Lucky Lulu.

"This idea is nothing new, Emma. No disrespect to your enthusiasm," Geraldine says, her tone and facial expression screaming *total* disrespect. "We've been through this already, and my position has not changed. I don't want all those people traipsing through our home. Imagine! What if they steal the silverware or leave their hamburger wrappers on the tables, or worse yet, relieve themselves in the bushes. It's all absolutely unthinkable."

Sebastian laughs as he shakes his head. "Granny, you have a very dim view of the general public. I can't imagine any of those things will happen."

"How do you know?" Geraldine replies rhetorically. "You don't, and therein lies the problem."

"Even the Queen opens her home," Sebastian says.

"For one month of the year when she's elsewhere for the summer," she sniffs. "We don't have a summer home anymore. Sebastian lost it, remember?"

I know what you're thinking. My fiancé somehow lost the Huntington-Ross's summer home. The thing is, Sebastian's father was called Sebastian. With the same name it can be very confusing. But most of the men and even some of the women in this family are called "Sebastian" (just kidding about the women), so I generally simply nod along and hope I can work out which one they're talking about at the time.

Sebastian's dad was a terrible gambler. Terrible in that not only was he a compulsive gambler, but he was really, really bad at it, too. Through his habit, he plunged the family into their current state of potential financial ruin. Sebastian has never told me how much his dad lost, but it's pretty safe to say it's a whole lot. And thanks to a fatal heart

Marrying Mr. Darcy

attack a while back, he's not around to deal with the consequences of his actions, either.

Not surprisingly, Sebastian has a complicated relationship with his deceased dad.

"Of course I remember, Granny. Now I want to ensure we don't lose *this* house, too. Emma and I think it's well worth revisiting the idea now that we know the show was never going to be enough. My feeling is we need to do it in spring."

Geraldine scoffs.

"What else would you have us do? We're already down to one cook and one housekeeper. I suppose we could give them their notice..."

"No!" Geraldine exclaims, her face aghast. "You can't do that. Who would cook and clean for us?"

Uh, we could do it?

"I think opening up the house is a fabulous idea," Zara says firmly. "Well done, you two."

"I have to agree. Although I know it will take work, it's better than the alternative." Jemima turns to Geraldine. "Mummy, what do you say?"

It always gets me when Jemima calls Geraldine "Mummy" for two reasons. 1. Geraldine isn't her mother, she's her mother-in-law, and I know people of that generation sometimes called their parents-in-law Mom or Dad, but to me it's plain weird, and 2. the word "Mummy" sounds so awfully, awfully British. *Mummy*. See?

"You all want to do this, do you?" Geraldine asks, and everyone nods.

This isn't *Crazy Rich Asians*. This is more Disapproving Impoverished Aristocratic Brits Who Don't Seem to Realize What a State They Are In. Geraldine needs to get on board with this. Period.

She exhales. "All right. I acquiesce."

I don't need to google "acquiesce" to know it means "accept." Doesn't it?

"You can open the house," she finishes.

Jemima claps her hands together. "Marvelous, Mummy."

"It's the right decision, Granny," Sebastian confirms.

"As long as no one steals anything, breaks anything, or stows themselves away in a cabinet to smother us in our beds at night," Geraldine warns.

I press my lips together to stifle a giggle. What planet does Geraldine live on?

"We'll do our best to avoid all such threats. I promise," Sebastian says, his eyes dancing. "There is another idea we've been discussing."

"What's that, darling?" Jemima asks.

"I'm in preliminary discussions with the *Dating Mr. Darcy* production company about doing another reality television show."

"You are?" Zara asks as Granny grumps, "Good Lord, Sebastian! Why on Earth would you do something as incomprehensible as that?" and Jemima looks at her son blankly.

"Because, Granny, we need to explore all avenues, and they're interested in making a show out of our efforts to save our home. We kill two birds with one stone and make some good money."

"I thought you might be looking for a new Miss Elizabeth Bennet," Granny says as she shoots me a pointed look.

Nice, Geraldine. Real nice.

Sebastian ignores the jibe. "Granny, I found my Miss Elizabeth Bennet already, and I'm delighted she has agreed to be my wife."

I glow inside. Sebastian is protecting me. Okay, it's only against the wrath of his eighty-year-old granny, but he's protecting me all the same.

"Well, I don't like the idea of more reality television one iota," she sniffs.

"It could be lucrative, Granny. Hear me out."

As Sebastian talks his family through the idea, I feel a growing sense of excitement. I might not be a Huntington-Ross or Lady of the Manor yet, but I've got a head on my shoulders, and together we're presenting a united front. We're a team. We're Lord and Lady of the Manor. Lord and Lady Martinston.

Nope, that still sounds weird to me. But I know I'll get used to it, and together, we will do our best to save this house.

Chapter Five

The following morning, I wake up determined to win Geraldine over. Once she gets to know me, she'll get past the fact I'm American and not from some aristocratic family. She won't be able to help herself from liking me. Well, that's the hope, anyway. I plan on dazzling her with my winning personality, my quick wit, and my high degree of worldliness.

And failing that, I'll just tell her how amazing she is every five minutes.

I throw on some Timothy activewear and head out into the refreshing morning air. The rest of the house is still sleeping, so I pad along the corridor and down the staircase as quietly as I can, shoes in hand. Once outside, I breath in the fresh country air and make my way through the ornate formal gardens, past the water fountain, and across the lawn toward the pretty pond.

I pull my phone out from my arm band and dial.

"Well, if it's not Soon-to-be Mrs. Darcy herself."

"Kennedy Bennet. It's great so to hear your voice," I say as I smile, thinking about my *Dating Mr. Darcy* bestie. "I'm back at Martinston, and it's made me think of you, like it always does."

"You mean you remember when you were sneaking around with Sebastian on *Dating Mr. Darcy* behind everyone's backs?" she teases. "I gotta tell you, I do not miss that show."

"Tell me about it."

"Babe, you ended up getting the guy. You've got nothing to complain about."

"You mean other than the fact the public wanted him to marry Phoebe and they think I'm a total idiot?"

She laughs. "Who cares what they think? You two fell in love. You're getting married. You got the fairy-tale ending, girl."

My mind turns to Geraldine. "I know I'm lucky, and I'm so happy."

"But?"

"It's Seb's granny. She's not my biggest fan. Actually, she's not a fan at all."

"How can she not be? You're awesome."

"Can you come stay with me here? I need a cheerleader," I joke.

"Actually, funny you should mention it. I've got a new job, and I've got some time off before I start. I was thinking of coming over a week or so before Phoebe's wedding."

"Here? Seriously?"

"If you think that'll be okay? I'll go to London and Paris and a bunch of places I've dreamt about all my life, too."

"Of course it's okay! I would love to have you here."

"It's a plan. What's his granny's problem with you, anyway?"

"Where do I start?"

She lets out a laugh. "That bad, huh?"

"Oh, yeah. Let's see—I'm American, I'm not from an aristocratic family, Seb met me on a dating show, oh, and the worst part, I'm marrying her favorite grandchild."

"Isn't it enough for her that Sebastian loves you?"

I pant lightly as I climb the rise to the pergola where Sebastian proposed to me. "That would be way too uncomplicated."

"What does she like to do?"

"Look down her nose at me and use words I don't understand."

"I mean other than that."

"I dunno. Regular rich person stuff?"

"Why don't you invite her to something she enjoys? She's got to have hobbies, right? I know you're real good at bowls," she says with a laugh.

My giggle ends in a snort as I think of the bowls game we competed in on *Dating Mr. Darcy*. I wasn't a natural, let's just put it that way. "Definitely not bowls, but you know, you might be onto something there with the whole hobbies thing."

"Good. Now, let's talk about when I can come visit. Just imagine Sebastian's granny with not one but two loud Americans in the house."

"She'll probably ask the British prime minister to declare war on the States and have us sent to a prisoner of war camp."

"OMG, girl! Is it that bad?"

"Maybe I'm being a touch dramatic."

We talk for a while longer as I make my way through to the forest before my tummy begins to rumble and I turn back toward the house. No sooner have I slotted my phone back into my arm holder when it beeps again.

How's my girl? I miss your pretty face xoxo

I smile to myself and fire off a quick reply.
I miss you, too, Mom. Everything okay?
Everything's fine, honey.
Will call you soon, I promise xoxo
Make sure you do. I miss you!

Right now, I've got some research to do. Operation Win Granny Over is locked and loaded, and I'm determined to make it work.

After breakfast, I grab Sebastian before he heads to the station to catch the London train. He's managed to take some time off this week, but he's still got his job at the bank in "The City" to go to.

"I invited Kennedy to come stay in a couple weeks. Is that okay?"

"Of course."

"Will it be weird to have one of the contestants from the show here again? I mean, you did take her on a date."

"Phoebe was here only a few days ago, remember?"

"Of course," I reply with a laugh. "Hey, changing the subject...what does your granny like to do? Like, her hobbies or whatever?"

"She loves to walk the garden. She tended to the roses for years before her hip replacement."

"What else? I'm thinking movies, I'm thinking shopping. You know, things I could do with her."

"Nice idea, Brady. She loves the opera, but I don't think she's been in some time, I think."

I swallow. "Opera?"

He chuckles. "Not your cup of tea?"

"Not exactly. But hey, it could be? I've never been before. I prefer soap operas to the real deal. Give me James Scott from *Days of Our Lives* any day of the week."

"Who is this James Scott guy, and do I need to have words with him?" Sebastian jokes.

I plant a kiss on his cheek. "No, you're good."

He slings his laptop bag over his shoulder. "Don't offer to watch a soap opera with Granny, whatever you do."

"No soap opera. Got it."

"Perhaps you could invite her to an actual opera. Now, I've really got to go." He leans down and kisses me. "See you for dinner tonight."

I grin at him. "Totally. And I'll look into what operas are on in London, too. You're coming as my back up."

"Anything for you. You know that."

With Sebastian gone, I google operas in London, and am excited to learn that not only are there operas playing at fancy London theaters, but there are still some available tickets. Score!

After getting changed into a pretty summer dress and cardigan, I read up on two operas and their composer so that I can come across as knowledgeable as possible, and then I set about to find Geraldine. This plan has got to work. She'll like how thoughtful I'm being by inviting her to something she loves, and I'll dazzle her with my newfound knowledge.

I find her and Jemima sitting together on one of the garden benches over by the fountain. I scrape my fingers through my hair and take a deep breath.

Rip off the Band-Aid, Emma.

"Good morning, ladies," I say brightly as I approach them. "Isn't it a lovely day?" As I say it, the sun slips behind a dark cloud, and we're thrown into instant gloom.

Come on, Mother Nature. Help me out here.

Jemima greets me with a warm smile. "Emma. How are you today?"

"Wonderful, thank you," I reply. "I wanted to ask you if

you'd both like to come to the opera with Sebastian and me. I can get four tickets for Friday, and I thought it'd be fun for us all to go together."

I turn to Geraldine in anticipation, hoping she'll be touched that I'm inviting her to something she loves. But, by the look on her face right now, the only thing that's touching her is the wooden seat below her bottom.

"Emma, that's so sweet of you," Jemima coos. "Isn't that sweet, Geraldine."

Geraldine arches an eyebrow, her watery blue eyes trained on me. "Very sweet."

"I'm so sorry to tell you I have a prior arrangement on Friday, so I won't be able to come. But you can, can't you, Mummy?"

I try not to giggle at her use of the word "Mummy."
Mature? Me?

"Which opera is it, and where is it being performed?" Geraldine asks as she rises to her feet.

"We've got a choice, actually, ma'am," I reply, pulling out the Texas manners my mom taught me. "There's a German opera called *Tannhäuser*, which looks quite long and serious, even though the name made me think it was about a spray tan business." I grin at them both, but when they don't return it, I add, "Get it? Tan house? As in a spray tan?"

I'd hoped for at least a small acknowledgement of my joke, which I thought was at least worthy of a smile. But I'm met with a look of curiosity from Jemima, and a further tightening of the lips from Geraldine. Seriously, if this woman were to tighten those already thin lips of hers any further, they'd disappear into her face altogether, never to be seen again. She'd be the Lipless Wonder of Martinston.

Yup, I'm feeling *super* mature today.

"That was a little joke," I explain, feeling increasingly awkward. And if you've got to explain a joke...

I press on. I'm on a mission here, after all. "In case you don't know the opera, it's by a guy called Richard Wagner. I'm not sure if he's related to Robert Wagner, but if he is, he's Hollywood royalty."

"Richard *Vah*-gner," Geraldine corrects in her superior tone, "was a 19th century German composer, my dear girl. I very much doubt he is related to anything to do with Hollywood."

"Of course. That makes perfect sense," I reply hastily, kicking myself for mispronouncing his name. And I suggested he's related to the bad guy on the *Austin Powers* movies! But seriously, why would they spell it *Wagner* if it's pronounced "*Vah*-gner"?

It's a trick for young players, that's what that is.

"Anyway, the other opera we can go to is called *Les Mamelles de Tirésias*. It's French, and I'm sure I've mispronounced it."

"Ah, Poulenc," Geraldine says knowingly, pronouncing the composer's name as though she were a French native. "One of the more unusual operas."

"Unusual good?" I chance.

"It certainly makes one think," she replies elusively.

"Well, both operas are being put on in London, and I thought we could choose one and go together." I look hopefully at Geraldine.

"Mummy?" Jemima enquires. "That would be lovely, wouldn't it? You could get to know Emma a little better and enjoy some opera while you do it. You haven't been to town for a while."

I would kiss Jemima right now if it didn't make me look too grateful—and too desperate.

Geraldine pauses for a moment, her lips making a brief appearance when she replies, "Thank you, Emma. I would like to go to *Les Mamelles de Tirésias*," she says, and I could punch the air. Which I don't do of course. I know such brash American behavior would go down with her about as well as a plateful of boiled Brussels sprouts would for me.

Ugh.

"I think you'll find the opera most illuminating."

"Okay, cool."

"With Jemima not able to attend, did you want to invite someone in her stead?" she asks.

"Oh, uh." I wrack my brain for an appropriate invitee. Phoebe will be too busy with the wedding, and Zara's not home this weekend. The only other friend I've made here is Jilly. "I might invite Jilly," I say and hold my breath.

"Oh, Jilly's a darling," Jemima says with a smile. "A wonderful choice, Emma. I know she enjoys the opera, too. What do you think, Mummy?"

"As Jemima says. A wonderful choice."

"Good. That's all set then," I say. "I'll arrange everything. All you've gotta do is throw on your Sunday best."

Geraldine regards me for a moment before she replies, "Quite."

Her English reserve firmly in place, I thank her and tell her I'll let her know all the details closer to the day. I trip away back into the house knowing Operation Win Granny Over may have stalled, but we're back on track. And this time it's going to work.

Chapter Six

Friday night swings around after days of me trying to get *someone* in this country to take a meeting to discuss carrying Timothy in their stores. I've sent emails and left messages for purchasing managers at a bunch of large sports stores, none of which have been returned, and I'm beginning to get seriously frustrated. Although we've had to work hard to get where we are in the US, at least we've gotten somewhere. Here it feels like I'm having to start again from the very bottom, a tiny tadpole in a pond of oversized frogs.

But tonight isn't about my career frustrations. I need to put all that aside. Tonight is about winning Geraldine over.

Just as I googled *Vah*-gner and Poulenc (still no idea how to pronounce that one right) to scrub up on my opera knowledge—okay, *get* some opera knowledge—I google what to wear to the opera in London. The search results are not overly helpful. The answer seems to be anywhere between floor length gowns to a tidy pair of jeans. But, knowing what a traditionalist Geraldine is, I plump for a borrowed ball-gown from Jilly, and a sparkly jacket that I think makes me look like a housewife out for her one big night of the year, but which Jilly assures me is completely appropriate for the opera.

I choose my opera outfit with great care. I'm not turning up to this thing looking all wrong. No way. I need to show Geraldine that I'm a composed, classy, refined young lady, totally worthy of her grandson's affections.

Well, that's the plan, anyway.

I check my appearance in the mirror and then turn to face Jilly. "How do I look?"

"Emma, you absolutely look the part," she says to me as she perches on the end of the four-poster bed. She's dressed in a gorgeous burnt orange silk gown, an impressive array of diamonds around her neck. "Although I think the tiara might be a bit much."

I touch the tiara atop my head. I'd bought it from a costume jewelry store for less than my updo cost at the local village hairdresser. It might be a little less Kate Middleton and more "little girl's princess birthday tiara," but I wanted to go all out to impress Geraldine. "I thought I looked a little like a princess."

"Exactly, darling. Tiaras are generally the preserve of royalty or brides in this country."

"Or beauty queens," I add.

"That too. Yours looks...well, my advice is to take it off."

I extract the tiara from my updo. "Done. Everything else okay?"

She sweeps her gaze over me. "Twirl," she instructs before she declares, "Perfect."

"Thank you so much for lending me this outfit. I've never been to the opera, so I had no idea what to wear. Wearing this fancy dress reminds me of the last time I wore a floor-length dress in this house. It was on the show. I was dressed as Lizzie Bennet in her Regency finery, right down to the bloomers."

"Bloomers?" She pulls a face. "How ghastly." She hops off the bed, adjusts the skirt of her dress, and says, "Let's go down to the others."

Downstairs in the reception room, Sebastian greets me with a kiss, telling me how gorgeous I look.

"Not bad yourself, fiancé," I reply, admiring how his tux fits him to perfection. "Is that the tux you were wearing the night we met?"

"It is, and although I thought you were cute in your activewear that evening, you look even more enchanting this evening."

"Doesn't Emma look just darling?" Jilly says at my side. "So appropriate for the opera. Don't you think, Geraldine?"

I shoot Jilly a look. I appreciate her support and all, but could she be any less subtle?

I smile at Geraldine. "Ma'am, you look beautiful tonight," I say to her. She too is in a floor-length dress, hers black velvet, highlighting her silver hair. She's got about twenty strands of pearls around her neck. Okay, not twenty exactly, but there are a lot. What can I say? Much like the Queen, she's a woman who's fond of pearls.

"Thank you, Emma," she replies stiffly. "You do look quite enchanting in that dress."

I blush at the unexpected compliment. Geraldine approves of something about me! "Thank you so much," I gush. "I feel like a princess in this."

"I imagine Jilly did, too, when she wore it to the Windsor gala evening last month."

Shot down.

"Right. Of course."

Sebastian kisses me on the cheek. "She looks gorgeous, Granny, and you know it."

She ignores his response. "My grandson tells me you've booked us a car. I had rather expected you'd want us to take the train and the Tube. I thought maybe public transport was more your speed, Emma, what with being an American tourist here."

I ignore the jibe. "Nothing but the best for us tonight."

Sebastian slips an arm around my waist. "Emma's not a tourist, Granny. She lives here now."

Granny's jaw tightens a fraction. "Of course."

"Shall we go? The car should be here any minute."

Luckily for me, it arrives as we step out of the house onto the front steps. Sebastian helps his granny into the car, and together the four of us are driven into the bright lights of the city. I sit holding my fiancé's hand as Jilly chats away to Geraldine about people I don't know.

"This is such a kind thing to do for Granny," Sebastian says quietly to me, his breath tingling my neck. "I know opera is hardly your thing."

"Who knows? It might be after tonight. I'm super keen to get in her good books."

"Oh, I'd say you're doing that tonight."

I shoot him a grin. "I hope you're right."

The car pulls up by the theater, and I gaze up at the building with its unlikely combination of traditional classical architecture and modern glass. "Wow, this place is amazing," I exclaim. Because it is. The old part of it looks like something from Roman times, even though I can tell it's in much too good a state to be two thousand years old. The rest of the building is all modern glass, the interior lights glowing inside.

"It is quite something," Sebastian says.

"It's preposterous what they've done with all this glass," Geraldine grumps. "This is an opera house, not Kew Gardens."

"Ignore her," Sebastian says to me. "My grandmother has got something against buildings made of glass. Haven't you, Granny? You think it should be the preserve of glasshouses in order to grow plants."

"Quite," she replies.

We join the throngs as they enter the building, and I notice many people are dressed in smart casual, but there are a bunch who are dolled up like us. And Geraldine seems to know each and every one.

"Darling, how are you?" Geraldine air kisses one woman who is so elderly and frail, she makes Geraldine look like a sprightly youngster. Well, relatively speaking. The woman *is* eighty.

"You would not believe how happy I am to see you well after all that frightful television business," the woman replies. "Did it take a dreadful toll on you, Gerry?" She glances up at Sebastian. "Oh, Sebastian. You're here. Are *you* quite recovered, too?"

"There was nothing to recover from, Lady Kirkpatrick." He greets her with a kiss to the cheek, and I swear the woman blushes. "I'd like you to meet Emma Brady, my fiancée. Emma, this is Lady Kirkpatrick."

Her barely perceptible eyebrows ping up as she regards me through widened eyes.

"How do you do, Lady Kirkpatrick," I say as though I'm Eliza Doolittle in *My Fair Lady* practicing her best rounded vowels. It sounds weird, even to my ears, and I catch Sebastian's lips twinge in amusement out of the corner of my eye.

"Oh. You're *American*," she replies.

So much for Eliza Doolittle.

Marrying Mr. Darcy

"She is American, Mary. You are quite right," Geraldine says. "Sebastian met her on that television show."

Her eyebrows leap up again to join her thinning hairline as her eyes bulge. Any more surprises and I suspect Mary Kirkpatrick's eyeballs will pop clean out of her face and slap onto some unsuspecting theatergoer. Keeping her focus on me, she clutches onto the suit fabric on one of Sebastian's arms.

"Are you quite all right, Lady Kirkpatrick?" he asks.

She pulls him down to her height—which is w*aaa*y low for the guy—and says, "My granddaughter, Bexley, has recently returned from a stint with some sort of computer company in India."

"Has she indeed?"

"She's awfully clever, you know, and very pretty. Well, in certain lights or when you squint a little, anyway."

It's clear Sebastian knows precisely what she's getting at when he replies, "I remember Bexley well. Do send her my best when next you see her." He takes my hand in his, and her eyes dart over to me briefly.

She lets go of his arm. "I see." Her gaze lands on me once more, and I resist the urge to shrink into my borrowed dress.

Instead, I shoot her my most winning smile, and say, "I'm looking forward to this opera tonight. Are you a fan of Francis Poulenc's, Lady Killpatrick."

"Kirkpatrick," Sebastian mutters under his breath.

"Kirkpatrick. Lady *Kirk*patrick. That's what I meant. Not *Kill*patrick. Who's that? No one I know, that's for sure."

Stop, Emma. For the love of God, stop.

"Of course I'm a fan," she replies in a tone that suggests no one in their right mind wouldn't be a fan of Francis

Poulenc's, a guy I'd never even heard of before I began my research.

She turns her back on me, and she and Geraldine begin to talk among themselves. Probably about how wildly inappropriate for Sebastian I am.

"Well, that went super well," I say to Sebastian.

"Forget about Lady Kirkpatrick. She's narrow minded and thinks the US should never have got away from the kingdom," he replies. "She disapproves of everything and everyone."

"Seb, she blatantly tried to set you up with her granddaughter. Right in front of me."

"She did do that," Jilly confirms. She's been hanging in the wings this whole time.

Sebastian rubs my arm. "Ignore her. Let's focus on having a nice evening."

I glance at Geraldine's back. She's now got another couple of elderly ladies in a huddle, and I bet I know the topic of their conversation.

Double, double toil and trouble.

Shakespeare's witches had nothing on this bunch.

A bell tolls, and the crowd moves toward the doors leading into the auditorium.

Sebastian—brave man that he is—interrupts his granny's gossipfest, and the four of us make our way into the auditorium to find our seats.

Inside, the place is incredible, and I can't help but stop and gawp at the surrounds. Everything is gold, red, and white, with a huge, ornate white ceiling with gilded details and rich red curtain over the stage. Standing here, it feels like stepping back in time, and I could almost expect to see the Darcys on a date here, out for an evening of opera in their Regency finery.

But then I remind myself they're fictional characters from a book, and I'm here to win Geraldine over, not get lost in an Austen-induced fantasy.

We take our seats in the Grand Tier with a direct, uninterrupted view of the stage, and I'm secretly ecstatic I managed to get such good seats. Of course, they cost me an arm and a leg, but I'm hoping the quality of their position won't be lost on Geraldine. I've got Sebastian on one side of me, and Geraldine and Jilly on the other.

"Have you seen this opera live before?" I ask Geraldine as I try to put the whole witches brew thing aside. But my nerves are heightened now, and I need to try to push through to make this evening a success.

"Naturally. I've made it a habit to attend opera as often as I can. My family has been great patrons for many years."

"Oh, I thought Seb's dad's foundation was for artists who paint and stuff."

Paint and stuff? *Smooth, Emma.*

"No, dear, I mean *my* family. I was a Pentiskew before I married into the Huntington-Ross family."

"Right. Pentiskew. Gotcha."

We fall into silence as I struggle to think of a topic that doesn't involve me sticking my big foot in it again.

Why does this have to be so hard?

Jilly comes to my rescue. "Do you know, I saw one of your grandnieces last week," she says to Geraldine. "Fenella. She's a darling, isn't she? So grown up now. Emma, you must meet Fenella. I'm certain you'll get on famously."

"She sounds great," I reply.

"She's in her last year at Badminton shortly," Geraldine says. "We're very proud of her achievements."

"She plays badminton, huh? I played it in high school. I

was quite good, actually," I say, glad they're talking about something I know about for a change.

"Badminton is a girls' boarding school, Emma," Jilly explains kindly.

"Oh, right."

"Tell me, Emma," Geraldine begins, "does your family patronize any of the arts?"

I think of my mom and my cat, Frank. "The only patronizing that goes on in my family is when Frank deigns to allow me to pet him," I joke.

"How charming," she replies, clearly not charmed in the least.

I exhale as I shoot Sebastian a look.

He takes my hand in his and gives it a squeeze. "I know she's not easy," he says quietly so only I can hear him. "Just relax and enjoy tonight, okay? I'll have a chat with her tomorrow."

"No!" I exclaim too loudly, and several people around us turn to stare. I throw them a sheepish smile and say, "Sorry. I'm just excited about this opera, I guess."

They smile at me as if I'm some kind of looney-tunes and turn back around.

"It's gone on long enough," Sebastian says. "I think it's only right I do something about this. I don't want you to feel unwelcome in my home. In *our* home."

"I don't, honestly."

"She's a stubborn old goat, and she needs a little coaxing to see what the rest of us already do," Sebastian whispers into my ear.

I beam at him, my heart contracting. "You're the best, did you know that?"

He gives my knee a squeeze. "I've been told."

I look down at my program and begin to read the synopsis. After seeing the translation of the opera's name, I turn to Sebastian in alarm. "Did you know *mamalles* is French for breasts?" I whisper.

"Yes."

"But this is terrible!"

"Why?"

Through gritted teeth I reply, "Because I've taken your granny to an opera about boobs!"

He chuckles lightly. "If you think that's terrible, you're in for a treat with this one."

"What? Why?"

"Brady, this opera is a farcical take on the French post-World War II stance on repopulation. It's fairly *avant garde*."

I cock an eyebrow. "Can you say that in English, please."

"People die in wars, right? And then you need babies. Read the synopsis."

Dang it! I was too concerned with learning what to wear to the opera and how to behave. I didn't even find out what this one was all about.

As I return my attention to the synopsis, the music begins, and a hush descends. I look up, nervous about what we're about to see. But it can't be that bad, can it? Sebastian or Jilly would definitely have told me if this opera was a mistake.

The overture plays for a while, and then, as the first performers enter the stage, I heave a sigh of relief when they begin to sing. It's just an opera, sung in a foreign language. I'm sure women's appendages won't feature all that much.

Wrong. Wrong. Wrong.

A woman in a full-body leotard that is doing nothing for her curves sings a long song with a couple of balloons stuck to her chest. And then, just when I thought that was about as weird as this thing was going to get, she detaches the balloons and waves as they float away.

"What was that about?" I ask Sebastian.

"The balloons represent her breasts."

"You're kidding me."

He shakes his head. "She's now going to pretend to be a man."

"Do you mean the guy she's tied up and is putting in a dress right now?"

"That's the one."

I glance at Geraldine. She's watching the stage avidly, a pair of elegant opera binoculars in her hand. At least one of us is getting into this, I think as I settle back against my seat. I've just got to hope there aren't any more balloon breasts floating around the stage.

The rest of the first act steams ahead with nothing stranger than a guy in drag who everyone fully believes is a woman (observant much?), and a couple of guys apparently killing each other.

Nothing to see here.

At the end of the first act we have a short recess in which Geraldine springs out of her seat—well, as much as an eighty-year-old can spring, which is more like a creaking rise on arthritic knees—and leaves us to chat with friends.

I stand up to stretch my legs, and Jilly asks, "How are you enjoying the opera?"

"It's very thought provoking," I reply, by which of course I mean it's totally out there and I wish I was at home, snuggled up to Sebastian and Frank on the couch, watching a normal movie in which women's breasts stay on their chests.

"Thought provoking is one way to put it," Sebastian says

with a laugh. "I've not seen this opera before, although I know the story, of course."

"Of course," Jilly confirms as though an opera about floating boobs and men in drag is part of every high school curriculum.

"Do you think Geraldine's enjoying herself?" I ask her.

"Oh, I'm certain she is. She loves all opera, even these, shall we say, more *avant garde* ones."

"And by *avant garde* you mean weird, right?"

"Less usual."

The lights flash a few times around us, indicating the second act is about to begin, Geraldine returns, and we all take our seats once more.

"Are you enjoying the opera?" I ask her as she settles into her seat next to me.

"I am, thank you. I'm interested to see how they handle the birth of the forty thousand or so babies in this next act, of course."

"Of course," I reply, working hard to keep my composure, while inside my head I'm screaming "forty thousand babies?! On a freaking stage?"

The curtain flies up to the sound of voices crying "Papaaaah! Papaaaah!" and I watch, my jaw slack, as a sea of grown men and women scatter across the stage, with caps on their heads that would make Mrs. Watson proud, balloons in their hands, and wearing nothing but adult diapers.

Adult diapers, people!

Balloon boobs floating away was one thing, but a guy singing about giving birth to tens of thousands of babies in diapers and holding balloons is a whole other level.

I begin to lose it. I'm not proud. Really, I'm not. I'm a fully grown woman, not a prepubescent tween giggling with her friends. But as the "babies" pop their balloons and fall to the ground, what was once a small snigger percolating away grows and grows and grows until it's an oversized laugh, eager to get out. I press my lips together in a vain attempt to stifle it, but that laugh is not giving up.

A weird sound, kind of like a cross between a hyena and a banshee, emanates from me. "*Hhhhhhhmmmmmmmm.*"

Sebastian shoots me a sideways look. "Are you okay, Brady?"

"Mmm-hmm," I reply. There's no way on this sweet Earth I'm opening my mouth right now.

"You sure? You're making strange noises, and you've gone all pink."

I fan myself with my hands. I want to tell him I'm fine, but then I want to *not* be having this giggling fit, as well.

Neither of these things happen.

Instead, I make the absolutely fatal error of glancing at the stage once more. And there they are, the man and his "babies," all still singing happily away, bouncing, crawling, and playing on the floor.

I'm done for.

"You're having a giggling fit, aren't you?" Sebastian whispers into my ear.

I nod as tears begin to fall down my cheeks, my stomach muscles aching. I make that weird noise again.

"I can't blame you. Go. Laugh it off. Come back when you're ready."

I give him a quick succession of nods before I do exactly as he suggests because I have *got* to get out of here before I explode. And *fast*.

Chapter Seven

Holding in a laugh that could shatter the Hoover Dam, I stand bolt upright from my seat between Geraldine and Sebastian. I clamber over my fiancé and a very grumpy looking couple—there's no way I'm going the other direction and have to crawl over my future grandmother-in-law—and into the aisle. I know Geraldine will be appalled at me getting up like this during a performance, but better that than a full-on laughing fit in my seat.

With my hand over my mouth in the hopes it can somehow stem the laughter flow, I rush up the steps as fast as my heels will take me, making my weird hyena-slash-banshee noises as I do.

I burst through the double doors and instantly the laughter that's been bubbling furiously inside me bursts out like the world's biggest sneeze. I laugh and laugh, all the tension and hilarity of the situation gushing out of me as I clutch my sides, deeply thankful to be out of the auditorium, away from Geraldine's judgmental eyes and, most of all, away from the lunacy on the stage.

I reach the bar, panting like I've run a marathon, where I lean as I try to recover.

"Are you all right?" an amused voice says beside me. "Only, you sound like you might need an ambulance. Or a double shot of vodka."

With my laughter still pouring out of me, I wipe my eyes and look up to see a guy smiling at me over a glass of something on ice, a perfect-teeth grin on his tan face.

"Excuse me?" I manage to ask, impressed I can form words once more rather than the "*Hhhhmmmmm*" of before.

"I'm just checking you're okay. You came rushing in here like a hurricane, and well, if I'm totally honest, you sound kinda hysterical."

I open my mouth to reply then shut it again.

"And now, you look like you're doing a fish impersonation. Yup, you need help." He gets the barman's attention and says, "She'll have one of these," holding up his glass.

"Right you are, mate," the server replies.

As he prepares the drink, Mr. Smiley moves over to me and plunks himself down on a barstool. "Have a seat."

I let out a relieved puff of air that I'm now back in control and gladly take the seat. "Thanks. I will."

"So, tell me your story. Are you a woman on the edge or just found something really, really funny?"

"You're American," I say in surprise, finally working out what's different about this guy—and getting past his movie star good looks. If you mixed DNA from Channing Tatum and Liam Hemsworth, and threw in Bradley Cooper's blue eyes, you'd get this guy sitting next to me right now.

"Smart, beautiful, *and* maybe a little crazy," he replies as he takes a sip of his drink. "My perfect combination in a woman."

Marrying Mr. Darcy

Is this guy hitting on me?

"Not crazy," I reply, feeling about as articulate as a snail.

The server places a drink on the bar in front of me. "Here you go, miss. Vodka on the rocks."

"Err, thanks." I reach for my purse. I'm not sure I exactly need alcohol after my outburst a moment ago, but it's ordered now, so I guess I should pay.

"I'll get it," Mr. Smiley says, giving the server some cash and instructing him to keep the change. He lifts his glass. "Cheers."

"Cheers," I reply lifting my own before I take a sip. "Thanks for the drink."

"You're welcome. So, tell me. If you're not crazy, you must have found something real funny. Can you tell me what it was?"

I let the cool liquid slip down my throat, relieved the overwhelming desire to laugh has subsided. "Tell me that opera is not insane. A man gives birth to forty-thousand or so babies, all on the same day. I mean, hello?"

"It is kinda out there, I've gotta agree."

"Out there? Oh, for sure. And the babies, which were people in adult diapers. What was *that* all about?" I let out a fresh giggle at the thought.

"I believe they're the man-mother's babies, who all came out as adults with careers."

"Seriously?" I shake my head. "That Poulenc guy must have been smoking something pretty mind-altering when he wrote this opera. Are all operas like this?"

He gives me a knowing look. "Ah. You're an opera virgin."

"I am."

"Figures."

"Why?"

"You're not an octogenarian for starters. There are a lot of them here, you may have noticed."

I think about Geraldine and her friends and of the rows of gray heads that were in front of us in the auditorium. "Oh, yeah. I noticed that."

"You're also not some British toff who thinks going to the opera will make them look super smart and educated. Plus, you were laughing like a hyena on caffeine a couple minutes back, so it's obvious to me this ain't exactly your jam."

"A hyena on caffeine?" I reply, thinking that's exactly what I thought I'd sounded like myself, only without the caffeine. "Thank you very much." I feign offence, but really I'm glad I've met someone who gets it.

"Would you prefer I said you laughed like a deranged witch around a cauldron?"

My giggle ends in a snort as I'm reminded of Geraldine and her friends. "No. That would be way worse."

"Then I suggest you take the hyena comment and run." He extends his hand. "I'm Chris Hampshire, by the way."

I take his hand and shake it. "Emma Brady."

"So, Emma Brady, did you also enjoy the soprano whose voice could shatter all The Gherkin's windows in one note?"

"What's The Gherkin?"

He raises his eyebrows. "You don't know what The Gherkin is? You *are* new around here. Fresh off the boat, huh?"

"I've just moved here from Houston, Texas."

"A Texan gal," he says, and I wait for him to make the usual comment about cowboys or *Dallas*, but he doesn't. "The Gherkin is the affectionate name given to that tall

Marrying Mr. Darcy

green glass building in the City, mainly because it looks like a giant gherkin."

"So, I take it it's not a trick name?"

He laughs, and his whole face lights up, his Bradley Cooper eyes twinkling. "You got it."

The volume of music coming from the theater grows as one of the singers reaches a particularly loud note, and I wonder if the second act is about to come to an end.

"Aren't you glad you're missing *that*?" Chris asks, gesturing at the doors. "Man, he's got to blow after that effort."

"I think I'll stay here for a while longer. I can't trust myself to go back in there and not get the giggles again."

"I'm with you on that, although I'm out here propping up the bar for an entirely different reason."

"What's that?"

"I think the technical term is 'boredom.'"

"So, you're not an opera buff either."

"Do I look like an opera buff?"

I size him up. In his navy suit and open-neck pale blue shirt, he looks stylish and modern. "Actually, you do."

"Ha! You don't even know me, and you're insulting me. Not cool, Texas. Not cool."

"Are you saying I need to get to know you before I can insult you?"

As the words fall out of my mouth, I realize how flirty they sound, and I instantly edge away from him. It doesn't matter that he's built like Channing Tatum, has Liam Hemsworth's jawline, with Bradley Cooper's eyes. I'm in love with Sebastian. There's no way I'm going to intentionally flirt with anyone else.

If he notices my sudden retreat, he doesn't mention it. Instead, he says, "Insult me all you like. I can take it."

I take a gulp of my drink, the cool liquid slipping down my throat.

"What brings a Texan gal to England? Other than your love of the opera, clearly."

"I came here for love," I reply simply, and instantly feel weirdly relieved I get to talk about Sebastian to this guy.

Where did *that* come from?

"Love, huh? I thought you might have moved here to work at The Gherkin."

"I just got engaged, actually." I flash him my ring, and to my surprise he takes my hand in his and examines it.

"Impressive. Who's the lucky guy?"

"His name is Sebastian. He's English. I'm here with him and his granny, actually."

Still holding my hand, he glances around the bar, empty but for him, me, and the server cleaning glasses. "Emma, I'm concerned. First you have a giggling fit then you tell me you're engaged to some guy called Sebastian who it seems is invisible. Tell me, is this fiancé of yours imaginary?"

I laugh as I pull my hand away. I'm not going to sit next to some guy in a bar, holding his hand. "Of course he's not. He's in the theater."

"I see. So, is he an octogenarian or just a toff who thinks liking opera will make him look smarter than he is?"

"He's neither, thank you very much," I sniff, although I admit I'm enjoying our chat. After the stress of trying—and failing once again—to impress Geraldine, it's nice to simply have some fun. Fun that's got nothing to do with the Huntington-Rosses. Even if things were getting a little unintentionally flirty a moment ago.

Inside the theatre, the music has come to a stop, and I can hear the audience applauding.

"Drink up, Texas," Chris instructs as he downs the rest

of his own drink. "We need to face the opera buffs, and take it from me, it's best to do that with some alcohol in your bloodstream."

The doors to the theater burst open, and people begin to pour out, their chatter filling the hall. I search the crowd for Sebastian, Jilly, and Geraldine.

"There you are, Emma," Jilly says, rushing over to me. She stops in her tracks when her eyes land on Chris. "Oh. It's you," she says, breathless.

"That's a fine way to greet your favorite ex," Chris replies with a cheeky grin.

Wait, *what?* Chris and Jilly dated?

He gets to his feet and kisses a bewildered-looking Jilly on the cheek. "You're looking gorgeous as always, Jill. I always loved you in orange."

"Err, thank you," she replies in an uncharacteristically timid way, color rising in her cheeks.

"You two know one another?" I ask them. Which is the dumbest question ever, considering they've just greeted one another and Chris said that Jilly's his ex.

Chris slings his arm around Jilly's shoulders, and she tightens up like a sailor's knot. "Jill and I know each other well, don't we?"

"Uh, yes, yes we do," she replies curtly as she removes his arm from her shoulders. "You've been out here practicing your lines on my friend Emma, have you? Because you needn't waste your time, you know, Chris. Emma's *engaged.*"

"And it's a stunning ring," he replies with a smirk, totally disarming her.

"Yes. Well. Quite," she replies, ruffled.

"Chris and I met when I had to leave the theater," I explain to her. "I didn't think I could go back in."

"Why? All I knew was you started to make strange sounds, and the next thing I knew you'd bolted like a horse from the stables."

"I had a giggling fit with all the opera insanity, and I *had* to get out of there. Chris helped me pass the time."

"He's good at that." She shoots him a disapproving look, and I'm dying to ask what happened between them. I've never seen Jilly thrown like this.

"Where's Seb?" I ask her.

"He got caught up with Geraldine and some of her acquaintances back there. I'm sure he'll be along in a minute."

A girl dressed in a black strapless, satin dress, who looks like she fell off the cover of *Vogue* magazine, appears behind Chris and drapes her long arms over his shoulders, leaning against his back. "Chris. Why did you have to leave? I was stuck in there with my parents when all I wanted to do was be with you."

He pulls her around, and she drops onto his lap, all fifty pounds of her. "You know me, babe. I can't stand all that insane bellowing."

"Buy me a drink, and I'll forgive you," she coos, so easily won over I can't help but judge her a little (and yes, I know I judged her as super skinny the moment she arrived, but that's only because I've never in my life looked like that and wish I could).

"Of course," Chris replies. "This is Clementine, by the way. Meet Emma and Jill, two of my dearest friends."

I blink at him. Dearest friends? I met the guy ten minutes ago.

We all say hello to one another, Clementine giving me the weakest, floppiest handshake of my life. With her appearance, Jilly seems to relax a notch.

Marrying Mr. Darcy

"Anyone else for a drink?" Chris asks, and we both shake our heads.

With his back turned—and Clementine draped over him once more, presumably because she's so long and willowy, standing for any period of time is super tricky—I whisper in Jilly's ear, "What's the deal with you and Chris?"

"I should be asking you the same thing," she whispers back.

"There's no deal. I just met him at the bar when I left, and he bought me a drink."

Her eyes widen. "Did he now?"

"Jilly, it's fine. It's just a drink. He was out here avoiding the opera, too."

"Actually, you need to know that Chris is not exactly what you'd call a good egg."

I lean in, eager to hear all about it, when I feel a warm hand on my shoulder. I look up into Sebastian's smiling face.

"I assume you've recovered from your giggling fit," he says as he brushes a kiss across my cheek.

"I'm fine now," I reply, genuinely happy to see him but frustrated I didn't get the dirt on the history with Chris.

"I thought of coming after you, but I knew you were going to survive it."

I scrunch up my face. "Do you think your granny noticed?"

He presses his lips together, his eyes dancing. "Darling, I wouldn't be at all surprised if the entire theater noticed."

My heart sinks. "Was it that bad?"

He kisses me on the cheek once more, making tingles shoot down my spine. "Let's just say I'm fairly sure everyone here knows you didn't exactly appreciate the nuances of the opera."

"I'm so sorry, Seb. Really, I am," I gush. "It just all got too much, you know? The weird singing and the adult diapers. I mean, what the heck was up with *that*?"

"That was quite odd, I agree. But that's the opera for you."

"I'm really annoyed. I was trying so hard to impress your granny, and all I did was embarrass myself in front of her. *Again*. Where is she, by the way?"

"She's chatting with some old friends. It seems she knows half the audience here tonight."

"Ah, the octogenarians. Or it could be the toffs."

His eyebrows ping up. "Excuse me?"

"This guy I was chatting with told me people who go to the opera are either ancient or trying to appear smarter than they are. I don't believe it for a second, of course," I loop my arms around his waist, "because you're here, and you're neither old nor—"

"Smart?" he offers.

"Not what I was going to say." I notice Chris out of the corner of my eye. He's still got Clementine draped over him like a human cape. "Come meet him," I say to Sebastian. "You might know him. In a weird coincidence, he's one of Jilly's exes."

"That is a weird coincidence."

I tap Chris on the shoulder. "Chris, I'd like you to meet my fiancé, Sebastian." He turns around, a big smile on his face.

Sebastian's grip on me tightens as Chris's features drop for a split second before he pastes on his dazzling smile once more.

"How are you, man?" Chris says brightly, sticking his

free hand out toward him. "Long time no see. Your fiancée is terrific. Great work."

I smile at the compliment and look up at Sebastian. His features are taut with tension as he stares at Chris.

Weird.

And then it dawns on me. This so-called "history" that Jilly didn't get a chance to tell me about. Something about him being a bad egg. *So* Jilly. Perhaps Sebastian is being loyal to his good friend?

"Yes," Sebastian grumbles at my side, "we, ah, we know one another." Sebastian looks down at Chris's outstretched hand and appears to be deciding what to do with it.

"Seb," I say under my breath. This is the first time *I've* got to be the one telling *him* about a social faux pas.

He straightens up and reluctantly takes Chris's hand and shakes it briefly before dropping it like a hot potato. "Emma. We really should leave. Jilly? Would you mind collecting Granny? We'll meet you at the entrance. I, ah, I need some air."

"Sure," I mumble, totally confused by his reaction. "Bye, Chris," I say as Sebastian takes me by the hand, leads me through the throngs of people, down the stairs, and out onto the street.

Chapter Eight

Once we're safely alone back at the house, I shut the bedroom door firmly behind us and say, "Okay, dude. Spill the beans. What was that all about?"

"What was what all about?" Sebastian replies, and I know he's playing innocent. What else would I want him to spill the beans on? What happened to all those people in adult diapers at the end of that insane opera? No thank you.

"Chris Hampshire."

"Ah. Him."

"You did not look happy to see him, and you took off faster than the Road Runner to get away from him."

"Did you talk with him for long?"

"Not really. He was at the bar when I had to leave because of my giggling fit." I scrunch up my face. "Man, why did *that* have to happen? And in front of your granny, too."

"Don't let it bother you," Sebastian soothes. "As I said, I'll ask her to ease up on you tomorrow."

I walk over and wrap my arms around him. "Thanks,

Marrying Mr. Darcy

but I want to try to win her over. You talking to her about me will only make it into a thing, you know?"

"The most important thing to me is that you feel like you belong here. Because you do."

"I know. Let me try first. Deal?"

He kisses me softly on the lips. "Deal."

"So, Chris...?" I lead.

He exhales. "Chris Hampshire and I do not see eye to eye."

"Because of the fact he used to date Jilly?"

He regards me in surprise. "Did he tell you about that?"

"Jilly mentioned it. She seemed as shocked to see him as you were."

"That's because it didn't end well between them, and I'm sure she didn't want to see him. He didn't have the best of intentions towards her."

"Love rat, huh? Poor Jilly."

"She got a lucky escape, if you ask me."

"We've all been crossed in love, I suppose. Mine was a guy in high school. Danny O'Hara. He invited me to prom then dumped me the day before to take Kira Ackerman. I was heartbroken."

He kisses me on the forehead and says, "I hate Danny O'Hara and Kira Ackerman."

"Who was yours?"

"Stephanie Moore while I was at Cambridge. She didn't want what I wanted."

"Which was?"

"To date."

I giggle. "You've always got to be on the same page about that in a relationship, I find." I give him a kiss and add, "It's sweet that you dislike Chris Hampshire because of how he treated Jilly."

"I'm nothing if not a good guy," he replies with a cheeky grin. "It was a long time ago."

"Maybe he's changed? He seemed like a nice enough guy, albeit a little flirty."

Sebastian's eyes widen. "He flirted with you?"

"I'm not sure. It might just be the way he talks to women. He made jokes about my laughing fit and bought me a drink I didn't ask for."

"That sounds like Chris Hampshire." He leans down and brushes his lips against mine in a tantalizing kiss. "How about we forget about him and focus on something far more appealing?"

I throw him a smile. "What did you have in mind?"

He pulls me closer to him and deepens his kiss, making every inch of me wake up and take notice. "Does that give you a clue?"

"No. I'm at a total loss," I tease. "I think you might have to give me more clues. Like, a *lot* more."

"Oh, I think I can manage that." He scoops me up in his arms and carries me over to the large four-poster bed, where he lays me down and kisses me once more, this time like he can't get enough of me, and any thoughts I had about Chris Hampshire vanish.

* * *

The following morning, I resolve to fix this whole Geraldine thing once and for all. It's crazy that the woman has made a snap judgment on me and not even given me a chance. So what if I'm not from some toffy-nosed British family? Sebastian and I are in love and we're getting married. That should be enough.

I fire off a text to Jilly, asking her to meet me at Mia's

Café for coffee. I've decided I need to bring in reinforcements to tackle this whole Geraldine situation, and with Zara living in London most of the time, Jilly's my only friend here. She knows how things "should" be done. She's easily my best bet.

When she replies with a yes, I do a little air punch. With Jilly's help, Operation Win Granny Over will be back on track in no time.

While I'm on a roll, I take some time to make some Timothy-related calls. I've been steadily working my way through the list of potential UK activewear retail outlets that Penny and I compiled, and so far all I've had in response is purchasing managers' polite disinterest.

But Penny and I didn't get where we've got in the US without being knocked back a bunch of times, and I'm determined to make a success of the label in my new home country. I've sent out a bunch of samples, and am now hoping like crazy that at least one of the purchasers is open to meeting with me to talk about the label.

I sit at an ancient walnut desk in the bedroom, with its green felt tabletop and ornate detailing, and I begin to dial. I work my way down the list, getting knocked back at every turn. Some of them have received the samples, some of them haven't. One even tells me she liked the shorts I sent her so much she wore them to her cardio tennis session yesterday, but although she personally loved them, she couldn't see her store stocking them at this time. Hopes raised and dashed, all within one sentence.

I try the guy at Body Sports, the biggest sports clothing chain in the country. He tells me once again that he's super interested in the label, but now isn't the time. Again. As I hang up with a sigh, I wonder if he realizes he's used that line on me before.

Eventually, I snap my laptop shut. I refuse to be defeated, even if no one seems to want to even give Timothy a chance. I know it's a great line. I just have to keep working at it to show these Brits that, too.

I glance at the time and realize I need to leave to meet Jilly. I find Sebastian at his desk in the large study downstairs. He's got his reading glasses on as he studies his laptop, looking utterly adorable. My heart gives a little squeeze at the sight of him.

Eat your heart out, Clark Kent.

"Brady," he says as I plant a kiss on his cheek. "Are you leaving?"

"Off to see Jilly at Mia's."

"Say hello to her from me. "I've got a wonderful day planned researching the intricacies of opening the house to the public."

"Do you need some help?" I ask, hoping he'll say no.

He holds up a wad of paper. "Do you want to read all about inheritance and capital gains tax?"

"As totally riveting as that sounds…"

He shoots me a grin. "I'm joking. Take the Aston Martin. She needs a blat."

"What is a 'blat'? Because it sure doesn't sound like it'd be good for a car. Or for me, for that matter."

He chuckles. "It means give the car a good run." He collects the keys from the chest of drawers and hands them to me. "Only please remember which side of the road we drive on here."

"How stupid do you think I am?" I tease as I take the keys from him. "I know we drive on the right."

"The *left*, Brady. The left," he says as I kiss him once more and I collect my purse.

"Just kidding," I call out as I waltz out of the room. I

rush down toward the front door only to come face to face with Geraldine.

"Emma," she says with a pleasant enough smile, by which I mean she's not throwing daggers at me with her eyes and there's only a hint of looking down her nose at me. It's a pretty low bar, I tell you. "Where are you off to in such haste on a Saturday morning?"

"Good morning, ma'am. I'm meeting Jilly in the village. Did you enjoy the opera?"

"I found it highly amusing, of course, as one should with any satirical performance, although I suspect my amusement was a little less than some."

"About that. I'm really sorry about the whole giggling fit thing. I'm not usually like that."

"I'm sure," Geraldine replies, her thin lips pulled tightly together.

We stand in awkward silence until I say, "Well, have a great day."

"Thank you," she replies and then brushes past me on her way down the hall.

I let out a puff of air as I make my way through the house to the large former stables that have been converted into garaging. I hop into Sebastian's old Aston Martin sports car, sitting low to the ground, and rev the engine. I've got no idea about cars, but I do know this is a pretty stylish one, and it's definitely got more power under the hood than a girl driving on the wrong side of the road should have.

Although driving stick on the wrong side of the road still has its challenges for me—you know, like remembering which side of the road I'm meant to be on in the quiet country lanes with their lack of road markings and other minor points—I feel very much the lady of the manor in this beautiful, classic car.

Despite it all, I manage to make it to the village, where I drive around for a long time, looking for a parking space—parallel parking this thing is a step too far for this American right now. Finally, I spot one, pull into it, and dash down the road to Mia's Café, where I'd agreed to meet Jilly.

I push the door open and am immediately hit by the tempting aroma of baked goods, and my tummy rumbles, demanding to be fed cookies, and now. The aroma reminds me of Penny, and I suddenly miss her. She would know what to do about Granny right now. And she'd help me laugh at myself, too.

I hear Jilly call out, "Yoo-hoo, Emma! Over here," and spot her at a table at the back, waving and smiling at me, looking as beautiful as always in a floaty dress and tailored navy jacket with gold buttons.

Jilly isn't one to dress down, even on the weekend.

I make my way through the coffee house, and we do the usual greeting, this time narrowly avoiding the dreaded cheek slap.

See? I'm becoming more English by the minute.

"Can I get you a coffee?" I offer. "I've got to get one of their chocolate chip cookies, too. They are so good."

"One of those would be lovely, although I am meant to be on a no-carb, no-sugar diet, you know."

I regard her size two frame. "That sounds terrible."

"You're right. It is terrible. Beyond terrible. Get me a biscuit and a cappuccino with chocolate."

I grin at her. "Good choice. BRB." I put in our order and return to the table. "Thank you so much for agreeing to meet me at such short notice."

"Oh, it's fine. I was doing boring solicitory things anyway, which is my life, really, even at the weekend. I could do with a break from all that, and you are a refreshing

Marrying Mr. Darcy

change of pace, Emma." She leans her elbows on the wooden table. "Tell me, how are you after last night's little debacle?"

I cringe at the memory. "That's what I wanted to talk to you about."

"Oh, I absolutely felt for you, Emma. A giggling fit is the worst. I remember once when I was in church for one of my sister's children's baptism—I forget which one—someone said something that had me in stitches, and I had to rush out of the church, my hand pressed to my mouth to keep from laughing. When I finally got outside, I burst into hysterical laughter, only narrowly avoiding weeing in my undies, and then realized too late I hadn't closed the door behind me. Everyone was gawking at me through the open doors. Ophelia wouldn't talk to me for weeks! Awful business." She toys with her hair before she adds, "At least you had someone to distract you once you left the auditorium."

Chris Hampshire.

"What's the deal with him? No one seemed exactly happy to see him. Well, other than that supermodel looking girl who couldn't take her hands off of him."

"With Chris Hampshire there's always a supermodel looking girl who can't take her hands off him. That's the way he is. Charismatic and adored."

I think of his good looks and smooth demeanor. The guy's definitely got it going on. "So, what's the story with you and him? Seb told me things ended badly between you."

She lets out a heavy sigh. "Back when we were at Cambridge, I met and fell in love with him. We were together for a year, and I thought he was The One. He's so charming and handsome, and we had so much fun together. He would tell me I was the one for him and he couldn't imagine life without me. I was totally deluded. I wanted a fantasy that was never there in the first place."

"I get it. We've all fallen for guys who have turned out to be something other than they seem."

"Well, Chris was definitely that."

Greg, the friendly café owner I've chatted with a couple of times, delivers us our coffee and cookies. "Enjoy, ladies," he says with a beaming smile.

With Greg gone, Jilly takes a sip of her coffee and says, "The problem with me and Chris was that the only thing we really had in common was we were *both* in love with him."

I chortle. "Oh, Jilly, I'm sorry. It must have been hard running into him like that last night."

"It was a bit of shock. You see, he, ah, he left me at the altar."

My eyes bulge. "As in he left you at the altar on your *wedding* day?"

She presses her lips together and nods. "It wasn't my happiest moment."

"I know about those," I mutter under my breath, my mind darting to that gut wrenching moment when Sebastian sent me home from *Dating Mr. Darcy*. "That's so horrible."

"It was all a bit silly, really," she says with a shake of her head. "We should probably just have had a mad affair and left things at that. But the problem is, he's like catnip and Jilly finds him extremely hard to resist."

"I can see that."

"Oh?"

"I mean, he's handsome and flirty. A lot of girls go for that."

"Indeed. Sebby was marvelous at the time. He is an incredibly loyal person, you know, Emma."

I nod and smile, feeling the warmth of our love. "He is."

"When things between Chris and I ended, your darling fiancé stepped in and told him never to come near me again. He was awfully heroic. I half expected him to challenge Chris to a duel to protect my honor."

I give her a sardonic smile. "But then you remembered this is the twenty-first century, right?"

"Right."

"What did he say? Do you know?"

"No clue. All I know is Sebby made everything okay for me, and I'll always hold him dear."

"He's a good friend to you."

"He is. And as for Chris Hampshire, he may be handsome and fun and charming and nice to chat with in bars at the opera, but he's not one of the good ones, as they say."

"Oh, I think I got that message loud and clear."

"Good." She takes a bite of her cookie. "My goodness. This biscuit is fab," Jilly pronounces after her first mouthful.

"I know, right? These remind me of home. I would go out with Penny—she's my business partner and best friend—and we would eat these amazing chocolate chip cookies at our favorite coffee house whenever we had a problem to solve." I think of how many cookies I ate after I thought Sebastian had dumped me. It's a miracle I can still fit into my Timothy leggings, to be honest. "These are almost as good."

"Well, I think they're splendid. I don't usually eat carbs, as I said. A treat for me is to have butter on my cauli rice."

"Cauli rice?"

"Cauliflower. Awfully nutritious. You should try it sometime.

"Sure," I reply, thinking I'll just stick with regular old rice. I take a bite of my own cookie, enjoying its crunchy, gooey, chocolatiness. "I wanted to talk to you about the whole Sebastian's family thing."

"You have my attention. Go on."

I look around the café to check no one is listening. Not that I expect them to, of course, but they are a well-known family in this area. "Can I ask you something confidentially?"

"I am the soul of discretion, Emma. I held all my friends' secrets at boarding school, and I tell you, I knew a few utter doozies about that bunch of cows."

I cock an eyebrow at the image of Jilly keeping secrets for a herd of cows. But at the risk of mixing my species, I've got bigger fish to fry right now.

"My life back in the States is nothing like it is here. I know the rules. I know how things are done. I get it."

"I imagine you live on a ranch in Texas. Do you? Surrounded by beefcake cowboys with their lassos and cattle?"

"Ah, no," I reply, doing in internal eyeroll at the stereotypical view of life in Texas a lot of the people here seem to have. It's either cowboys or the TV show, *Dallas*. Neither bear a whole lot of similarities to my actual life.

"No?"

"I live in a rented apartment in a city of over four million people, Jilly. Not too many cowboys in my neighborhood."

She seems deflated. "Oh. Shame. I was going to suggest a little trip there so you could introduce me to burly cowboys called things like Maverick and Gunner." She seems to swoon a little at the idea.

"No can do, sorry."

"Pity."

"What I want to ask you is whether you can help me out? You know, train me up so that I fit in a little more around here."

"Train you to be English?"

"I guess," I reply with a shrug.

"Or more specifically, help you navigate the intricacies of the British upper classes."

"There's more than one upper class?"

"Oh, darling. You have so much to learn."

"I know," I say, my heart sinking. "I need help with someone in particular."

She leans in conspiratorially. "Do you mean who I think you mean?"

"That depends. Who do you mean?"

"Who do *you* mean?"

I'm not going to be the one to say it. "I mean someone in particular."

She gives me a knowing look. "You mean You-Know-Who."

Do I, though?

"Who would that be, exactly?" I ask.

This beating about the bush is getting old, real fast.

Her eyes dart around the room then land back on mine. "Geraldine Huntington-Ross," she says under her breath, and I give a short, sharp nod. "You were trying to impress her at the opera, so it's not a giant leap for me to come to that conclusion now. But you need to know, Geraldine's a pussy cat."

More like a sabre tooth tiger out for my blood.

"Is she though?"

"Oh, yes. She can be a little prickly, granted, but she's a real brick."

I know what that means now. It's a good person you can rely on. Nothing to do with red rectangular building blocks. Weird, I know.

I press my lips together and give a brief nod. "The problem is, nothing I do seems to meet with her approval. Granted, I messed up at the opera, but I she knew I was trying to relate to her by taking her to something she loves. Although how anyone can love that kind of thing is beyond me."

"Poor Emma." She leans back in her seat, her eyes trained on me. "You're not good enough for her darling grandson. You're not from the right stock. Not only that but you don't even have the good graces to come from money. And what's more, you're American."

"That's right," I say in a small, strained voice.

Could she get any blunter? I mean, it's one thing to think all of that to myself, but it's another to hear it come from someone's mouth. Spelled out it makes me feel as though there's a snowball's chance in Florida she'll ever accept me, let alone actually *like* me. Although I don't like it, I know everything Jilly says is true. Granny doesn't think I'm good enough for Sebastian or her family, and the fact I have no "breeding"—I mean, what am I, a freaking horse?—no money, and I have the audacity to be from someplace other than England, makes me just about the least desirable future Lady Martinston she could ever imagine.

"What did you have in mind?" she asks as she lifts her coffee cup to her lips.

"Well, I thought you could help me with things like dress codes, for example."

"Easy. What else?"

"How to behave, appropriate topics of conversation, I guess. Oh, and how to use some of the totally weird silverware y'all have here, like grape scissors. Who's ever heard of them? And why the heck do you need them in the first place?"

She giggles. "You said 'y'all.'"

"Focus, Jilly."

"Grape scissors are only rarely used, you know."

"Like when you eat grapes?"

"Exactly. I wouldn't go worrying about those. You've got a few social engagements coming up. There's the exhibition opening for Sebby's father's foundation and Johnathan and Phoebe's wedding—"

"I'm a bridesmaid at that."

"Oh, lovely. Will Geraldine be there? What am I saying, of course she will. Johnathan Bentley's family and the Huntington-Rosses have been friends for centuries. Well, other than the time around Charles II's reign when some of them tried to poison the other to take their land. I'm not sure whether it was the Bentleys poisoning the Huntington-Rosses, or the Huntington-Rosses poisoning the Bentleys." She looks at me questioningly, as though I should have the answer.

I shrug. "No idea."

"Oh, well. That's all water under the bridge now. Or poison in the bloodstream, you could say. The point is, Geraldine will be there, so you'll need to be the perfect BM."

"The perfect BM," I echo, my tummy doing backflips.

She studies me across the table for a moment before her face breaks into a smile. "Emma, I would love to help you. I will train you up to be the very best Lady Martinston you can be, and together we will win Geraldine over. You mark my words."

Relief washes through me. "You are an absolute lifesaver, Jilly. How will I ever repay you?"

She waves my question away with a flick of her wrist. "Make darling Sebby happy. That's enough for me."

I grin back at her. "*That* I can do."

"Now, the first thing on the agenda it would seem to me should be how we clean up this opera debacle."

A fresh wave of mortification pounds up against me. "Oh, yes. That."

She grins at me. "We may need some more of those yummy biscuits for that, darling girl."

"I'm on it." As I make my way over to the counter, I feel a huge weight lift from my shoulders. I have a plan, I have an accomplice, and I'm going to show Geraldine that I'm worthy of her grandson and the title Lady Martinston.

Chapter Nine

"What's Heather McCabe like?" I ask Sebastian as he skillfully backs his car into a parallel park on a busy street in Shepherd's Bush. It's an area of London that, by the looks of the traffic clogged streets, the buildings, and the streams of people going about their business, has got absolutely nothing to do with sheep. Or bushes, for that matter.

It's something I've noticed in my time here in the UK. They've got some pretty funny names for places. Point in case, the word "Bottom" appears in a ridiculously large number of place-names, from Shepherd's Bottom to Wild Church Bottom, to my personal favorite, Loose Bottom, which sounds like the sort of place no one would want to visit *ever*.

And don't even get me started on all the place-names that involve words that describe parts of the anatomy, because things can go downhill pretty fast, I can tell you that. (Titty Hill, anyone?)

Back in Shepherd's Bush, Sebastian turns the ignition off and says, "Heather is good at her job, that's for certain."

"Meaning?"

"Meaning she's blunt. She calls a spade a spade. You know where you stand with her."

I climb out of the car and close the heavy sports car door with a *clunk*. "She sounds a little scary."

"She's harmless. She just knows what she wants."

"Well, for the sake of Martinston, let's hope she wants us."

He takes my hand in his. "Who wouldn't?"

We walk together along the bustling city street for a couple of blocks until we arrive at a nondescript mid-century modern brick building that looks like it could do with a serious upgrade. Standing outside the building, talking animatedly on her phone, is Jilly. She's here in her official capacity as the Huntington-Ross's lawyer, but I'm glad to see a friendly face.

"All right, darling. Okay. Just don't let it go pear shaped, ya? I'm relying on you. All right. Bye bye, now." She hangs up the phone and greets me as though she didn't just see me at the café on Saturday and she has in fact been starved of my attention for far too long. "Sebby, Emma! Darlings!" *M-wah, m-wah*. You know the drill.

Gotta love Jilly.

"Are you ready to go in?" Sebastian asks her.

"Wild horses could not keep Jilly away," she replies. "Oh, and Emma, don't you look scrumptious in that divine pants suit of yours? What is it, gaberdine?"

I'm pretty sure my suit is a crappy polyester mix of some description with maybe something vaguely resembling a natural fiber in there somewhere, but I'm not going to share that detail with Jilly. If she thinks my suit is high-end wool, I'm gonna let her. "Yup. Gaberdine."

"Nothing like the real thing, is there? Why wear some

dreadful man-made material when you can wrap yourself in a little luxury?"

I shoot her a sideways look. "Sure."

Sebastian pushes the glass door to the building open for us to enter through, where we're met by a thoroughly bored looking receptionist. She can't be a lot older than eighteen, with heavy eye makeup and false lashes that reach above her eyebrows. Her hair is tied so tightly on the top of her head, she looks like a pineapple.

"'Allo. Welcome to Upfront Productions. 'Ow can I 'elp you today?" she asks in her broad accent, the nametag on her lapel telling us her name is Shaznaay with two *a*'s.

Despite her dull monotone and the fact she barely bothers to look our way, I want her to keep talking. That accent is freaking fantastic!

"We're here to see Heather McCabe," Sebastian replies, his own accent sounding super hoity toity in comparison with Shaznaay's with two *a*'s.

"Awigh'. Sign in, will y*aaaaa*?" The last syllable is stretched so long, I wonder when it's going to end. She points at a screen, and we enter our details.

"Can I get you anyfink?" she asks with a heavy sigh that tells us getting us "anyfink" is the very last thing she'd want to do for us. "Tea, coffee, a glass a wa'er?"

I smile at her. I could listen to her butcher the English language all day.

"No, I think we're all quite all right, thank you," Sebastian replies. "Unless one of you would like something?" he asks us.

"No, no," Jilly replies, and I shake my head.

"In that case, take a sea' n'all. 'Evver'll be 'ere soon enough. It's no' a big place, 'ere. Know wha' I mean?"

I gawp at her before I snap out of it. I've got absolutely

no clue what she's saying. All I know is I want her to keep talking.

"How big is the place, exactly?" I ask as the others sit down.

"I dunno, do I?" she says with a shrug. "Big enough for about twen'y of us, innit."

"Gosh. Okay," I reply.

"Emma? Come and sit down with us," Sebastian suggests, and I take a seat on the firm couch next to Jilly.

"Is she a Cockney?" I whisper.

Jilly looks over at the receptionist. "I have absolutely no idea, but she does need to do something about that truly dreadful hair of hers. It looks like something died of fright on top of her head."

I stifle a giggle. I had enough bitchiness as a contestant on *Dating Mr. Darcy* to last me a lifetime, but I've got to admit Jilly's description is quite funny.

"Oi!"

Startled, we look up at Shaznaay with two *a*'s. She's holding a phone in her hand and looking at us.

"'Evver's on 'er way down. She'll be 'ere in a mo'."

"Thank you," Sebastian replies.

"A mo'?" I ask Jilly.

"A moment," she explains.

"Got it."

Literally a "mo" later, a tall woman with dark brown shoulder-length hair dressed in a bright red suit strides through a door behind the reception desk, making a beeline for us. "Sebastian Huntington-Ross, as I live and breathe." She wraps her arms around him and pulls him in for a hug. "My God, you look hot. And you smell divine. You do not change, do you?"

"Always the charmer," he replies as he steps out of her grasp.

Jilly extends her hand. "Heather. Good to see you again. Jilly Fotherington, Sebastian's lawyer."

"I remember you. Tough negotiator, if I recall correctly."

"I do what's best for my clients," she replies.

Heather turns to me. "And I know who you are. You're Emma Brady. The little contestant that could."

What the heck does *that* mean?

"Err, hi," I say insipidly.

"Well," she says as she claps her hands together, "let's get this show on the road, shall we? Follow me." She strides away, past Shaznaay with two *a*'s and her pineapple—or dead furry animal, depending on whether you subscribe to Jilly's grizzly metaphor or mine—through an open-plan office, and into a brightly lit boardroom. "Take a seat," she instructs as she closes the door behind us. "I assume Shaznaay offered you refreshments?"

"She did," Sebastian replies.

"Good, good. Now." Still standing, Heather slaps her hands down heavily on the table, and I elevate in my chair. "I'm coming straight to the point. The idea of following you on your journey to save your house is interesting to us. It's got legs, and we like ideas with legs."

I can't help but imagine a lightbulb on little legs, walking through the room.

"I'm thinking *Saving Pemberley*. I'm thinking you on a horse, dressed as Mr. Darcy. I'm thinking heartfelt scenes of you baring your soul about how much Pemberley means to you, how much history there in the place, how your family will be homeless without a cash injection. And, I'm definitely, definitely thinking pond scene."

"Pond scene?" Sebastian asks.

"Oh, she means in the BBC production with Colin Firth," Jilly explains. "Very famous scene. Rather sexy, in fact."

I nod. "Yup, it sure is. Mom's favorite."

"I'm sorry, what exactly did Colin Firth do in a pond, and why would I want to replicate it?" Sebastian looks thoroughly confused.

"I'll explain," Jilly offers with her hand in the air as though in school. "Colin Firth dived into a pond in a white shirt at Pemberley and came out with the shirt virtually translucent, molded to his manly chest, looking all brooding and sexy as he tried to deny his raging feelings for Elizabeth Bennet. Which of course he couldn't do, because they were so raw and forceful that he could think of little else but her." Jilly leans back in her chair with a satisfied sigh, looking all pink in the face. "It really was quite something to behold."

"Bit of a fan, eh, Jilly?" Sebastian teases.

"She's a woman, isn't she?" Heather replies with a laugh as Jilly fans herself to cool off. "Really, I don't know how we missed doing the pond scene on *Dating Mr. Darcy*. But we can make up for it now when we do *Saving Pemberley*." She sits down at the table opposite us. "With your consent, of course, Sebastian," she adds as an afterthought.

"You're telling me you want me to dive into the pond at Martinston wearing a white shirt, so you can film me getting out of the pond?"

Jilly and Heather both nod with enthusiasm, and I've got to admit the idea is more than a touch appealing. Particularly as I know exactly what that white shirt would mold to.

Sebastian crosses his arms defensively. "So, I'm a sex symbol now, am I?"

Marrying Mr. Darcy

"Oh, Sebastian, of course you are. You became a sex symbol the moment you first stepped on the *Dating Mr. Darcy* red carpet," Heather replies. "You sent American and British women's hearts racing, believe me. You're the reason we're interested in *Saving Pemberley*. You and you alone."

He purses his lips. "I see."

"So it's a yes to a pond scene. Good," she says.

"I'll consider it," Sebastian replies stiffly.

"Sebastian, I'm sure you're familiar with the notion that sex sells. You doing the pond scene will definitely increase our viewer numbers, which can only be a good thing for you and for me."

"Maybe we should focus on the other details of the show first?" Sebastian suggests.

"I do have an idea on that front. We need a George Wickham character, too. You know, a love rat, scoundrel type who's impossibly gorgeous and gets the women's hearts afluttering. We couldn't do that on *Dating*, but we could work it into *Pemberley* somehow. We'd just have to work out the angle."

"Oh, I do like that idea. George Wickham is the ultimate handsome cad," Jilly says.

"You're so right, Jilly," Heather replies.

"Getting back to the house," Sebastian says pointedly. "We have plans to open the house up to the public already in play. What do you need from us to make this idea work? *Other* than me in a pond, that is."

"Well, for starters we'll need you to give us some background on the place. How long it's been in your family, if anything of any historical interest has ever happened there, that sort of thing. All interesting background stuff."

"Oh, there's plenty of that, Heather. Believe me," Jilly

says. "You won't be disappointed on that front. Will she, Sebby?"

"It's true Martinston has a long and varied history. There was once a castle on the land, although it's long gone now."

Heather nods as she stares intently at Sebastian. "Excellent. Mind if I whiteboard this?"

"Be my guest," Sebastian replies.

Heather springs out of her seat, grabs a pen, and begins to write on the whiteboard on the wall. "Interesting backstory," she says as she writes just that. "Tick." She turns back to face us. "Look. Our viewers love a good story, especially about privileged people facing their inevitable downfall. Gone are the days of these huge estates, populated by the lucky, powerful few with literally dozens of underpaid staff catering to their every whim. We need to dig around in the Huntington-Ross family past and find some juicy stories our viewers can get their teeth into."

"Wasn't there that ancestor of yours who had an affair with Henry VIII, Sebby?" Jilly asks.

"Err, I'm not sure, actually," he mumbles, clearly uncomfortable.

"Now, that's the sort of thing we're looking for here, although I think half the female aristocracy slept with Henry VIII at some point, didn't they? He was hardly picky, although you did run the risk of losing your head." Heather laughs uproariously at her joke as she writes "Henry VIII affair" on the whiteboard. "Anyway, my point is we need some salacious stories, and we need a human interest angle as well. What will happen to you if you lose the house? Where will you live? How will you survive? *Will* you survive at all? These are the questions that will propel the viewers to watch."

Marrying Mr. Darcy

"Well, that's going a little far, don't you think?" Jilly scoffs. "Of course they'll survive. This is about preserving our uniquely English heritage, not whether the Huntington-Rosses will end up on the streets."

Heather writes the word "survive" with a big question mark on the board. "Let's circle back to that one."

"Jilly's right. That's where the focus needs to be," Sebastian says.

"But we need the human interest angle," Heather protests. "I mean, why now? Why are you facing the potential loss of your house now and not, say, fifty or one hundred years ago when a load of landed gentry lost theirs?"

My eyes dart to Sebastian. I'm certain he won't want Heather to know that his father's gambling debt is what's put his family in their precarious current position. Some things are too personal to get aired on television.

"We simply managed to hold out longer than others, I suppose," he replies smoothly. "There's really nothing more to it."

She raises her eyebrows. "No scandal, no skeletons in the closet?"

"Nothing like that," Sebastian replies swiftly.

Heather turns to her board and begins to scrawl once more. When she turns back, I read the words "family tragedy" with a large question mark.

She's clearly not convinced. I give Sebastian's hand a squeeze under the table. "Blunt" is definitely the word for Heather McCabe. He shoots me a brief smile. This can't be easy for him.

"How would you see the show working?" Jilly asks, thankfully changing the subject.

"Oh, that part's easy. We'll film Sebastian in the house, going about whatever it is he's doing to save it. You said you had some things going on already. What are you planning on doing?"

I see my chance to enter the conversation. I've been a bystander up until now. The little contestant that could. Whatever that means. "We're going to open the house and the gardens up to the paying public in spring," I announce, feeling proud of the decision we've reached. "We might also consider opening a café on the grounds, but we've not worked the details of that out with the family just yet."

Heather stares at me blankly for a moment, as if wondering who I am and what I'm doing in the room.

"Oh, of course," she replies. "You two are engaged, aren't you?"

I can't help but smile as my eyes find Sebastian's. "We are."

"Hmmm." She twists her lips and studies me across the table.

I shift, uncomfortable in my seat.

"Look, I'm going to be honest with you here," she says, and instantly my back straightens as my nerves up. When do people ever have anything positive to say following the words "I'm going to be honest with you?"

Answer: never.

"As you know, the way *Dating* ended riled a few people up to say the least. Sure, your whole speech about messing things up and wanting Emma back was dead romantic, Sebastian, but the audience didn't get to *see* your reunion. That's why they're having a hard time buying into you guys together. Well, that and the fact Emma was seen as the comic relief on the show."

Wow. Just wow.

Sebastian leaps to my rescue. "That's a bit harsh, Heather."

"Falling out of the limo onto her bottom? That dreadful rendition of *Old Town Road* of hers where she replaced the lyrics with the word 'horse' repeatedly?"

I cringe at the memories.

"Come on, Sebastian, she was hardly the romantic lead." She turns her attention briefly to me. "No offence, Emma."

Offence! Offence!

"My point is, in the eyes of the viewers, it was either Camille—who, let's face it, no one wanted you to end up with, and I thank the stars you didn't choose her—or Phoebe. The audience clearly wanted Phoebe, but mostly they wanted a proposal from you. On air. For everyone to see. Preferably to Phoebe."

I know everything she's saying is true. Sebastian may have asked for my forgiveness and told the world he wanted to be with someone he'd already sent home publicly on the show, but he didn't name me, and there were no cameras when he turned up on my doorstep in Houston to declare his love for me. A fact I was very happy about at the time.

"Everyone wanted Seb to end up with Phoebe," I say dully.

"They did. And, I hate to say it—" she begins, and I wonder does she actually hate to say it? My guess is no. "—you were never a frontrunner, Emma. You were what we refer to as an 'also ran.'"

An "also ran"? How to make a girl feel super special. I swallow down a rising lump in my throat. The memes, the headlines, the jokes. It all comes flooding back. No one wanted me to end up with Sebastian.

No one but him.

Under the table, Sebastian takes my hand in his and gives it a reassuring squeeze. "Heather, I need you to know I fell deeply in love with Emma on the show, but the audience didn't see it because it happened when the cameras were off."

"Exactly! Because you were breaking the rules and sneaking around behind everyone's backs," Heather quips. "We know, Sebastian. We know."

"I don't see the issue here. The fact of the matter is Emma and I are engaged to be married, we are incredibly happy together, and we are both committed to saving my family home. *Together*." He's so firm and manly in his delivery, a tingle shoots up my spine as I gaze lovingly at him.

That's *my* man.

Heather taps her chin while she studies us across the table. "I see where you're coming from. I get it, I do. Love is unpredictable. The heart wants what the heart wants."

"That's right," I say, my spirits bolstered. Perhaps she's open to me being included on the show?

"Shame the heart didn't want someone the public wanted, though, isn't it?" Heather poses it as a question, but I know it's rhetorical.

"Look, Heather," Jilly says, adjusting her seating position, "Sebastian has made his decision. There is no other woman for him. Isn't that right, Sebby?"

Sebastian nods. "That's right. My mind is set."

Heather narrows her eyes at Jilly. "Are you just the family lawyer, or something more?"

"Oh, ah," Jilly stumbles, "we've known one another since we were in nappies, I suppose. Our mothers are great friends, you see. And we went to Cambridge together, too, of course."

"A lifelong connection, eh?" Heather says. "That might be an angle the viewers could get on board with."

"I'm sorry, what?" I sputter.

Marrying Mr. Darcy

Is she suggesting what I think she's suggesting?

"Picture this." Heather gestures with her hands. "Sebastian, you went on *Dating* to find the love of your life. It didn't work out, not because you didn't want it to. You did. Badly. Because you're harboring a secret. A big, juicy secret." She shoots us a knowing look.

"What secret is that, exactly?" Sebastian asks, a mixture of curiosity and trepidation in his voice.

"You've been denying your feelings all along. And now that your house is in peril, *wham!*" She bangs the table with her fist. "It hits you like a lightning bolt—you, Sebastian Huntington-Ross, are in love with your childhood sweetheart. You are in love with Jilly."

Jilly instantly bursts into frenzied giggles, probably from the sheer shock, while Sebastian and I blink at Heather in total disbelief.

"I'm sorry, what now?" I ask.

She leans back in her chair. "It's simple, really. The person you were talking to during that last episode of the show was Jilly."

"But it wasn't," Sebastian refutes.

"But it could have been."

"It was Emma."

"How does anyone know that?"

"How about the fact that I mentioned I sent her home from the show? Jilly wasn't on the show."

"He's right. I wasn't," Jilly adds unnecessarily.

"Then there's the fact your production team gave me the go-ahead to speak directly into the camera to deliver my message. You knew all about my plan. Don't pretend you didn't, Heather."

Heather exhales loudly. "Yes, all right," she says, annoyed. "Let's do it."

He leans forward in his chair, his elbows resting on the table. "What are you saying?"

"I'm saying as long as we can fulfil my list," She gestures at the whiteboard, "*Saving Pemberley* is a go."

"It is?" Sebastian's face lights up as my heart soars.

We're saving the house! We're saving Martinston!

"Oh, that's brilliant news. Just brilliant," Jilly gushes, her face still flush from all her giggling.

Heather raises her hand in the *stop* sign, halting our celebrations. "On one condition."

Sebastian's gorgeous smile has my heart melting all over again. "What condition?" he asks.

Heather's voice has a steely edge when she replies, "No Emma."

Wait, what? What does she mean, *no Emma*?

"We cannot agree to that," Sebastian replies through gritted teeth.

Heather pulls her lips into a line. "Think about it before you give me your final response."

Sebastian squares his shoulders. "No need. We're a package deal. It's either both of us, or neither of us."

Heather's eyes flick between Sebastian and me. "You're throwing away a big opportunity here, Sebastian. You can capitalize on your popularity with this show. Who knows where it could lead you?"

Sebastian stands, and Jilly and I follow suit. "With all due respect, I would say *you're* the one throwing away the opportunity, Heather." He slips his hand into mine and says, "Let's go."

As the three of us turn to leave, I feel like adding "In your face!!" to her, but I restrain myself. I'm working on my maturity here, even if I've been insulted by this woman.

Heather doesn't budge from her seat at the table. "Suit yourselves," she says.

As we make our way to the door, I hear her call out, "Give me a ring when you change your mind."

We walk out without a backwards glance.

Chapter Ten

Sebastian crunches the gears of his old Aston Martin sportscar for at least the seventeenth time as we round a corner of a tree-lined, suburban street, almost drowning out the music from the stereo.

"It's okay, Seb," I say for the umpteenth time.

"It's not, Emma. It's not okay," he growls as he takes a corner too fast, and we narrowly miss a car parked on the side of the street.

"Can you at least slow down?" I say, panic beginning to rise. "You're freaking me out right now."

He slows the car and pulls into a parking space. He switches off the ignition and lets out a heavy breath. "I hate the way she treated you in there."

"It wasn't exactly my favorite moment, either, but I'm sure it wasn't personal." I give him a sardonic smirk. I'm putting on a brave face, and I'm sure he knows it, because it felt pretty darn personal to me.

"It felt like she was telling you that you weren't good enough for her stupid show. That made me angry."

Marrying Mr. Darcy

"Really? I hadn't noticed." I nudge him playfully on the arm.

It would have been impossible *not* to notice. After Heather made it clear I was the last person she'd want on *Saving Pemberley*, Sebastian stood bolt upright and declared there would be no show without me and then proceeded to storm out of the room, trailed by Jilly and me.

I'd be lying if I didn't say it felt amazing to be defended like that by the man I love. In my mind, Heather was the horrible Miss Bingley from *Pride and Prejudice*, telling Mr. Darcy how beneath him I am. But instead of agreeing with her, he turned on her, saying how much he *ardently loved and admired* me, to quote Mr. Darcy himself.

#Swoon.

So, even though I'm crestfallen that the show won't go ahead and therefore we'll lose the financial boost we so need to save the house, I'm glowing with love for my handsome defender.

He, on the other hand, has been boiling over the whole drive back to Martinston.

"How dare she say that about you. You're more than good enough, Brady."

I reach over, cup his face with my hands, and plant a kiss on his lips. "Someone drank the Emma Brady Kool-Aid."

He smiles at me. "Guilty as charged."

"Look, she's a businesswoman, right? She knows I wasn't the most popular contestant on *Dating Mr. Darcy*. I was the class clown, the light relief while you got on with the serious work of finding your lady of the manor. If she thinks that not having me on the show means it can go ahead and be super popular, then I will gladly step aside."

He raises his eyebrows at me. "Gladly?"

"Okay, not 'gladly' exactly, but you know what I mean. I'll do it for you and your family. I know what. I'll hide out in the attic like Rochester's crazy wife in *Jane Eyre*. Good job I read that novel in high school."

He kisses me once more. "You're amazing, you know that, Brady?"

"In what way?" I bat my eyelashes at him and milk the compliment for all its worth.

"Too many ways to count. She treated you like you were nothing, and you're not. You, the future Lady Martinston, are everything to me."

My heart swells with love for him. "Ditto," I reply.

He turns on the ignition and the stereo springs into life, playing a popular song from a while back. Sebastian turns to me and says, "I think of you whenever I hear this song, because you are amazing, and I love you just the way you are," he says, quoting the famous line.

"Ditto," I say, beaming at him. "Bruno Mars sure has a way with words."

We sit and listen to the song.

"Beautiful lyrics," I say.

"Maybe we should have it as our wedding song?"

"Although I love the idea, your granny has made it clear to me that we should only have classical music played on an organ and probably by a woman called Mabel who needs bottle-thick reading glasses to see the sheet music."

He rolls his eyes at me. "That sounds like Granny."

He pulls the car away from the curb and drives a lot more sedately the rest of the way back to Martinston, London suburbia giving way to small, quaint villages and fields with old stone walls.

"You know what? Maybe I'll go back to Houston while you're filming the show? Penny is always telling me how busy she is, and by then I might have found us some retailers here to stock Timothy. That way I won't have to creak around in the attic the whole time."

Not that I'm seriously considering hiding out in the attic, of course. I might be bowing out gracefully here, but I'm not a masochist, or clinically insane (sorry, Mr. Rochester's wife).

"That won't be necessary," he says as he pulls into Martinston's long, tree-lined driveway.

"It's for the best, Seb. I'd feel weird being here while they were filming, trying not to get spotted. And you need the money from this show."

He drives the length of the driveway in silence, turns the car to the back of the house, and parks in one of the garages. Turning to me, he says, "I'm not sending you away like some embarrassment. You're the woman I love. The woman I'm marrying."

"I love that you're being so gallant and honorable about this, really I do, but it's no big deal. I'll get a lot done back home, and then I can come back here in time to become your wife. See? It'll all work out."

He shakes his head. "I'm not going to do the show."

"I know you *said* that, but you didn't mean it. You were just being all manly and defending my honor. Which I totally appreciate, by the way."

He shakes his head, his lips pulled into a thin line. "I meant it. I refuse to allow the woman I love be treated like a second-class citizen."

I knit my brows together in confusion. "But...the house."

"We've got a plan already. We'll just open in winter instead of waiting for spring. I've been doing a lot of research into how to do it. We will need to put off having a café, but we can at least start to get the house working for us."

Worry rushes through my bloodstream. "Will that be enough?"

"It'll have to be." He shoots me what he thinks is a confident smile, but I know better. Losing *Saving Pemberley* means the house is still in jeopardy. And I cannot help but feel responsible.

* * *

"Well, I'll say one thing for the guy, he's a total gentleman," Penny says over the phone after I've recounted the story of the reality show disaster meeting to her. "Probably shortsighted but a total gentleman all the same. I mean, is opening the house to the public enough to save it?"

Anxiety churns in my stomach. "The debts are big, Penn. Seb's family has consolidated all his dad's debts into one sum, and from what I know it doesn't make for fun reading. I think the guy was the worst gambler ever."

"I thought when you fell for an English aristocrat, it'd be all champagne and private jets. Maybe even a private island."

"No such luck, Penn."

"Just as well. He's a great guy, then."

"Oh, yeah. He's a totally great guy."

"How's it going talking with the people at Body Sports? Have you got a meeting yet?"

"I've been talking with the Apparel Purchasing Manager there. He says he's interested, but so far, he won't take a meeting with me. He says he likes our line but it's 'not the right time.' It's like he's dangling a carrot and I can't get a bite."

Marrying Mr. Darcy

"That is so frustrating."

My phone beeps, telling me I've got another call. I check the screen. It's Mom.

"Hey, Penn? Can I get back to you later? My mom's calling, and I've not gotten to talk to her for a few days."

"Sure. Love you."

"Love you, too."

I hang up and instantly answer the call from my mom. "Hey, Mom. How are you?"

"Oh, I'm great, honey. How's life as a soon-to-be Lady? Is it everything you hoped for?"

I think of Geraldine's obvious disapproval of me. I think of my schoolgirl giggling fit at the opera. I think of Heather McCabe not wanting me on the show.

I'm not going to tell my mom any of that.

"It's great, Mom. Really great."

"I am so happy for you, honey. You deserve all the happiness you can get. Now, where are my photos? I want to see the house, I want to see you and Sebastian together, and I especially want to see Frank frolicking in some gorgeous meadow somewhere."

"That I can do. Frank does love a good frolic."

"With you taking Frank with you, it all feels so...final." I think I detect a note of sadness in her voice.

"Final how?"

"As in that's it, you've moved to England. End of story."

"I'll be back to visit. You know I will."

"I know, it's just—" She breaks off as her voice cracks.

Concern twists inside me. "Mom?"

"It's nothing, honey. I'm being emotional, that's all. My only baby is far away from me for the first time. But you know what? Everything's fine, and you're following your heart. I could not be happier for you."

"Are you sure? I'm worried about you now."

"Don't be. It must be my dang hormones or something," she says with a laugh. "Now, how's work going? Have you got your label humming over there yet?"

I exhale. "I'm not sure the British are ready for Timothy. No one will take a meeting, let alone stock the line. It's kinda demoralizing."

"You're not one to feel beat. Remember what your dad always said? Never give up until the thing is done or dead."

I smile at the memory. That was something Dad and I had in common, relentless pursuit of something until either we achieved it or knew it was never meant to be ours in the first place. "Good old Dad."

"He'd be so proud of you."

I feel a sting of sadness at his loss. "I know he would, Mom."

"So don't you go giving up. Someone will want your label, and then it'll snowball. You mark my words."

"I hope you're right, Mom. I hope you're right. Now, tell me what's going on in H-town."

As Mom shares news of friends and family, to my surprise my eyes prick with tears. Although being with Sebastian is a dream come true and he means the world to me, I miss my mom and the familiar surrounds of my home. There I know how things are done. There I know that I belong.

As hard as I might try, and as much as I might want it, it hurts to know I don't yet have that here.

Chapter Eleven

There's a knock at the open door to our bedroom, and I glance in the mirror to see Zara standing in the doorway wearing a simple black dress, her dark hair in a messy side-ponytail that looks totally gorgeous on her. She does look like the British actress Gemma Arterton, after all, so practically everything looks gorgeous on this girl.

I rush over to her and give her a hug. "Zara, it's so good to see you. How's life in London?"

"Busy but fun. It's nice to be home, though. Seb tells me he's getting all the ducks in a row to open the house."

"He's been working really hard on it."

"He also told me we're not doing the TV show now. What gives?"

"Yeah. Sore topic. I want him to do it, but he's against it because the production company doesn't want 'the little contestant that could' in it."

She leans up against one of the bed posts. "The what?"

"Me. I'm the little contestant that could, apparently.

According to Heather McCabe, I'm not the right fit for Sebastian's fiancée."

"But you *are* Sebastian's fiancée."

"Semantics." I turn to face the mirror once more. "She wanted Jilly to pose as his fiancée. Can you believe?"

"Seriously? That's ridiculous."

"I know, right?" I slide my lipstick over my lips and smack them together. "I think Seb should do the show, but he won't hear it." I turn to face her once more. "He says he won't have me slighted by the production company."

"My brother, the hero."

I collect my purse from the chest of drawers and hook the strap over my shoulder. "The problem is, he runs the risk of being a homeless hero if he doesn't do the show."

"There's one thing I know about my big brother, Emma. When he sets his mind to something, that's it. Decision made."

"But if I'm okay with it, he should be too." I shake my head in frustration. "Anyway, am I dressed right for this thing?" I do a little twirl. In my red sleeveless dress, I feel pretty and demure.

"What do you usually wear to exhibition openings back in the US?"

"Like I go to them all the time," I reply with a laugh.

"No, but when you do?"

I shift my weight before I admit, "Ah, this is my first exhibition opening, actually."

She grins at me. "All the more reason to wear whatever you like, then."

Sebastian walks into the room, looking adorably cute in a pair of navy shorts and a white T-shirt. "It's an exhibition opening, Brady. You could wear a potato sack and people would think you're just being creative."

"But I want to look like the future Lady Martinston," I protest.

He takes me in his arms. "You *are* the future Lady Martinston. That's all that matters to me."

I gaze up at him as my heart dances. "I like hearing you say that."

"It doesn't freak you out anymore?" he asks, and I shake my head. He brushes a kiss against my lips. "Brady, you look beautiful."

"Ugh!" Zara exclaims. "How many times do I have to tell you two? Sister here. Enough with the mush."

"When you find the love of your life, you'll be just as mushy, little sis."

"If I am, I'll make sure you never have to see it. I'm in serious need of therapy because of all your PDAs, you know."

I giggle. "Maybe we should consider covering your sister's costs? After all, we're the ones responsible for her need for therapy."

"The only therapy Zara has involves falling out of nightclubs at three in the morning. Isn't that right, my wild, tearaway sister?"

"I'm hardly a tearaway," she replies with a roll of her eyes. "Come on, future Lady Martinston. We should go. Granny and Mum have already gone."

"Have they?" I ask in alarm. I give Sebastian a quick kiss. "Bye, fiancé. Ooh, I do like saying that. *My fiancé.*" I grin at him, and he shakes his head in good humor. "I wish you could come tonight."

"I need to finish some paperwork. I'm due back in the office first thing tomorrow, which means the early train for me."

"Another wild and crazy night in, eh, Seb?" Zara teases.

"If I'm a tearaway, I guess that makes you a middle-aged man with his pipe and slippers."

"One of us needs to be sensible." Although he says it in a lighthearted way, I pick up on a definite edge to his words. He's feeling the pressure of not only holding down his job at a bank in London but trying to save his family's home and deal with his granny not accepting me, too. It's a huge amount for one person to handle, and the fact he's forced to handle it plays on my mind.

* * *

In the car on the way to the gallery, we giggle ourselves silly over Zara's impersonations of her stiff older relatives. She's helped lighten my mood, and I'm so grateful to be out and having some fun, even if it is without Sebastian.

"Granny told me you had a giggling fit at the opera. Did you really have to leave the auditorium to get a hold of yourself?"

"It was horrible. I was so embarrassed." I shake my head at the memory. "What did she say about me?"

"Oh, nothing much. Just that you're clearly not an opera aficionado. I think it was meant to make me think badly of you, but it totally backfired because I told her you're clearly my kind of girl. I cannot stand the opera. So screechy and boring."

"And weird. This opera was off the charts."

"You know, Granny doesn't like new people all that much, so don't take it too personally. If she had her way, we'd all get married off to our cousins and no one would have to deal with anyone new."

I make a face. "That's kinda weird, isn't it?"

"She comes from an era when that sort of thing wasn't

at all uncommon. Upholding the family name mattered so much more than it does now."

"Was that the Dark Ages?" I ask with a wry smile.

"Granny's not that old. Well, if eighty is the new seventy. We had her big birthday bash while they were filming *Dating Mr. Darcy* in Texas. Granny was most put out that Sebastian, her favorite grandchild, wasn't there." She rolls her eyes at me.

"How big a 'birthday bash' does an eighty-year-old have, exactly? I mean, was it a tea and crumpet affair or something more *Girls Gone Wild*?" I giggle at the thought of Geraldine in a bikini, hanging off some buff guy at a beach, spilling her beer onto the golden sand as she laughs.

"OMG, stop! It was a cocktail party. Granny sat on a chair like she was the Queen receiving her guests. It was actually quite fun, considering I lowered the average age of the partygoer by a good couple of decades."

The cab comes to a stop, and as I peer out the window, my nerves kick up. "We must be here. Why am I suddenly nervous?"

Who am I kidding? I know exactly why. Geraldine is going to be there along with all the Huntington-Ross clan and their circle of friends, all judging me and finding me wanting.

It's going to be a super fun night.

"Come on," Zara says as she swings her legs out of the cab. "Let's get a quick G & T into you and you'll feel a lot better about everything, you'll see."

Once inside, Zara takes my hand and leads me to a makeshift bar where a server dressed in a white shirt and black waistcoat greets her like an old friend.

"Zara! How've you been?" he asks as she kisses his cheek.

"Fabulous, Jimmy. This is Sebastian's fiancée, Emma."

Jimmy raises his eyebrows at me. "The famous Emma, eh?"

"Not famous," I reply as I paste on a smile. "Just Emma."

"Well, Just Emma, what can I get you to drink?"

Zara chimes in with, "We'll have two G & Ts, thanks, Jim, and make them extra strong, okay?"

He flashes her his handsome grin. "I've got you covered."

As Jimmy fixes our drinks, I ask quietly, "How do you know Jimmy?"

"Somewhere or other. I can't really remember. Once you've lived here as long as I have, you get to know everyone, even if you get to escape to London as often as I do."

"Well, you have got a job there."

"That's the fabulous thing about being my own boss. Za-Za Interiors operates when and where it suits me."

Oh, to be from the *right* side of the tracks. If Penny and I had that attitude, Timothy would never have got off the ground, and I'd still be stuck in a dead-end job that sucked the life from me on a daily basis.

Zara points out some people in the crowd. "That's Uncle Hector. He's on Mum's side of the family, so not nearly as cray-cray as the Huntington-Ross side. He's married to Serafina, the gorgeous Italian woman over there in the black sequin dress."

I look in the direction she's pointing. "Zara, half the room is in black."

I glance down at my own dress. It's red and pretty and, up until about ten seconds ago, felt appropriate for a fundraiser slash exhibition opening slash impress the relatives event. What had felt colorful and fun when I got dressed now makes me feel like the poor cousin in a dress her mom sewed on her rickety, old machine.

"Serafina's the one that looks like Amal Clooney. She's next to the guy who's channeling Rick Astley."

"Rick who?"

"80's popstar. Total British icon. *Never Gonna Give You Up?*"

"I'm never gonna give you up, either, girl," I jest.

She nudges me with her elbow as my eyes find a tall, willowy woman listening closely to something a guy in coral-colored pants hitched up almost to his nipple line is saying.

"See the guy they're with? The one in white with the silver puffer jacket and eyepatch? He's the artist. His name is Rasmus."

"Does he have a last name?"

She shakes her head. "Just Rasmus. Come on. I'll introduce you."

We collect our drinks from Jimmy, who grins and winks at Zara, and make our way through the crowd.

"Emma! Zara! Hello, you two gorgeous things, you," Jilly says, greeting us both with her trademark *m-wah, m-wah* air kisses. She's also dressed in a black dress, hers with a silver trim and skinny belt. "Zara, I'm with your mummy and granny over here. Come and join us."

My nerves hop around at the mention of Geraldine.

"We were just going to meet Uncle Hector," I say.

"Uncle Hector can wait. He's deep in conversation with Rasmus, anyway."

I take a deep breath and steel myself. We make our way through the crowd. Geraldine is propped up on her walking stick, a glass of what looks like sherry in her hand, talking to a man I've not met before as Jemima listens in.

"Hello, Granny," Zara says as she gives her a kiss on her cheek.

"Zara, darling." She sweeps an appreciative eye over her granddaughter. "Divine as always, if the skirt is a little short." She looks pointedly at Zara's bare knees. "Couldn't you at least have worn a pair of pantyhose?"

"Granny, no one under sixty wears pantyhose anymore. And besides, pantyhose are just plain weird."

She presses her lips together. "If you're going to deride an item of clothing, dear, at least try to make better use of the vernacular. 'Weird' is an utterly ubiquitous term that's come to mean next to nothing."

"Weird means weird, Granny," Zara replies, unperturbed.

I, on the other hand, am feeling thoroughly perturbed. My dress is just as short as Zara's, and not only did I *not* consider wearing pantyhose tonight, I don't even own a pair.

"Hello, ma'am," I say to her with a nervous smile. "You look terrific. In fact, I love the way you're all dressed in black. It's like it's Team Huntington-Ross's color tonight."

And I'm the only one left out.

She throws a look in my direction. "I find the best eveningwear is black," she replies.

Right.

I try a different tack.

"I also love the way you've combined pearls with...more pearls."

Yes, I know, I'm a total suck. I feel no shame. A girl's gotta do what a girl's gotta do.

And as a side note, she is wearing a *lot* of pearls right now.

She regards me for a moment before she turns toward a piece of art on the wall. I've been so busy dealing with the people side of things, I haven't given a second thought to the art.

"I do find this piece intriguing. Don't you, Emma?" she says.

I run my eyes over it. It's a white canvas with what looks like a hair on it, one not from your head, if you catch my drift. "Sure is. Real intriguing."

"What do you think it says?"

Someone wipe this hair off me?

"Oh, I, ah, I imagine it's a comment on soap," I say, grasping at the first thought that pops into my head.

She arches her thin eyebrows. "Soap?"

"You know, how if you use a bar of soap after your roommate there might be something stuck to it that you don't want to be stuck to it?"

Beside me, Zara snorts. I shoot her a look.

"How very...*original* of you," Geraldine replies.

She was testing me, and I failed.

"Well, I think it's just splendid," Jilly says. "And Emma's very astute. Although it's my understanding the artist is making a commentary on the impermanence and transitory nature of 21st century life, I can absolutely see how soap can be a part of that conceptualization."

I nod along as though whatever Jilly just said made perfect sense. "Indeed," I say, touching my chin as though deep in thought. Which I am. It's just I'm thinking "What the frigging heck is she rattling on about?" rather than anything about "conceptualizations" and the like.

Geraldine widens her eyes and shoots me a look that suggests I add something more to Jilly's assessment.

"Jilly's totally right. That's what I meant about the soap thing."

I flash her a grateful smile. It's so good to have Jilly on

my side, someone who's close to the family but not *in* the family, someone who can help me navigate these new, murky waters.

Geraldine's smile is pleasant and totally unconvinced. "Tell me, what do you think of this piece?" She gestures at something behind me, and I turn to see a toilet bowl, filled with some sort of goopy pink liquid. It looks like it's been plunked in the middle of the room for no good reason.

What the heck do I say about that? If the last one looked like an errant hair stuck to a bar of soap, this one is a step w*aaa*y too far into the bathroom for me.

"Oh, this?" I ask, and I notice in horror as a couple of other people have joined our group around the toilet bowl, awaiting my *expert* assessment.

"Yes. This," Geraldine replies, and I'm sure I spot a glint in her eye.

"Right. Well, as you can see, it's a toilet bowl, used for... what you do in the, err, bathroom," I begin, my mind racing around, trying in vain to land on the artist's thought process behind sticking something like this in the middle of a gallery. I hope it's brand new and not—*ugh.* I can't even.

I swallow, my mouth dry. Remembering the gin and tonic in my hand, I take a large swig, stalling for time. I wrack my brain for some of the expressions Jilly had used moments ago. "It's a conceptualization," I begin, excited I remembered one of Jilly's words, "of the way in which humanity has ah, developed." My wobbly smile firms up.

Yup, that's good.

Well, not *good*, exactly, but it's better than what I really think.

"What do you mean by that, exactly? Developed in what way?" someone I haven't met asks, and if I could make him shut the heck up right now, I *so* would.

Marrying Mr. Darcy

"Developed to, ah...use toilets." I scrunch up my face, hold my breath, and await the response.

"As opposed to *not* using toilets?" the man asks.

Who *is* this guy, and what is he trying to do to me?!

"Mmm, yes. Yes, that's right."

Zara nudges me. I'm sure she knows I pulled that out of a hat. "Well said, Emma. You clearly understand this piece extremely well."

I don't look at her for fear of giggling. I've already had one giggling fit in front of Geraldine. I don't want a repeat performance.

"Oh, absolutely," Jilly adds, and I could collect both of them up in a grateful hug.

And then leave. I would very much like to leave.

"Although you did leave out the fact it's an *homage* to Marcel Duchamp's 1917 work, *Fountain*," Jilly continues, "and the way in which he altered the meaning of a urinal by placing it in an exhibition space as a piece of art. But I'm sure you meant to mention that."

"Well, *of course* I was going to say that," I reply. "I just hadn't got to it yet. Marcel Marceau—"

"Duchamp," Jilly corrects.

"Duchamp," I repeat. "Thank you for that Jilly. Marcel Duchamp deserves as many *homages* as he can get." Did I use that word right? "In fact, he is—"

"Was."

"—*was* a great artist. One of the best, particularly when it came to...toilets." I finish with a broad smile, hoping to dazzle them all with my straight teeth. You see, this is England. Orthodontists don't seem to feature much in their requirements for a good life here.

Jilly winks at me. "Quite."

"Well, thank you, Emma, for that enlightening soliloquy," Geraldine says. It feels like a compliment until she adds, "And thank you, Jilly, for filling in *all* the gaps."

I let out a defeated huff of air. I know I messed up. I know I came across as a bumbling idiot.

Geraldine turns to leave, and I'm gripped by a sudden panic. I need her to see me as Sebastian's equal, not some dithering philistine who doesn't know the differences between a couple of guys called Marcel.

"Please! Wait!" I call out as I dash toward her. I've got no clue what I'm going say, but I know I've got to say *something*. And it needs to be now.

I don't get the chance. The next thing I know, I walk *smack* into something in my way. On my uncharacteristically high heels, I begin to lose my balance, my arms flailing as I search desperately for something to hold onto. All I find is thin air, and the next thing I know, I've spun around and have landed heavily on my butt, cool liquid spraying out around me.

The room falls quiet as everyone gawps at me.

"What have you done!" Rasmus comes pushing his way through the crowd in his silver puffer jacket. He lifts his eyepatch and blinks with both perfectly functioning eyes at me in astonishment. "You have utterly soiled my masterpiece!"

I don't need to look. I know exactly what I landed on.

Humiliation seeps through every pore as my belly drops.

I'm sitting on a toilet, covered in pink goop, in the middle of an art gallery, surrounded by all of my future in-laws.

Chapter Twelve

Mr. Darcy's Emma makes a splash in the loo!

I clutch my phone tightly as I gaze at an image of me from last night, my butt firmly sunk into Rasmus's toilet. There's pink goop splattered all over me, the floor, and some of the bystanders, too. The look on my face says a bewildered "what the bleep just happened?" the very moment before the truth came crashing down.

Not content with simply fading away, Dating Mr. Darcy's *Emma Brady—the one no one wanted sexy Sebastian to choose—was spotted last night doing a one-up on her red carpet arrival on the show last summer.*

This time she made sure she was surrounded by a big crowd, some of whom she splattered with the pink goo artist Rasmus told us was meant to raise awareness of pig farming in this country. By the looks of things, clumsy Emma feels a certain affinity with our swine cousins. Oink oink.

I look up at Sebastian as mortification fills my bloodstream. "They said *oink oink*."

"Brady, don't torture yourself," he says as he gently

pulls the phone from my hand and switches it off. "It's not worth it."

"But it was so humiliating. And in front of your friends and family, too. And your granny!" I bury my head in my hands. "I cannot catch a break with that woman."

"My family probably barely noticed it," he soothes.

I let out a sardonic laugh. "It was a little hard to miss. The one good thing is that you weren't there to see it, but that really is the only good thing." I scrunch my eyes shut, willing all of this to go away. I feel his warm hand on my back, and I look up at him.

"You certainly found the most dramatic place to land," he says with a small smile.

"I know, right? A freaking toilet!"

His attempt to stifle a laugh is unsuccessful.

"Don't laugh," I sulk, not ready to make light of this just yet.

He slips his arm around my shoulder and places a soft kiss on my lips. "Brady, if anyone can look utterly charming while their bottom is wedged in a toilet bowl in the middle of a crowded room, it's you."

"Like that's a thing."

"I think you just made it one. I fully expect to see images of many celebrities posing in Rasmus's toilet bowls in the future. He'll love this publicity."

I begin to soften. "Do you think?"

"Are you kidding? You made his artwork frontpage news today."

"I guess," I concede.

"Before long, everyone will be accessorizing with a Rasmus bowl," he jokes, and I begin to soften.

"Maybe Gigi Hadid will appear in one on the next cover of *Vogue*?"

Marrying Mr. Darcy

He grins at me. "I have absolutely no idea who that is, but it seems highly likely to me."

"She's only one of the biggest models right now, Seb." I shake my head at his lack of pop culture knowledge. "I know what. They'll call it 'bathroom chic,' and everyone will be doing it, from the Kardashians to royalty."

"Lady Gaga at the next Met Ball."

My eyebrows jump up in surprise. "You know about Lady Gaga? And the Met Ball?"

"I'm English, Brady, not dead."

"Is that so, Mr. Darcy?" I tease as I place my hands on his face and pull him in for another kiss.

"Mmm," is his only reply.

A fresh thought has me pulling back. "What about your family? They all saw it. Even Uncle Hector and his beautiful Italian wife."

"For starters, I wouldn't worry in the least about what Uncle Hector thinks. He's not exactly done the family name any favors with his string of wives and dodgy businesses. And as for the rest of them, Zara and Mother both think you're the bees' knees. You falling into an artist's toilet bowl isn't going to change that."

I make a face. "What about your granny?"

"I admit, Granny's a different kettle of fish altogether."

I slump in my seat. "She already hates me. Now she thinks I'm a total idiot as well."

"She doesn't hate you," Sebastian mollifies.

"Fun fact, Seb, she does."

"Give her time. She's old-fashioned, sure, but she's also just trying to protect me. She's a lioness with her cub."

"She wants to protect you from the gold digger American reality show contestant who humiliates herself in the media."

"Well, when you put it like that..." he teases, and I bat him lightly on his arm.

"Look, I need to find a way to show her I'm here because I love you and I'm totally worthy of you."

"Brady, you are more than worthy of me. I'm the one grateful to have you in my life."

I melt a little at his words, but I don't let them distract me. Well, not until we've had a really good make out session for a while, anyway.

Eventually, I pull away from him with as much reluctance as a naughty kid called in to see the principal. "I've got to go. I'm meeting Jilly for a post-falling-in-the-toilet-disaster debrief, as long as I'm happy to "muck out" her horses. Whatever that means." I hop up and straighten out my clothes.

"Well, it can't be any worse than falling in a loo," he teases, and I narrow my eyes at him.

"Very funny." I extend my hand. "Keys, please."

"Drive on the left side," he reminds me.

"I know," I reply, pretending to be offended. Although I admit I do need to remind myself every time I get in the car. "Catch you later."

I give him a quick kiss and head down the hallway. Making the assumption the word "muck" is quite literal, I sneak into Zara's room and borrow her most serious looking raincoat. It's an oilskin that almost reaches the floor on me but is probably only thigh length on her. Okay, I'm exaggerating here, but she was genetically gifted the most fantastic pair of long legs. They make mine look like stubby fingers in comparison, thanks to my feeble five feet and three inches.

Not that I'm in any way jealous, of course.

To be extra careful, on my way out the door, I grab a pair of Sebastian's rubber boots—or Wellingtons as they're referred to here for reasons unknown to me—and although they're a gazillion sizes too big and come up to my knees, I throw them in the trunk of the car.

Once at Jilly's stables some forty-minutes' drive later, I slip on the boots and stomp over the cobbles, my feet bouncing around as though they're trying to escape from their roomy rubber incarceration. The distinctive aroma of hay and horse pee hits me between the eyes as I venture inside the stables.

"Jilly?" I call out when there's no sign of her.

A couple of horses' heads poke out of their stalls to check out who's disturbing them.

"Hey, horses," I say to them, their liquid brown eyes watching me. "You're all looking very…horsy today."

"Well, I would expect they'd look 'horsy' everyday, what with being horses. Wouldn't you?" Jilly says with a laugh as she walks toward me. She's dressed in a pair of riding pants and a black slim-fitting T-shirt, a pair of fitted boots on her feet. "Oh, Emma. What *are* you wearing?"

I glance down at my oversized coat and boots. Next to Jilly, I look like a toddler playing dress-up in her mom's clothes. "You said 'muck out,' so I thought I'd come prepared."

"You look like you're expecting the deluge of the century. Come on, take off that ridiculously large coat. You'll boil over."

I do as instructed, folding Zara's coat over one of the stalls.

"And the Wellies?"

"Seb's."

"I suppose they'll have to do. Now, pop into the empty stall here and help me move some things. I've just put Basil out to graze."

"You called a horse after an herb?"

"Oh, they all are. We've got Basil, of course, and these darlings are Rosemary and Tarragon down at the end." She points down the stalls at the horses who are still watching us.

"That's cute."

"Help me with the food tub."

As we set to work removing the items from the stall and then cleaning it out, I complain to Jilly about how I embarrassed myself once again in front of Geraldine.

"Do you mean when you fell into the toilet or when you referred to the Dadaist Marcel Duchamp as Marcel Marceau, the famous mime?"

"Marcel Marceau was a mime? Huh. I didn't know. I just knew his name."

"Oh, yes. Did all that stuck in boxes thing people seem to like so much." She flays her hands around, doing a very poor impersonation of a mime stuck in a box, and I let out a giggle.

"You'd make a great mime, Jilly."

"Maybe I could give up the law and pursue a life on the stage? Silently and dressed in a Breton shirt, of course."

I smile at her. Jilly is quirky and more English than the English, and her heart is in the right place. I'm so lucky to have her as a friend here.

"Did Geraldine say anything to you?" I ask.

"Nothing of any consequence."

Her tone tells me she did.

My heart sinks. Of course she did. The girl you don't want your grandson to marry made a public fool of herself. She must be enjoying every moment of this.

"Give it to me straight, Jilly."

"Only that you'd made a bit of a spectacle of yourself,

Marrying Mr. Darcy

and it was a little worse than the whole giggling fit at the opera thing."

My heart sinks. I know she's dulling Geraldine's words to soften the blow. "Oh, no."

She leans the broom she's been using to sweep the floor with against the wall of the stall. "But that's something, isn't it?"

"Jilly, I think I've hit rock bottom when we're discussing which of my humiliations is better than the other."

"Oh, buck up, darling. Tomorrow is another day, in the words of the great Scarlett O'Hara. Although I don't suggest you go making any clothes out of curtains to prove yourself."

"No plans."

"You can show Geraldine how truly perfect you are for her grandson at the house opening. I have got this gorgeous green jungle-print dress that you would look simply divine in with a darling fascinator hat to match."

"A green jungle print dress?" I ask dubiously.

"It's J Lo meets the Queen, darling. Sexy but buttoned up. You'll love it. You'll look like the perfect wife-to-be."

Although I've got no clue what "J Lo meets the Queen" could possibly look like, I reply with a smile, "You're a total godsend."

Thank goodness for Jilly.

Chapter Thirteen

"Penn, I so miss you," I say down into the phone from the window seat in our bedroom. Outside, the flowers are in full late-summer bloom despite the gloomy, gray day. I watch as Geraldine and Jemima walk slowly through the rose garden together, and I can guess what they're talking about.

Me.

Me and my huge social gaffe, to be specific.

"Uh-oh. That doesn't sound good."

"It's not. I hit a stumbling block and ended up firmly stuck in the toilet."

"Do you think you could be less cryptic? I've got so much to do to get this next order ready to go out, and I was up until two in the morning last night." She adds a yawn to emphasize her point.

With a pang of guilt that I should be there to help, I fill her in on the art gallery disaster.

"You fell in a toilet?" she asks as she lets out a hearty laugh. "Oh, Em, that is hilarious!"

"No, it's not," I rebuke. "It's a disaster."

"Oh, you're right. I'm sorry. I just had a funny image in my head, that's all."

Penny's laugh is infectious, and before long, despite myself, I begin to giggle.

"*Everyone* saw it, this girl falling backwards into a toilet filled with pink gooey stuff that squirted all over everything."

"There was pink gooey stuff?" she asks with a fresh chortle.

"Oh, yeah. You should have heard the deeply embarrassing sucking sounds my thighs made as they got detached from the sides of the bowl as Zara and Jilly pulled me out."

Penny loses it once more. "Sucking sounds? Oh, Em!"

"Not elegant and not ladylike. I need one of those memory erasing sticks from the *Men in Black* movies."

"Sure, I'll send one right over."

"It got in the media here."

"Oh, no. Not after all the bad press you've got for Seb choosing you."

"Oh, they loved this, I can tell you that."

"Don't read it. That's my advice."

"Well, that's not all." I tell her about the fact Heather McCabe won't do *Saving Pemberley* with me in it, and she's appropriately outraged on my behalf. As she should be. Penny's been my bestie since our first week at college.

"To sum up, the media thinks I'm a laughingstock, Seb is refusing to do the show without me, which means no show, and I've got his granny out for my blood. It's super fun to be me right now."

"Oh, girl. That sucks. Maybe you could use the whole falling into a toilet thing to market Timothy."

"What, like, if you're gonna fall into a toilet bowl in

front of your future in-laws, make sure you're wearing activewear by Timothy?"

Her giggle ends in a snort. "I was thinking you could be self-deprecating about it all, you know? Leave voicemails for these purchasing managers who refuse to take your calls, asking them if they want to meet the girl who famously fell in a toilet full of goop."

"I'm not sure I want to be known as that."

"Emma Goop Brady sounds so good to me."

I let out a resigned puff of air. "Jokes aside, I just don't know if I can come back from this with Seb's granny. Every time she even looks at me, she'll remember I'm the girl who fell butt first into the pink goop filled toilet in front of everyone."

"Have you seen her since?"

I notice Jemima looking in my direction, and I shrink back from view. "I've been hiding."

"Well, that's mature."

"Penn, if I had my way, I'd never see any of them again."

"Yeah, that would work. Marry a guy and not see his family. Oh, hold on, he *lives* with them. You're gonna see them every freaking day. Unless you perfect your ninja skills, of course."

My insides twist. "No ninja skills."

"You're just gonna have to rip off that Band-Aid. Remember when I first met Trey, and his mom hated me? That was all because I told her I found football boring."

"Which it is. How did you win her over?"

"I pretended to love football, and then I got myself a Texans shirt."

"I'm not sure me buying a soccer shirt is gonna help them get past me falling into a toilet in front of them all."

"Does she have a sense of humor?"

"That would be a big, serious, stiff upper lip *no*. My friend Jilly's helping me make sure I look and play the part at the big event we're having to kick off opening the house."

"Oooh, that sounds fun."

"As long as I don't fall into anything, have a giggling fit, say the wrong thing, or all of the above."

"Answer me something, is Seb worth it?"

I think of my handsome fiancé, and my heart fills with love. "Totally worth it."

"Then you've got this, girl."

"I guess. At least I've got Jilly. She's training me so I don't make a fool of myself at the opening. Jilly knows how things work here. She is an absolute godsend."

"Good for Jilly."

I think I detect a note of jealousy in her voice. "Don't be like that, Penn. She's really great. You'll love her when you meet her."

"Like when you get married back here at home?" she leads.

"I, ah, I think we'll get married here at Martinston. It's a family tradition, and it only seems right."

"What about your little chapel? You've always wanted to get married there."

"It's fine," I reply with a shrug. "That was just some silly fantasy. Martinston is so much grander and more amazing, anyway." I think of the beautiful grounds at Martinston where we could have a massive marquee, the ballroom where we could dance the night away, the pergola on top of the rise overlooking the house where Sebastian proposed to me. It would be the picture-perfect wedding. "I might have once wanted a small, simple wedding in a sweet little chapel, but that was before I agreed to marry a Lord. Things have changed, Penn."

"Heck yes they have, girl! Lady Huntington-Ross shall have the best of everything!"

"Actually, I'll be called Lady Martinston when we get married."

"You're named after the house? That's like calling me Mrs. 12156 Memorial Street."

I giggle. "Well, Mrs. 12156 Memorial, I need to go help the others. We're moving a bunch of stuff around for the opening, and that means packing boxes and choosing which of the priceless antiques to put where."

"Nice for some."

"I know, right?"

"Em? I hope Seb's granny is nice to you. You deserve nice."

"Thanks, Penn. You're the best."

"That is very true," she jokes. "I hope you have some success with getting a meeting this week. I cannot wait to get Timothy into some UK stores."

My heart sinks as I think of my complete lack of success on that front to date. "I hope so too, Penn. Wish me luck."

"You got this, girl."

I hang up and make my way downstairs where Sebastian is busy going through boxes of stuff. You know how you move from a small place to a larger one, and you think "wow, so much space!" and then you end up filling it all up? Well, it turns out it's the same with oversized English manor houses, only on a much, much larger scale, thanks to the generations upon generations of family who have lived there.

"What can I do to help?" I ask.

"Why don't you see what's in those boxes over there," Sebastian says as he points at a stack of old cardboard boxes in the corner. "Granny thought there might be a few things

Marrying Mr. Darcy

in there we could put on display, but I've got no idea what's in them."

"For sure." I work my way through the boxes until I come across one filled with old toys. "This one's interesting."

"Let me see." Sebastian pushes himself up off the ground and walks over to me. He reaches into the box and pulls out a wooden cup and ball. "Did you ever play this game?" The red paint around the rim is chipped, and the string holding the ball is grey and fraying. It looks like it was made about a hundred years ago, which knowing Martinston, it probably was.

I shake my head. "I was more a Barbie and Ken kinda girl. Trying to catch a ball in a cup was never my thing."

He hands it to me. "Give it a try."

"I guess." I untwine the string and begin to flip the ball at the end of the string into the cup. It hits my arm, my hand, and the cup's rim, but it doesn't go in. I pass it back to Sebastian. "Not my jam."

He flips the ball into the cup the first time and grins at me. "It's my jam, it would seem."

I nudge him with my shoulder. "Show off."

"I played with this exact one when I was young. It was my great grandfather's, I think."

I roll my eyes. "Of course it was. Everything in this place has history."

"Which is why the task of clearing out is so hard." He reaches back into the box and pulls out a bronze tin. Opening it, he says, "Look at these. I bet you they're made of lead." He holds up a toy soldier.

"Better put it back, then. You don't want to poison us all."

He places the soldier back in the tin and clips it closed. "Good point."

"Now," I say as I clap my hands together in an I mean business kind of way. "What's next?"

"You could take that toy box up to the attic. It's not too heavy. But first I'll hold onto these." He pulls the tin box with the lead soldiers out. "They can go in one of the display boxes in one of the bedrooms. I read that people love that kind of thing."

"Gotcha." I turn to leave when Jemima comes sailing in. Suddenly nervous to see her following my embarrassment of last night, I say, "Jemima. Hi."

Her face lights up in a smile. "Thank you for helping with this."

"Of course. I'm going be part of the family, after all. I want to do what I can."

"Oh, you are sweet. I hope you're okay following that incident last night. I thought maybe your bottom might be a little sore."

I shake my head, my cheeks flaming. "All good. Just humiliated, that's all."

"Don't be. It was nothing. I'm glad you're okay," she replies kindly, and if it wasn't for the box in my arms, I'd hug her.

"Thank you. I'd better take this up to the attic."

"Lovely," she says to me as she turns her attention to her son. "Seb, I finally have that list of items my friend Joffrey from British Historicals said we should display." She holds up a printed sheet.

"Wonderful. That will definitely save us some time."

I make my way down the hallway to a flight of stairs that leads up to the attic. I clamber up, glad at least this box isn't too heavy. When I reach the top of the stairs, I find Zara leafing through a photo album.

"Hey, Zara," I say, embarrassed to be a little breathless after climbing the stairs with a light box.

She looks up at me, blinks, and dabs at her eyes. "Oh. Hi."

"You okay?" I ask as I place the box with a stack of others on the floor by one of the angled walls.

"Yeah, I'm just looking at some old photos of us with Dad."

"Can I see?"

"Of course you can. Come, sit."

There are several photos of Sebastian Huntington-Ross Senior around the house, and of course a very large portrait of him hangs in the grand hallway, looking down on you as you walk by. Naturally. Haven't we all got one of those in our grand hallways?

I sit down cross-legged on the floor next to her and look at the album. There are a bunch of family photos taken at Christmas one year when Sebastian must have been about ten or eleven. There are photos of them in the living room together, all dressed up in their Sunday best. I point at a particularly sweet one of Seb looking extremely cute in a shirt and tie tucked into a V-neck sweater. "He looks super proud there."

"I bet it was something Dad said. Seb used to hang on his every word."

"He did? I had no idea. He doesn't talk about your dad all that much, really, only to say he was quite formal and standoffish."

"Oh, he was that too. But if being a daddy's boy is a thing, that would have totally been Seb. He would do anything to get our father's attention. He studied hard and was always a bit of a Goody-Two-Shoes in my opinion. All for Daddy." She turns the page, and I see another photo of the family together. Sebastian is gazing at his father with love in his eyes, and my heart squeezes for him—for the boy he was and the man he is today.

"It must have been so hard for him when your dad died. Hard for all of you."

"It wasn't a lot of fun. But then, you know all about that, don't you?"

I feel a stab of pain worm across my chest. "My dad was the best."

"You miss him."

"I do. I find myself wondering what he'd think of me here, set to marry your brother, and the very different life I'm going to have." I smile at her, my heart aching. "I wish he could have met you all."

"Do you think our dads would have got on?"

"I'm not sure. From what Seb has told me, your dad was quite formal and not that warm. My dad was the total opposite. The only formal thing about him was the suit and tie he'd wear on Sundays for church. The same one, every week."

Sebastian walks in with two boxes stacked on top of one another and places them heavily down on the ground. "Why do we have so many books?" he complains, panting lightly.

Zara puts her hands up in the air. "Not guilty."

"Oh, I know *that*," he replies as he walks over toward us. "What are you two looking at?"

"Photos," Zara replies simply. She turns the page over. "Oh, my gosh. Look at this. These are from that Christmas when Uncle Hector came with that dreadful woman who had that horrendous high-pitched laugh and smoked cigars after dinner. Remember?"

Sebastian arches an eyebrow. "Do I want to?"

"She sounds fun," I say.

"She must have thought you were either a girl or into girly things because she gave us both Bratz dolls. Remember?"

"She did?"

"Yup. She gave me Cloe, and you got Jade. I was thrilled because I was only six or seven, but you were much older."

"And a *boy*," he adds with a laugh.

"I remember Bratz dolls," I say. "Did you play with your doll much, Seb?" I tease. "Actually, if you were a tween at the time, I don't know if I want you to answer that. Those dolls were pretty sexy. You know, for dolls."

He sits down next to us on the floor. "Sexy dolls, huh, Brady? Is there something you need to tell me?"

I shake my head as I giggle. "You were a totally cute teenager." I point at one of the photos of him in the album.

"I was deeply self-conscious and won friends by acting the clown."

"Oh, that makes me feel so sad," I exclaim.

"Show me a thirteen-year-old who's totally self-assured and knows their place in the world, and I'll show you a liar," he replies with a smirk. "We all go through phases. I gained in confidence through my teenage years."

"But you never rebelled," Zara comments. "You never let loose and got drunk and threw parties and smashed priceless vases."

He raises an eyebrow. "Zara's describing her teens, Brady."

"You were pretty wild, were you?" I ask her.

She shrugs. "No more than your average. Daddy was pretty strict, and there were so many rules at boarding school. A girl has got to let loose every now and then, you know."

"So, you never did anything outrageous? Never broke the rules, got in trouble, did something you'd never do again?" I ask Seb.

Zara answers for him. "Seb was always a good boy. Always looking for Daddy's approval. Whether he got it or not, I don't know."

"Did you?" I ask.

"He was a hard man to please," he replies, and my heart goes out to the young boy wanting desperately to win his father's approval and falling short. No matter how hard he tried.

"I'm sorry." I place my hand on his knee, and he shoots me a grateful look.

"Look at Father in this photo," Seb says as he points at an image in the album. "He looks so young and happy there."

"He probably was. He adored Mum."

"He did. A love that stands the test of time is valuable indeed." Sebastian's eyes find mine, and we share a smile.

Sure, our love has only stood the test of four and a half months, but we both know what we have is real. We both know what we have is precious.

We flick through some more photos, both Zara and Sebastian sharing stories of their upbringing, until we agree it's high time we got back to work, or the house wouldn't be ready for its grand opening. Zara hops up and returns to the stack of boxes downstairs.

With Zara out of the room, I pull Sebastian in for a hug. "I cannot imagine how hard it would have been for you to not only lose your dad but to find out that his gambling had put your home in peril."

He looks down. "It wasn't easy. He surrounded himself with the wrong people, people who saw him as a bottomless pit of cash."

"I'm sorry, Seb."

"We're righting the wrongs now. Together. That's all that matters."

An hour later, with Jemima's help, we have managed to move most of the family's personal effects out of the soon-to-be public section of the house and have fulfilled most of Joffrey's list.

"Who needs a snack?" I ask.

Zara wipes her forehead and grins at me. "Oh, I could kill for a coffee, and I'm in serious need of some sugar."

"I've got you covered. Seb?"

"A cup of tea would be great."

"I'm on it."

Chapter Fourteen

I head straight to Mia's Café. I got seriously addicted to their chocolate chip cookies when I first arrived in this country, and it's a habit I just cannot break now. They're crunchy on the outside and chewy on the inside with enough sugar to induce a diabetic coma. But sometimes you've got to treat yourself, and with the number of things we've had to rifle through and boxes we've had to lug around Sebastian's massive house today, I think we more than deserve it.

"Hi, Emma," the owner, Greg, says as I arrive at the counter. He's a sweet man in his fifties, always with a smile on his round face. His bushy moustache and red bow tie always make me think of the Pringles chip guy. He told me once that he named the café after his late wife, and I always detect a hint of sadness in his eyes whenever he talks about her. "Let me guess, some of my lovely Mia's chocolate chip biscuits?"

"You got it in one, Greg," I reply with a smile. "I'll take eight, please. They're too good not to, and we've been working pretty darn hard today. Plus, some beverages, too. Two large flat whites and a cup of tea, please."

"My pleasure." He opens the large glass jar filled with cookies and uses some tongs to pull them out. "Not long now until the house opens up. It's the talk of the village."

"Yeah, I heard." I chew on my lip when I think of everything that needs to be done before then. "Thanks again for having the poster in your window."

"Of course. Martinston has been a part of this village for centuries. It's about time we all got to enjoy it. I don't think it's been open to visitors for decades."

"I totally agree with you."

"How's business? You make that gym kit, is that right?"

Gym kit?

"No, I have an activewear line," I correct.

"That's what I meant, love," he says with a chuckle. "Gym kit means clothes."

"Huh. I did not know that. Well, Timothy—that's my label—is pretty much dead in the water in the UK right now. For some reason I can't seem to even get a meeting with any of the big sports chains or the department stores here, even though it sells super well in the States. I don't get it."

"Have you tried any of the smaller places? My sister-in-law, Denise, she runs a shop in the neighboring village. Specializes in sports kit for ladies who want to hold things together, if you know what I mean. I can put in a good word for you, if you like?"

Although I know a boutique that caters to a small demographic isn't exactly going to set my world on fire, it's a kind offer and one I won't say no to. "That's so sweet of you. Thank you, Greg." I open my purse and pull out my business card. "Here's my card. It's got all my contact deets on it, including our website."

"Oh, I'm not sure Denise is much for the internet, love, but I'll pass this on all the same."

I give him a weak smile. That doesn't sound promising. "Sure. Thanks."

"Anything else today?"

"That's all."

I pay, and he says, "Take a seat while I rustle them up for you."

I glance around the busy café and spot a vacant seat at a table in the window bathed in the warm sun. I plunk myself down heavily in the chair, a wave of exhaustion washing over me. You know how you can keep going with something and not even notice you're tired until you stop and then it hits you like a steam train? Well, that's me right now, the hard work of the past weeks catching right up.

I lean back against the comfy cushions, take a deep breath, and close my eyes, enjoying the warmth of the sun streaming through the window and the hum of the chatter around me.

"Things have got to be pretty bad if you're choosing to catch some Zs in public," a voice says.

I ping my eyes open to see an extremely handsome face I've seen once before grinning down at me.

"Chris," I exclaim, taken totally by surprise. "What are you doing here?"

He pulls a chair out from the table and sits down opposite me. "Well, I can tell you what I'm *not* doing here, and that's falling asleep in the sun."

"I wasn't sleeping. I was resting my eyes."

He laughs, his face lighting up. "I see. Well, I suppose

that's an improvement on a giggling fit at the opera, anyway."

"True."

"It seems to me you urgently require some caffeination. Might I assist with that?"

"Is that a weird way of asking if I'd like a coffee?"

"Did I sound like Sebastian? 'Cause that's what I was aiming for."

"Actually, you kinda did."

He leans closer to me, and I catch the aroma of his scent. "Although, between us, I could never be like your fiancé."

"Why not?" I shift uncomfortably in my seat. This guy is getting a little overly familiar—again. And now that I know how he treated Jilly and how much Sebastian dislikes him, I wish he'd just leave me alone.

"Seb's English, for a start. I mean, I've been here since I went to college, and they still confuse the heck out of me."

"I can relate to that."

"What is with calling someone a Muppet as an insult? Being a Muppet is cool. I so wanted to be Kermit as a kid."

I giggle despite my determination not to like this guy. "No, you didn't."

"Okay, I wanted to be a Power Ranger, but seriously, they've got some weird expressions and ways of doing things. Have you noticed the queuing?"

"Queuing?"

"Lining up. They do it whenever and wherever they can. I was in London last week, and I saw a line of people just standing there on the sidewalk. I asked one of them what they were doing, and they said they were queuing up but had no idea what for. They just joined the queue."

"No, they didn't."

"Okay, that was a total lie, but they do love a good queue here."

With his fun, cheeky personality, I can't help but warm to him a little. Maybe it's having a fellow American to talk to in this new and unfamiliar world? Whatever it is, it still feels a little wrong to enjoy the company of the guy who broke my friend's heart.

"Here's another one for you," he continues. "How about the way they talk about butts as 'bums'? That's weird."

"I know, right? A bum is a homeless guy who smells bad, not a part of your anatomy."

"I went on a super steep learning curve when I moved here for college."

"Why did you come to college here?"

"My mom's British. She had this idea that her offspring should go to universities here because she did. Cambridge is her alma mater."

"Where did you grow up?"

"Boston."

"Right. Because they don't have any good colleges there."

He shakes his head as he laughs. "None I've heard of, anyway. Going to Cambridge was a major stretch for my family financially. We're not like the Fotheringtons or the Huntington-Rosses."

"Who is? I didn't exactly grow up in the lap of luxury myself."

He smiles at me, his Bradley Cooper blue eyes soft and warm. "Something else we've got in common, Texas."

Greg arrives at the table with a cardboard tray filled with our drinks and cookies. He gives Chris a sideways look before he says, "Here you go, love. Hope it all goes well with the house this week, and I'll pass on your info to Denise."

"Thanks, Greg. These cookies will help for sure." I stand to leave as Greg returns to the counter. "Well, it's nice to see you again," I say to Chris.

He rises to his feet too, and I notice how tall and broad he is. "I'll walk you out."

"Didn't you come in here for coffee?"

"What can I say?" he replies with a shrug. "I'm fickle."

Outside the coffee house, I pause and say, "Well, see you 'round."

"Before you leave," he says, and I turn to face him. "One word of advice—whatever you do, don't butter your toast with the butter knife."

Random.

"Err, okay."

"I figure you need all the help you can get marrying a stuffy English aristocrat."

"What do you know about marrying a stuffy English aristocrat?" I ask and then catch myself. He almost married Jilly. I take a different tack. "Not that Sebastian is stuffy."

His tone changes when he replies, "I came close to marrying one myself. Jilly, your new BFF."

"Right."

"She told you about that, did she? What did she say?"

"Only that you're a total love rat and need to be avoided at all costs, which I guess makes you a Muppet."

He gives a sudden laugh. "Gotta love Jilly." He directs his thumb at his chest. "And I was a Power Ranger, remember?"

"You're not exactly Sebastian's favorite guy because of it, either."

He pauses for a moment before he says, "You do know there are always two sides to any story, don't you?"

"So, you didn't leave Jilly at the altar?"

"I'm not saying that."

"What kind of answer is that? You either did or you didn't."

He takes a step closer to me. The atmosphere has changed around us from light chat to something else entirely. "Look, I think you're great. A little naïve but great all the same."

I open my mouth to protest, but he puts his hand up in the *stop* sign.

"Let me finish, okay?"

I nod. I have a feeling I'm not going to like what he's got to say—or believe it, for that matter.

"Sebastian and Jilly, the whole lot of them? They come off like us—normal, regular people with normal, regular lives. But they're not. They're different, and they've got a different way of doing things, too. It's something that took me a long time to realize."

I narrow my eyes at him. "What are you saying, exactly?"

"You seem like a great girl, and I don't want you to get hurt by them."

I'm beginning to get irritated now. "I'm not going to. And anyway, my relationship has got nothing to do with you."

"Just hear me out. Please?" He puts his hand on my arm, and I look from it back up at his face.

"Seriously, dude?"

He removes his hand straight away. "I loved Jilly and had every intention of marrying her. That is until your fiancé turned up and began to threaten me. He said that if I went through with it, bad things would happen to me. Seriously bad things."

"What?" I shake my head vehemently. "That does not sound like Seb at all."

He shrugs. "How long have you known him? A year?"

It's a lot less than a year, but there's no way I'm going to tell him that.

I raise my chin. "I know Seb. He wouldn't threaten anyone, not without a really good reason."

"Maybe you don't know him as well as you think. He wanted me gone, and he turned Jilly against me."

"But you left her at the altar!"

He shakes his head. "*She* was the one who left me. And it was because of Sebastian."

"I don't believe you," I reply with conviction. "What could Sebastian want to gain from stopping your wedding to Jilly?" A thought occurs to me. "Unless he felt he had to *protect* her from you."

"That's exactly what he thought he had to do, Texas. Because he didn't think I was good enough for her."

I try not to let that familiar feeling show on my face. Not that Sebastian has ever, ever made me feel like that. His granny is another story, though, of course.

He inches closer to me. "You see, Texas, Sebastian always hated that Jilly loved me—and not him."

"That's ridiculous," I scoff.

"Is it? Look at them. They've known each other forever, they're from the same world, they fit. Sebastian was always going to be a better choice for Jilly than me."

"Are you trying to tell me that Sebastian is in love with Jilly? Because that is seriously messed up."

"All I'm trying to do is open your eyes. I'd hate what happened to me to happen to you."

I regard him for a moment, unpleasant things twisting

inside. "I think this conversation is over," I say with a strong, calm voice. I turn on my heel and walk away.

"I get it. I've upset you. Just bear what I've said in mind, okay?"

Without turning back, I call, "I'm going now."

"Take care, Texas," he calls out behind me.

Clutching my tray of drinks and snacks to my chest, I make my way back to the car. I don't respond. Instead, I get in the car, and I drive off, back to Martinston, back to my fiancé.

Chapter Fifteen

We spend the rest of the day knee-deep in boxes, reorganizing the house and getting it ready for professional cleaners to come in and make it shine. Marie Kondo would be proud of us, although I wonder how many of the dusty old books, worn out furnishings, and unusual artifacts would spark any joy. Still, we boxed a bunch of stuff up, and it's now tucked away out of sight, so that's enough joy for me.

On top of getting the house ready to be seen, we're hosting an invitation-only garden party to celebrate the house opening, and it's only a matter of a week away, so there's still a lot to do. Lucky for us, Jemima has taken the reins on organizing the day, with a very willing Jilly as her second in charge. Sebastian has agreed to speak, and we're all getting dressed up in our garden party attire, including hats.

I don't get any time with Sebastian alone to ask him about what Chris had told me. That and the fact I know it's a sensitive subject, and I don't want to upset him during a time when he's so worried about losing his home, means I'm not rushing to do it, either.

But Chris's words keep running through my mind, leaving their footprints to linger. Although I trust Sebastian one hundred percent, Chris is right that I've not known him all that long. Sure, I feel like I know him really well, but I can't possibly know everything there is to know about him. We all have things in our past we're not proud of. Perhaps the way he treated Chris is his? Perhaps he was in love with Jilly at the time?

I resolve to talk to him about it when the time is right, and then I shelve it and get on with the job at hand.

Midafternoon, a call comes through on my phone, and I welcome the chance to grab a few minutes break.

"I'm gonna get this," I say as I walk out of the room and press answer. "Hello?"

"Oh, 'allo love. Is this Emma?"

"It sure is."

"I'm Denise Johnson from Vestiti da Donna. Me bruvvah-in-law, Greg, gave me your number. Said you might have some things you'd like me to look at stocking?"

Although I know Denise only runs a small boutique that caters for a market we've not sold into before, the fact someone in this country is interested in stocking Timothy makes me want to leap for joy.

"Yes! Hi, Denise. Great to hear from you. I've got an activewear line called Timothy I'd love to show you."

"How about this afternoon, say about half four? The shop's usually pretty quiet then."

I glance through the door at the others still working hard. "This afternoon? I'm not sure I can make that work. I'm sorry. Can you suggest another day?"

"I'm leaving for Ibiza for two weeks tomorrow. I'm

rekindling love with my man. Things have been a bit quiet on the bedroom front, you see. You've got to do that when you've been married forever and a day, believe you me. You'll see, once you've been married to that lord of yours for a few years."

TMI, anyone?

"Thanks, I'll, ah, bear that in mind."

"So, what do you say? Half four?"

I know Sebastian needs me to help out here, but equally, I've been finding it impossible to get anywhere with stores here. I'm sure he'll understand.

"Denise? You got it. I'll be there then."

"Lovely. TTFN."

I walk back into the room where Zara, Jemima, and Sebastian are all sorting through linens. Man, are there a lot of linens. Hundreds of years' worth, I guess. Did these people never throw anything out?

"Hey, guys," I say. "Do you mind if I shoot off for an hour or so this afternoon? I've finally got a shot at getting Timothy into a store here, and the woman can only see me today."

Sebastian straightens up and walks the obstacle course of boxes toward me, grinning. "Brady, that's amazing! Of course you have to go. We'll manage without you."

"Totally," Zara confirms. "Go get 'em, Emma."

"That's wonderful news, Emma. Which shop is it?" Jemima asks.

"Vestiti da Donna. Do you know it?"

"Oh, yes. All my friends buy their Zumba clothes from there. They've got the best support bras and control briefs of anywhere in the county."

"Mum!" Zara protests as Sebastian says, "Can we please *not* talk about your underwear?"

Jemima waves their complaints away with a flick of her wrist. "Believe me, once you get to my age, you need a little extra help in keeping things from going too far south."

Zara exclaims, "Ugh!" and promptly holds her hands over her ears as Sebastian looks vaguely ill. Jemima gives a cheeky laugh, clearly enjoying their discomfort.

Well, I guess that proves it. It's universal. Even aristocratic Brits find the thought of their parents in their underwear super embarrassing.

"Even though it's small fry, I'm super excited to finally get to talk to an actual British shop owner. I may as well pick up my bridesmaid's dress for Phoebe's wedding while I'm in the village, too."

Sebastian plants a kiss on my lips. "Good luck."

I paste on a brave smile. "I don't need luck. I need a miracle."

* * *

I walk through the door of Vestiti da Donna with a suitcase filled with Timothy. I know I'm being optimistic in bringing more than just samples, but who knows? Maybe this Denise person will love the label so much, she'll take some stock today? Yeah, I know, I sound desperate. But really, I kinda am. Denise is the first person to even talk with me about Timothy, let alone meet me.

I look around. The store is smaller than I was hoping, but it's bright and filled with stock, all the usual suspects of the activewear world. *It's a start*, I tell myself as I spot a couple of middle-aged women at the back of the store, talking and laughing together. I wait, hoping they'll be done soon. I take the time to leaf through the stock, working out which products Denise carries that will be in direct competition with Timothy.

Finally, the customer makes her purchase and leaves.

I approach the slim, almost skinny woman wearing a purple jumpsuit and pair of killer heels. "Hey there. Are you Denise?" I ask.

"I am, love, and you're Emma Brady. We don't get a lot of Americans through here, you know, and I'll admit, I recognize you from the telly."

I brace myself for the judgment. Anything from "he should have chosen Phoebe" to "you were hilarious" to my personal favorite "it's hard to believe Sebastian Huntington-Ross chose someone like you." Seriously, I've got that before. Charming, right?

She doesn't give me any of them. Instead, she says, "I always liked you on that show from the very start. I felt awful bad for you when you fell out of that limousine. Why didn't they let you redo your entrance? It only seems fair to me."

I grin at her, warming to her immediately. "Thank you! Finally, someone who sees it from my perspective. They did allow me a do-over, but they didn't use it on the show in the end."

"Ooh, those devious whatsits. I always wonder about reality telly."

"Believe me, it's not that real."

She smiles at me. "I bet it's not, love."

"Paula!" she calls suddenly, giving me a small fright.

"Yeah?" a bored voice calls from out the back of the store.

"Come and mind the shop. I've got a meeting with Emma."

"Do I have to?" the voice groans back.

"You do."

Denise rolls her eyes at me. "Teenagers."

I hear a huff and an "Okay," and the next thing Paula herself appears in the store. She's the same build and size as Denise, and she can only be about seventeen or eighteen. The look on her face tells me this is the last place she'd ever want to be.

"Paula, this is Emma Brady. We might stock her label. Paula's my daughter. She's learning the ropes here at Donna."

"Hey, Paula. It's great to meet you," I say with an outstretched hand.

"All right," she replies in the English expression for "hello" (although why they can't just say "hello" is beyond me) with as much enthusiasm as I had when faced with a plateful of Brussels sprouts as a kid. Not that Mom ever did that to me, because that would be straight up child abuse in my opinion.

Paula gives me a limp handshake then slinks past me and plunks herself down on a stool behind the counter, her shoulders sagging.

Denise shoots her a look. "Help anyone what comes in here, Paula. No sitting around and being all teenager-y, thank you very much."

"If I have to."

"You do." Denise turns her attention back to me. "Come on then, Emma. Let's have a wee chat, shall we? Greg says you're a top bird."

I've never been called a "top bird" in my life, but I can only assume it's a good thing, and nothing to do with actual birds. I blush at the compliment. "Greg's the best. And those chocolate chip cookies of his are out of this world."

"Oh, I wouldn't know about those. I'm strictly paleo. Have been for years."

I regard her out of the corner of my eye. She hasn't got an ounce of fat on her, rendering her middle-aged face lined and a little gaunt.

"Now, take a seat," she says, doing so herself among the boxes and racks at the back of the store. "I used to be the size of a lorry, you know," she says, and I remind myself a lorry is a truck, "until my friend Rhonda suggested we try it together. Changed my life. I got into the lifestyle, you know? Going to the gym and whatnots. That's when I opened up this shop. I wanted to help women like me who once lived on carbs to smash that habit." She punches her fist into her hand to illustrate her point.

"Well, you look great, and your store is just terrific."

"Tell me all about your label. Greg says you've had some success in America and want to expand into the UK?"

"That's right." I tell her all about how Penny and I set up Timothy, that our philosophy is to provide women with comfortable clothing in quality products that look good, too, and then show her some of our products.

"You wore that one on the show." She picks up the tank top I was wearing when I fell out of the limo the first day of filming. I remember trying desperately to pull it up over my thighs as the limo came to a stop, my dress tangled up in my hair.

"I sure did. It has a built-in bra for support and comes in a wide range of colors and sizes."

"Mum!" Paula calls from the shop. "A little help here? I've got a queue."

My mind immediately darts to Chris's comment about how the Brits love a good line. I push it away. I don't want to think about him and the things he said.

"Coming, love," she calls back. "I'd better go and help her. My girl's a sweetheart, but she's not much of one for customer service."

"Sure, no problem. Mind if I come with?"

"Be my guest."

We walk back into the bright store, and I wander around as Denise helps an overwhelmed Paula deal with the line of women purchasing various activewear items.

I'm rifling through some shorts when an older woman says, "'Allo, love. I need a bit of help here, if you don't mind."

I look up to see a woman of about sixty with dyed auburn hair and a floral nylon blouse and matching pants.

I glance at the line at the counter and Paula and Denise working to service them, and I reply, "Sure thing. What can I do for you, ma'am?"

She blinks at me a couple of times. "Oooh, you're American."

I smile. "I sure am. I'm Emma. What can I help you with?"

"Well, Emma, I'm Doreen, and I need some of them tights what you young things wear for the yoga."

I press my lips together. Her accent is fantastic, and "the yoga?" Too cute.

"I think you might mean yoga pants. Those comfortable, stretchy leggings that hug your legs."

"Them's the one."

"All righty, Doreen. Come with me." I take her to the pants section I spotted on the other side of the shop, take a guess at her size, convert it to American in my head, and suggest she try on a few pairs in the changing room.

"Do you do yoga?" I ask her.

She shakes her head, her coiffure bouncing. "Not yet,

but me and me neighbor, we're tryin' to get back in shape. 'Er 'usband left 'er, see. I've told 'er she wants to get out there and find herself a new fella. One what's got a bit of class, you know?"

Although I'm finding her accent super hard to decipher, I reply, "Good for her."

"Doing the yoga did it for my Doris."

"Doris?" I ask.

"Me daugh'er. She were right podgy until she took it up. Now she's stick fin."

"You gotta use it or lose it, right?"

"That's the truth, love. It was either the yoga or Zumba, and I didn't fancy all that jumpin' and bouncin' around they do. It's me boobs, see. They're too big, and I don't want to go riskin' 'em slappin' me in the face."

Immediately, an image of this nice older lady with the amusing accent getting hit in the face with an errant breast pops into my head, and I've got to bite back a smile.

"You need a good sports bra. They help keep everything where it's meant to be.

"It's either that or I could tuck 'em under me arms," she says with a laugh that ends in a loud snort.

I smile at her, enjoying her humor. "That might be a little uncomfortable."

"Ooh, don't I know. Can you get me one of them sports bra thingies, then? I've not 'ad one before, and I've got no idea where to begin with 'em."

I glance at the line once more. Denise and Paula are still busy serving customers. Surely me helping this woman into a sports bra isn't part of the "please stock my label in your store" brief?

But then I look back at Doreen. What harm could it do to help this nice lady out while I wait? It's not like I've got a sea of retailers banging at my door to stock Timothy. I really do need Denise's business. Maybe she'll see it as a good thing I helped a customer out today.

"For sure," I reply. "I'd be happy to help you. What size bra do you wear?"

"No idea."

"How about you go into one of the fitting rooms and look at the label of the one you're wearing?"

She smiles at me. "You're a clever one."

I walk her over to the fitting rooms where she pulls the curtain over and gets changed. After a moment, she calls out to me and thrusts a slightly graying, tattered old bra out at me. "'Ere you go, love. I'll try on the yoga tight thingies while you get me one of them sports bras."

"Sure." Reluctantly, I take it in my hand. It's still warm. As nice as this woman seems, I'm not mentally prepared to manhandle her warm bra right now.

I flip it over and try to make out the size, but the thing's so old, any sign of it is long gone. I chew on my lip. I've got no clue how to measure for a bra, and I'm not excited about learning.

Instead, I wander over to the sports bra section and begin to pull bras out and try to fit the cups of Doreen's one inside them. It's not exactly scientific, I know, but all I can do is work with what I've got. I come up with a few options, which I pass through the curtain to her.

After a few minutes of grunts and groans emanating from behind the curtain, I call out to her. "Everything okay in there?"

"I'm not sure, love. I think I might need some 'elp with this 'ere bra."

Before I can stop her, she pulls the curtain back, and I'm met with a sight I cannot unsee. She's not wrong that the bra doesn't fit, and she's got some serious boobage going on, all bulging out at the top and the sides.

"How about we close this curtain up to preserve your modesty, Doreen," I say hastily as I do just that. "I'll go get you some more sizes. Okay?"

"Right you are."

I grab a bunch more, this time paying closer attention to cup sizes. I return with some options, and after a couple more failed attempts, we find one that fits Doreen perfectly with no sign of spillage anywhere.

At the checkout, she thanks me and tells Paula how helpful her new "shop girl" was.

Once Doreen's made her purchases and left the store, Paula arcs an eyebrow at me.

"You fitted Doreen Sanderson in a sports bra without a measuring tape and not even knowing her size?" she asks.

"There was a lot of guesswork involved. I hope that was okay. You and Paula were both super busy, and she asked me for help." I hold my breath. Is she annoyed with me? Did I overstep the mark?

The edges of her mouth twitch. "Actually, I think it's just brilliant! I best stock some of your line, now shouldn't I?"

"Seriously?" I ask excitedly. "Thank you!"

"Thank me when we manage to sell some. Now, let's sit down and work it out. Paula, you're on the till."

"If I have to," she moans in a bored monotone.

As I follow Denise to the back of the store, I do a little air punch. It might be small, and I did have to see more of Doreen than ever I'd expected to see, but it is most definitely a start in the right direction.

Perhaps I can make a success of Timothy here after all?

Chapter Sixteen

Leaving Vestiti da Donna behind, I arrive at the sweetest looking olde-worlde bridal shop I have ever seen for my bridesmaid dress fitting for Phoebe and Johnathan's big day. With me in the States a lot of the time, the dress had been made from measurements I sent Phoebe, so this will be the first time I see it in the flesh. Or in the fabric. However you say it for clothes.

A bell tinkles as I push the door open, and I enter a world nothing short of bridal heaven. There are rows and rows of gorgeous bridal gowns lining the pale pink walls, a chandelier glinting in the weak sun overhead, and soft, romantic music playing in the background.

Without even realizing what I'm doing, I reach out and run my fingers over the fabric of the dresses, imagining myself gliding down the aisle in a satin or silk confection with a skirt billowing behind me as everyone gazes at me in my full bridal splendor.

My romantic side runs away with itself as I imagine Sebastian dressed as Mr. Darcy at the end of the aisle,

Marrying Mr. Darcy

gazing at me with love in his eyes as I make my way toward him as though on a cloud.

Yup, I may be getting a little carried away here.

My fingers find a beautiful ivory dress with a deep V-neckline, tapering into an Empire waist. Chiffon fabric falls in soft folds to the floor. It's nothing short of exquisite—an elegant, modern dress with a nod to Lizzie Bennet in her Regency fashion, perfect for the bride of Mr. Darcy. Instantly, my heart rate kicks up, and I hold the dress against my body, imagining myself in it.

Could this be *The Dress*? Could I have found it before I've even begun to look? I mean, I've heard about this happening to brides—they walk into a bridal store and get hit between the eyes by their fantasy dress. Well, not literally hit between the eyes, but you get what I mean.

The weird thing is I never would have taken a second look at an Empire line dress until I did *Dating Mr. Darcy*. On the show, the contestants had to wear clothes, right down to the uncomfortable stays (read: primitive bra) and bloomers (yup, just what you might expect). Despite my reticence, when I first saw my reflection dressed up as Lizzie Bennet, I *felt* something, something I never expected to feel. I felt romantic. I felt whimsical.

I felt like Lizzie Bennet herself.

Since Sebastian and I got engaged, I've had a secret desire to wear a Regency style dress. Perhaps this could be it?

"Hello?"

I'm vaguely aware of a voice punctuating my daydream. "Miss?"

I come around to see an older woman with greying hair pulled into a French twist and a pair of glasses on string around her neck.

"I can only assume everything is all right?" she enquires, a knowing look on her face.

"Yes, sorry," I stammer, totally busted in my wedding-inspired daydream. "I was just looking at this dress."

"It's beautiful, isn't it?" she says as she collects the long skirt and holds it up. "I love the detailing around the Empire waist. So pretty."

I touch the twist tie and instantly feel embarrassed.

"You're a bride to be."

"I am," I reply, more sheepish than a lamb "But not until next year."

She smiles at me and claps her hands together. "How wonderful. You know, I recognize that look in your eye."

"You do?"

"Oh, yes. I've been in this business long enough to recognize when a bride finds *The Dress*. I'm going to assume you would like to try it on?"

"It's beautiful," I say as I gaze at it.

"I think someone like you would look simply marvelous in this dress. Have you ever worn an Empire line?"

I think of my costume on *Dating Mr. Darcy*. "Once or twice." Try virtually every waking hour of the day for what felt like a lifetime.

"Well, it's lovely to meet you. I'm Susan."

"Emma."

"Emma, come with me." Holding the hanger in one hand, she folds the dress delicately over her other arm and walks to the back of the shop. She hangs it up on its own rack and pulls a heavy, whipped cream-colored curtain back for me to enter the changing room.

"Just slip off everything down to your knickers, and I'll help you into the dress," Susan instructs.

I have a flashback to the last time someone had to help

me into a new dress. It was Margaret, the person in charge of wardrobe on *Dating Mr. Darcy*, and it was a Regency period dress complete with an uncomfortable nineteenth-century answer to the push-up bra and "knickers" (don't you love the British?) so voluminous you could use them to make a tent for the entire family to sleep in.

This time it's different. Despite the fact I'm not meant to be here to look at bridal dresses but rather to collect my bridesmaid dress for Phoebe's wedding.

But come on! I've just got engaged to the most incredible man, *and* I'm in a gorgeous bridal shop. A girl can only take so much bridal fantasy shoved in her face before she'll succumb.

And yes, I know I began rifling through the dresses the moment I stepped into the store. But still.

With my hands covering my modesty, I step into the dress, and Susan does it up behind me, adding some industrial-sized clips to the back to hold it in place. She pushes the curtain open, and I step up onto a small, round step surrounded on three sides by mirrors, just like on that show *Say Yes to the Dress*.

I gaze at my reflection. Well, reflections, as I can see myself from nearly all angles. The dress is every bit as stunning on as I'd expected it to be. My waist looks tiny against my amped-up bust, the ivory chiffon falling to the floor in soft, pretty waves around me. It's simple and elegant and totally gorgeous.

"You'd need to have it taken in, of course, but we can do that for you here," Susan says. "What do you think, dearie?"

What do I think? I'm Cinderella at the ball. I'm the bride of my dreams. I'm a modern-day Elizabeth Bennet marrying her handsome and dashing Mr. Darcy.

"I love it," I breathe.

The bell tinkles at the other end of the shop, indicating another customer has arrived, and Susan excuses herself. I turn to look at myself in the multiple mirrors, loving the way the skirt forms its own train at the back.

I hear a familiar voice. "Susan, how are you?" *M-wah, m-wah* air kisses.

Jilly Frotherington.

"You are looking radiant as always. Is that a new dress?"

"Well, yes—"

"Gosh, I hope I look like you when I'm older. Not that you're old, of course. Sorry. Jilly sometimes blurts things out she shouldn't, you know. Her tongue runs away on her sometimes."

Susan's tone is unsure. "Oh, right. Well, welcome to the shop. What can I do for you, Lady Fotherington?"

"Can I go back? Don't you worry. Emma will be delighted to see me," Jilly says. Around the corner she comes, a bright smile on her beautiful but flushed face. She's trailed by Susan who looks like she's still recovering from being told she looks old.

"Emma, darling." She air kisses me. "Sebby told me I'd find you in the village, although I didn't know you were dress shopping."

"I'm not," I reply, although it's obvious that's exactly what I'm doing, what with me standing in front of her in a wedding dress and all.

"I thought you might need some help, you know, after our little chat the other day." She shoots me a meaningful look.

I give her a grateful smile. It feels good to have someone on my side. "Thanks, Jilly."

"Of course." She winks at me. "Look at you. Engaged

for five minutes, and you're already wedding dress shopping. How utterly exciting!"

I look down at the dress, and I'll admit to feeling a little thrill. "I didn't mean to. It just kinda happened."

Susan gives a sage nod. "We get that a lot here, love."

"No, I mean I'm meant to be here to be fitted for a bridesmaid's dress for my friend's wedding. I guess I got sidetracked."

"Who's wedding is it?" Susan asks. "I'll go and get the dress for you, dearie."

"Phoebe Wilson and Johnathan Bentley's."

Susan's eyes get wide. "Oh, you're *that* Emma."

Thrown, I reply, "That's right. I'm Emma Brady. My friend Phoebe's getting married."

"Oh, yes. We know all about *that*. It was the talk of the town. Now that I look at you, I can see exactly who you are."

I'm not sure how to respond.

"I loved *Dating Mr. Darcy*," she continues. "We all did here in the village, although we did think Lord Martinston would end up marrying Phoebe."

This again? How awesome.

"It was such a shock when she proposed to his best friend. I tell you, I nearly spilt my cuppa all over my settee when that happened."

"It really was quite a moment, wasn't it? A bolt from the blue." Jilly throws me a wink because of course *she* knew Sebastian was announcing Phoebe was in love with Johnathan. She thought Sebastian was going to propose to Camille and sail off into the sunset with her and her wads of cash. As his lawyer, she'd helped set up the whole deal, after all.

I was the wrench in the works that stopped the plan in its tracks. Love can do that to your plans.

"Well, sorry to disappoint you, but he's marrying me, and Phoebe's marrying Johnathan," I say brightly, enjoying absolutely nothing about this conversation.

Jilly picks up on my tone. "Emma's an absolute treat, Susan. Really, she is. She's been very unfairly represented in the media. Haven't you, Emma?"

"I have," I sniff.

"Oh, they were cruel," Susan agrees. "Saying you were like Bozo the Clown and all those 'butt of the joke' memes of you falling out of the limousine. Although I've got to admit, some of them had me and my Paul chortling over our cornflakes."

Jilly lets out a giggle but immediately presses her lips together to stop it when she takes in my glare. "It was very hard on poor Emma."

"It was big news here, particularly since Lord Martinston is a bit of a local hero. You could not have expected to find a more suitable man to be Mr. Darcy, could you?"

"Oh, I absolutely agree," Jilly gushes. "Sebby is one in a million."

As the two discuss Sebastian and me as though I'm not standing right here in front of them both, I begin to feel beyond ridiculous in this dress. Part of me wishes I'd never even tried it on.

Jilly pulls the conversation back on track when she says, "But of course darling Emma is getting her happily ever after with her very own Mr. Darcy, and we're all thrilled for them," Jilly finishes.

"Aren't you the lucky one, then, love?" Susan says.

"Now. This dress," Jilly says, negating the need for me to respond to Susan.

Marrying Mr. Darcy

"Isn't it divine?"

"It does look gorgeous on you, but I wonder if it's a little too...flashy for certain members of the family."

She means Geraldine.

I regard my reflection. "It might a be a bit of deep *V*, but I think it's super classy."

"We Brits feel that one doesn't want to show too much flesh on one's wedding day. It's just not the done thing. Not in our social circle, anyway. Footballers' wives are a whole other demographic."

"I don't think it's too revealing. Sure, it's a little low cut, but it's not like I've got massive cleavage or anything." Not that I've ever got any cleavage on show, well, not without the help of a couple of slippery chicken fillets to stuff down my bra, that is.

"Oh, it's revealing in what it's not revealing, if you catch my drift," Jilly says with a head nod that's meant to be meaningful.

I blink at her dumbly. "I don't catch your drift at all."

"Let's put it this way. We don't want to excite the vicar now, do we? Make him all hot under the collar? That simply wouldn't do at all."

I chew on my lip as I regard my reflection once more. Although I do love the dress, I did ask Jilly to help me navigate the mysterious and confusing world of the English aristocracy. I know I need to go with what she suggests to fit in here. "Should I try something else? Wedding dress shopping is super fun."

"Why don't you let me find something for you that would be more appropriate for a Martinston audience."

"Thanks, Jilly," I reply, glad she's here. Although I love this dress, the last thing I want to do is stand out like a footballer's wife (whatever *they* look like), excite the vicar, or the worst of the lot, upset Geraldine.

Jilly begins to rummage through the racks as Susan helps me out of the Empire line dress.

"Can she try this one, Susan?" Jilly's holding up another dress, this one with long sleeves and a neckline that looks like it's just that, coming right up to the chin.

It's no pretty deep *V* dress with a delicate, floaty skirt, that's for sure.

"Of course she can," Susan replies.

I eye the dress. "I'm not sure. It's a lot of material."

"Oh, it'll look simply divine on you, Emma darling. Just you see," Jilly says. "Very Lady of the Manor." She leans in closer to me and says conspiratorially, "Geraldine won't be able to help but approve."

I trust Jilly, and she knows how things work in this social set, so I reply, "Sure. Why not?"

"That's the spirit."

Behind the heavy curtain, Susan helps me into the dress. Once she's put some clips in place like she did with the first dress, she says, "Pop up onto the step again, and you can show Jilly. I'll be right back with that bridesmaid's dress." She holds the curtain to the side for me to walk through.

I step up onto the little platform once more and regard myself in the many mirrors.

"Splendid!" Jilly declares. "Much more appropriate. Nothing revealing. Very, very classy, Emma."

I screw up my face. Whatever "splendid" means in England, it sure as heck doesn't mean that where I'm from. The dress might be slim-fitting and show off my curves, but that's its only redeeming feature. It reaches so high up my neck, down my arms, and all the way to the

Marrying Mr. Darcy

floor, that the only skin on show is my face, knuckles, and fingers.

This dress makes the Amish look daring in their fashion choices.

"Well?" Jilly asks hopefully.

I scrunch up my face. "I'm not feeling it."

"Look. I imagine Americans like to look their absolute best on their wedding day, stopping at nothing to have the perfect dress, the perfect hairdo, the perfect makeup."

"Don't you?"

"Oh, no," she replies. "That's all rather OTT to us aristocratic Brits. We are much more understated than Americans. We wear our money and breeding on the *inside*. We like to look nice, of course, and a wedding dress will certainly cost the same as a car. But it's all about looking classy. Covering up rather than bursting out."

I gaze in the mirror. I look like a big white cotton ball. "But...Meghan Markle looked beautiful when she married Prince Harry."

"American," Jilly dismisses.

"Right." I chew on my lip. "What about Kate Middleton? She was picture-perfect gorgeous in her wedding dress, and that one didn't reach up to her ears."

"Royalty," Jilly replies with a delicate wave of her hand. "Entirely different set of rules."

"Right." I slump my shoulders. I've never been one of those girls who's planned every last detail of her wedding before she's even met the guy. I don't have a Monica from *Friends* scrapbook full to the brim of all things weddings. I don't google bridal dresses or buy wedding magazines, dreaming of my big day. The only thing I've ever really thought about is that someday I'd like to get married in that cute little chapel back home.

But even if I've not been one of those wedding-obsessed types, I'd still like a wonderful wedding, and part of that is not looking like I'm wearing a white tablecloth from head to toe.

Susan returns with the bridesmaid dress draped across her arm. "Oh." She stops in her tracks as she takes in my appearance. "That's a different look for you."

Different? Try *nun-like*.

"Look," Jilly says. "I can see you're not loving the dress right now. We can have it tailored to fit, can't we, Susan?"

"Of course. We tailor all our dresses to meet our client's needs."

"Marvelous. Isn't that marvelous, Emma?"

"Sure," I reply, not meaning it at all. I glance at the gorgeous Empire line dress hanging against the curtain. Although it's perfect in every way, I do need to try to fit in here, and apparently my taste in wedding dresses is all wrong for the family I'm marrying into.

I look from Jilly to Susan and then back at my reflection. I want more than anything to feel a part of my new world, to win Geraldine over, to be the Lady Martinston that is expected of me.

Perhaps a dress like this one can be a small step in the right direction?

Chapter Seventeen

Today, there's no time to think about wedding dresses. Today, the day of the official opening of the house has arrived. Really, you'd think it was the inauguration of a president, the stress levels are so high —and so are expectations. Well, to be clear, *Jilly's* stress levels are high. She's been heavily involved with Jemima in running the event, giving us all time to concentrate on getting the house ready to be seen by the public. And now, everyone is focused on the fact that today is a huge day in Martinston's history. Views differ on how, though. On the one hand there are the people who think life will be different but better because we will be one small step closer to ensuring the house will be safe (Zara's, Sebastian's, and Jemima's view). And another's view is that the Huntington-Ross name will be forever soiled in the name of profit (guess who?). Needless to say, tensions are high.

But I do not care because today is the day that my reality show BFF and all 'round awesome chick, Kennedy Bennet, arrives.

I am beyond excited. Kennedy was my lifeline on the

show, the only one I trusted with knowing Sebastian and I were getting to know one another off camera, the only one who knew my original intentions for coming on the show. She's smart and funny and snarky. A lot like me, really, although with her shoulder-length brown hair and perfect olive complexion, she's far more beautiful than me.

Straight after breakfast I drive to the train station to collect her. As the train pulls into the station, I spot her through the window. In her jeans and tee, she's a southern California girl in a sea of pale English faces.

She disembarks the train with her backpack slung over her back, and I collect her in a hug. "OMG, girl! It is so good to see you."

"You, too, Em. I've got to tell you, it's so weird to be back in England."

"And not dressed like a Regency lady?" I ask, referring to the chosen attire for contestants on *Dating Mr. Darcy*.

"I could happily live my life without ever having to see a pair of bloomers again."

"Oh, I don't know. They kinda grow on you," I say before we both burst into laughter.

"It's great to have you here," I say.

"You'd better take me to Martinston so I can really feel like the third wheel in your love story."

We walk down the platform arm in arm toward the parking lot.

"Did you bring a dress for the garden party?" I ask.

"Dress, heels, hat. The works, girl."

"Awesome. We can get ready together. It's going to be mayhem at the house today with the caterers and everything going on with the setup. I'm so pleased I'm not involved in organizing it. I just get to be the eye candy in my garden party-appropriate attire."

We reach the house, and Kennedy greets everyone with smiles and a hostess gift of California's See's Candies, which Geraldine looks singularly unimpressed with, of course.

Up in her room, she asks, "Is Seb's granny always like that?"

"Oh, yes. She's been a challenge, that's for sure. She's not exactly excited about me and Seb."

"Is that because she's got a huge carrot up her butt?"

I giggle. "Totally. I'm gonna let you freshen up and get ready for the party. Come to my room when you're ready, okay?"

"Which one of the gazillion bedrooms in this place is your room?"

"How about I come get you? It'll be easier that way."

"Rich person's problems," she replies with a sigh.

If only.

"More like big house problems. I'll give you an hour, okay?"

"Deal."

An hour later and I arrive at Kennedy's door fully decked out in my Jilly-approved dress and fascinator hat. I feel a little ridiculous all decked out as I am, but if Jilly thinks it's the right way for a future Lady Martinston to dress, then I'm not going to argue.

I knock on her door, and she calls out, "Come in."

I take in her slim-fitted navy dress with a scoop neckline and floral clip in her hair. "You look stunning, Kennedy," I say, because she really does. Classy and understated.

She takes one look at me and exclaims, "Wow, Em. That's quite the look you've got going on there."

I glance down at my dress. Sure, it's virtually nun-like in how much skin it hides, but it's pretty and floaty, even if the neck ruffles, poufy sleeves, and ankle-length skirt are not exactly my style.

"It's garden-party chic with a subtle nod to J Lo. That's what Jilly said."

She raises her eyebrows at me. "Babe, that dress J Lo wore back in the day was cut down to her belly button. Yours is cut to your chin."

"It's classy," I protest.

"If you say so. But I tell you one thing—I don't know who this Jilly person is, but by the looks of things, she sure doesn't like you very much."

"Jilly's great. She's been helping me try to fit in."

"Into what? The Amazon Jungle?" she says with a snort.

I shoot her a sardonic smirk. "Not helping, Kennedy."

"Look, I'm not trying to upset you. I mean, it'd be fine on someone less, I dunno, less *you*."

"But that's the whole point, Kennedy. I'm trying to be the future Lady Martinston. I'm trying to fit in, to make Seb's family feel that I'm one of them."

"Do you want to be one of them?"

"Of course I do. I'm marrying him, aren't I? I'm trying hard here."

"How's that working out for you?" Kennedy asks.

"Not great," I reply with a resigned shrug as my mind turns to all the disasters that have befallen me—one quite literally. "But I'm sure today is going to be different. I've got the outfit, Jilly's given me the lowdown on anyone who's anyone at this party, and I've been working on how to play the demure, elegant, and above all appropriate future Lady Martinston."

She chews on her lip as she regards me. "Em, can I be straight with you?"

"As long as you're quick. People will be arriving soon."

"When we met on the show, the thing I loved about you was that you were you, no apologies. You were there to promote your label, and when that looked like it couldn't happen with the whole dress-like-it's-1813 bombshell, you did what you could to get sent home."

"Kennedy, I know all this. I was there, remember?"

"The thing is, you didn't compromise for anybody. You were Emma Brady, straight up. Take her or leave her. Now?" Her eyes flick over my outfit. "Now you're falling over yourself to be something you're not."

"I'm still me. I'm just trapped inside this green jungle-print tent with a fascinator hat stuck to my head," I joke.

"Are you sure? I don't want to lose Emma. She's awesome, and I love her. She shouldn't have to change for anyone."

I give a firm nod. "I know I don't look like the girl I was back on *Dating Mr. Darcy*, but I'm still me. Promise."

"Good. Shall we get this party started?" she asks with a cheeky glint in her eye.

I grin at her. "Let's do this."

As Kennedy walks out into the hallway, I give myself a final once-over in the full-length mirror. Although I don't look anything like the girl I was back then with my Timothy activewear and hair tied back in a practical ponytail, I know I'm still me. All I'm doing is bending myself a little to fit in here. Nothing more.

As we walk out onto the lawn, I take in the picture-perfect view before me. It's a gloriously sunny and warm day, albeit a little breezy, which means I've got to hold my full skirt down every now and then, à la Marilyn Monroe in that famous subway wind scene. Well, not that bad, but you get the picture. It's a little breezy.

"Oh, Em. This is gorgeous!" Kennedy exclaims.

She's right. The white tablecloths and chairs with their pretty pink bows look stunning against the green of the grass. Behind the tables, the pond glistens, and the trees are in full verdant bloom. I take a deep breath of the fresh country air as I take it all in.

Arms snake around my middle, and I turn to see Sebastian grinning down at me. "What do you think?" He pecks me on the cheek and smiles at Kennedy. "It's great to have you here for this, Kennedy."

"Thank you so much for having me. It's wonderful to be back here. And a little weird, I've gotta admit."

"I can well imagine," he replies. "We've been lucky with the weather. I'm not sure holding this in the ballroom would have been quite so romantic."

"You live in a stunning place, Sebastian," Kennedy says. "A garden party at my place would be three people squashed onto my tiny balcony that overlooks the neighboring building."

"Mine would be standing around my window box," I reply with a laugh.

"Not anymore," Sebastian says as he gives me a quick squeeze. "There is one pressing question I need to ask you, however, Brady."

"What's that?"

"Why you decided to have what looks like a giant lily pad on your head?"

My hand flies to the fascinator hat Jilly lent me to go with the dress. I'd also wondered about the whole lily pad thing, but she assured me it didn't even have a whiff of frog to it and that all the ladies would be wearing hats. She is my official adviser on all things English, so I went with it without a second thought.

Marrying Mr. Darcy

"Does it look bad?" I ask him. "I've never worn one of these things before. They're kinda weird."

"You look adorable, but might I suggest you avoid standing too close to the pond this afternoon in case any frogs need a new home?"

Kennedy giggles, and I smack him lightly on the arm. "Ha-ha. Very funny. Tell me honestly, does it look okay? Between you and Kennedy, I'm beginning to second guess myself."

"Don't!" Kennedy says.

"Brady, you could wear a potato sack for all I care, and I'd still think you were the most beautiful woman in the room." He turns to Kennedy. "No offence, Kennedy. You look gorgeous, too."

She raises her hands in the surrender sign. "No offence taken. Compliment your wife-to-be all you like."

Happy, I give him a quick kiss on the lips. "Keep those compliments coming, and I promise I'll marry you."

"Come on you two lovebirds," a voice trills beside us. "There's plenty of time for that sort of carrying on after the opening."

It's Jilly, looking a little frazzled, her usually tamed curls sticking out at angles, the bow on her dress unraveled.

"Here," I say as I tie it up for her and attempt to smooth down her hair. "You're looking a little wild." I gesture at Kennedy as I retie her bow. "Jilly, this is Kennedy."

"The famous Jilly, huh?" Kennedy says. "It's great to meet you."

"You too, although I do remember you from the show," she replies. Returning her attention to me, she says, "You'd look a little wild too if you had to deal with Portia Fortescue-Seymour and Cecily Parker-Smithston. They couldn't organize themselves out of an open box with a map."

"Why do you have to deal with...them?" I ask, their names too much of a mouthful for me to remember them in the correct order.

"Because ever since that exhibition opening—the one you'd rather forget, Emma—those two women have clearly made the rather irritating decision that I'm 'one of them,' and they can rely on me for everything. Really, it's quite exhausting." She places the back of her hand theatrically against her forehead as though she were an old-fashioned lady about to faint. "Thank goodness I've got your mummy, Sebby."

Kennedy shoots me a look and mouths *Sebby*.

"Well, thank goodness they have you, Jilly," Sebastian replies with a smile.

She glances at her watch and almost levitates off the pristine lawn. "I must go. Are you ready with your speech?" she asks Sebastian.

"I am," he assures her.

"Good, because you've got to be more than just the eye candy for all the ladies today," she says as she bustles away.

"I like to think I'm a little more than that," he calls after her, but all she does is raise her hand in the air and wave.

Thirty minutes later, the flowers have been delivered and placed on the tables, the catering staff have placed the tables in the approved spots, and the auction items and technology have all been set up, ready for the big event.

People begin to pour in, dressed in their garden party best, the women in pretty floral dresses, some with hats, some with parasols. The men are dressed in white or beige linen, many with dapper Panama hats. Never having been to a garden party—because as Sebastian pointed out, tailgating in the stadium parking lot during football season doesn't count as a garden party for many reasons, including the fact that it's not in a garden—I'm mesmerized by the romance of the surrounds transformed from a rolling lawn and simple but pretty pond into a scene worthy of an Impressionist's work of art.

And that's when I see him, dressed in khaki pants, a white shirt, and navy blazer, looking like he just stepped off the fashion section of a men's magazine. He saunters across the lawn as though he owns the place, a champagne flute in hand, a broad smile on his movie star handsome face.

Chris Hampshire.

I leave Kennedy to chat with some of Sebastian's distant relations and make my way through the crowd. I grab Jilly by the arm.

"What is it?" she asks. "Is there a problem with the flowers? The food? Did the violinists all break their bows and now the music's stopped?"

"Jilly—"

"No, it can't be that. They're still playing. I can hear them. Can you hear them?"

I say firmly, "Chris Hampshire is here."

She blinks at me a couple of times in response, but she doesn't look surprised. "Oh, him."

My eyes widen in surprise. "Did you know he was going to come today?"

"Look, Emma. I told you, he's catnip to me, and I'm the kitty cat who simply can't resist him."

Seriously? Ugh.

An image of a Chris Hampshire-shaped toy filled with catnip and Jilly as an oversized feline pops into my head. I push it away. It's just too plain weird.

"Not that I'm going to go there with him again, of course," she continues. "That would be totally insane. No, we're trying something new right now. We're trying to be friends."

"Good for you," I reply hurriedly. "But the thing is, this is Sebastian's *home*. I'm not sure he'll want him here. You might be trying something new with him right now, but those two are not exactly in the friend zone themselves. Are they?"

"Ah, now, that's where you can come in, Emma. Chris told me you had a lovely, cozy chat the other day, and I thought since you've become such good chums, you could break the news to Sebby."

"We didn't have a cozy chat."

She shoots me a look that tells me she doesn't even begin to believe me. "Emma, I understand. Believe me, I do. Chris Hampshire is a hard man to resist."

What?

"But I didn't need to resist him," I protest.

Her eyes bulge. "Oh? Now you'll have to tell me everything, but it'll need to wait until after the fundraiser. And I also need to say that I'm upset on behalf of Sebby, too, of course."

Exasperated, I reply, "You've got the wrong end of the stick here. I meant there was nothing to resist because I didn't need to resist him."

I'm confusing myself now.

"What I mean is I'm in love with Seb."

"Of course you are. But you know, ladies of the British aristocracy have been having affairs for years. It's quite accepted in some circles, even expected, I dare say."

Frustrated, I reply, "Argh!" as I throw my hands in the air. "There was no 'cozy chat,' no flirting, and certainly no affair!"

Marrying Mr. Darcy

"This sure sounds like an interesting conversation," a deep voice says behind me.

I squeeze my eyes shut before I turn around. I know exactly who it's going to be, and his timing is just perfect.

"Hey, Chris," I say with a stuck-on smile, hoping he doesn't realize we were talking about him—and suspecting he absolutely does.

"If you do decide to have an affair with anyone, Texas, be sure to give me a call," he says smoothly, his suggestive smile stretching across his face.

"Oh, no. I wasn't saying that at all. I was…err…you know, talking hypothetically."

Smooth, Emma.

"It's too early to be thinking about affairs, anyway. I would have thought you'd need to have been married to the stiff for at least six months first."

The stiff?

"If you're referring to Sebastian, I'll have you know he's not 'stiff,' as you so politely put it."

"Well, that is unfortunate for you," he replies with a cheeky glint in his eye.

I open my mouth to reply then it dawns on me what he means. I promptly close it again.

His eyes glide up to the fascinator hat clipped onto my head. "That's quite a hat you've got there. I see you've taken the Kermit conversation we had at the café to heart."

"It's not a lily pad," I reply in exasperation. "Tell him, Jilly."

"Of course it's not. It's a hat by renowned London designer, Paul Henri. It cost a small fortune. It's awfully *de rigueur*."

I shoot Chris a satisfied smile even though I've got no idea what *de rigueur* means. Something to do with oil rigs?

"See? Nothing to do with frogs."

"I was gonna add that it was a super sexy lily pad, but if you insist it's not..."

Does this guy never give up?

I choose to ignore his comment. "Chris," I say firmly with an I-mean-business tone. "Do you think it's a good idea that you're here? I mean, you and Seb aren't exactly friends these days, right?"

He waves my concern away with a flick of his wrist. "It's fine. There are so many people here, I doubt he'll even notice me. And anyway, that's all ancient history. If he's got a problem with me, he should just come out and tell me."

I scrunch up my nose. Today is a big deal for the family, and the last thing I want is for Sebastian to see Chris and feel uncomfortable. "Is it, though? He didn't look exactly pleased to see you at the opera that night."

"Texas, no one's pleased to be at the opera. You of all people should know that."

I let out an exasperated puff of air. This guy is the limit!

He places his hand on the bare skin of my arm, and I instantly tighten. "Look, Emma. You're real sweet worrying about how your boyfriend—"

"Fiancé."

"—*fiancé* is going to react to seeing me here this afternoon, but trust me, he won't care."

"I think he will."

"Why?"

"Because of what happened with Jilly." I look to her for confirmation. "Right?"

"If I can move on from that, so can Sebby," she says.

I'm aware Chris hasn't removed his hand, and I pull my arm away. "I guess." I look up to see Sebastian making his way through the throngs of people with Kennedy, smiling and chatting with people.

"Emma, there you are," he says as he sidles up beside me. "We've been looking for you." His face drops when his eyes land on Chris. "What are *you* doing here?" he says, clearly thrown.

Chris, on the other hand, looks completely unfazed. He extends his hand and says, "Sebastian Huntington-Ross. Twice in one month. What have I done to deserve this? Because whatever it is, I'll undo it. Now." He laughs at his own joke, and my eyes dart between Sebastian and Chris, landing on Kennedy who shoots me a questioning look.

Sebastian ignores his hand. "You weren't invited," he says frostily.

"I'm here as Jilly's plus-one."

Sebastian raises his brows at Jilly.

"We're trying to be friends," she explains.

"Good for you," he seethes.

I bet I know what he's thinking. He's thinking Jilly won't be able to resist him. She'll fall for his charms once more, and he'll be left to pick up the pieces, just as he did before. He's a good, loyal friend.

Either that or there was some truth to what Chris said about Sebastian having been in love with her in the past.

I slip my hand into his. "It's okay, Seb."

"Emma and I were just having a catch-up," Chris says. "She's a great girl, this one, Seb. You'd better hold onto her."

"Thank you," he replies, his features tense. "I fully intend to." He gives my hand a squeeze and says, "I thought we could take our seats."

"And who might you be?" Chris says to Kennedy, taking his hand in hers.

"I'm Kennedy, one of Emma's friends," she replies.

"It's great to meet you, Kennedy, one of Emma's friends," he replies smoothly.

"See you later," I say as I take Sebastian by the hand and begin to lead him away from this potentially combustible situation. "Let's go take our seats, Kennedy."

With the tension in the air so thick it could block out the afternoon sun, I'd be more than happy not to see Chris again this afternoon—and judging by his reaction, I'm sure Sebastian would be, too.

"Be sure to keep that lily pad well watered, Texas," Chris calls out as we turn on our heels and walk away.

"He calls you Texas?" Sebastian asks in surprise.

"He's that kinda guy, I guess. Do you think Jilly's making a big mistake by bringing him back into her life?"

"Jilly's a grown woman. She can make her own choices."

Confused, I reply, "But I thought you hated Chris because he broke Jilly's heart?"

We come to a stop beside one of the tables by the podium.

"Kennedy, why don't you take a seat?" Sebastian suggests.

"Sure thing."

As she sits, Sebastian says to me, "Chris Hampshire is the kind of man people want to be around. He draws them in and makes them feel special, important. Then, when it suits him, he moves onto the next. Emma, he uses people for his own purposes, and he doesn't care how that impacts others."

"This is about more than just Jilly, isn't it?"

He exhales heavily. "Chris and I were friends at Cambridge."

"When he was dating Jilly?"

"I introduced them."

"That's why you felt responsible for her."

"It is. Watch yourself around him, Brady. He comes across as a charming guy, but he's got a dark side."

As Sebastian takes his seat at the table, I glance over at Chris. He's got his arm slung around Jilly's shoulder, and they're laughing at something together. Sebastian's right, he is charming, and confusing. Given how much he's hurt the people I care for, I would be more than happy if he were to disappear from our lives for good.

Chapter Eighteen

People are finishing up their afternoon tea of scones with raspberry jam and cream and dainty finger sandwiches as Sebastian gets up to speak. I lean back in my seat and watch him at the podium. He looks so dapper in his garden party wear of a white shirt and navy blazer over khaki pants, the light breeze tousling his hair, making him look even more sexy than he usually does. He looks a touch Mr. Darcy, now that I think about it.

I feel like I could burst with pride and love for him.

"Ladies and gentlemen," he begins, and there's a general titter from Portia Fortescue-Seymour and Cecily Parker-Smithston's table nearby. "My family and I welcome you to Martinston on this historic day, the day we open the house to the public for the first time in decades."

There's a ripple of polite applause.

"We know how very lucky we are to live in such a picturesque part of the country, in this beautiful historic building behind you all. We are excited to be able to offer a large part of the house and the gardens for viewing. Sharing our family heritage is as much about the wider county community as it is about the Huntington-Ross family, and we are thrilled that we are the generation to bring this to you all."

There's more applause, and I beam at him.

"I'm sure you don't want me to stand up here doing all the talking, so—" he continues.

"Yes, we do!" a female calls out from behind me, and laughter rolls through the audience.

"What's it like being engaged to a sex symbol?" Kennedy asks me.

"It's a tough job," I reply with a grin.

"As the most senior member of the family, I would like to invite my grandmother, Geraldine Huntington-Ross, to officially open the house. Granny?"

At the neighboring table, Geraldine rises slowly to a stand and begins to make her way to the podium. As she passes by our table, I notice her slightly unsure on her feet. Perhaps it's the uneven grass or perhaps she sampled a little too much of the accompanying champagne. Whatever it is, I see my chance to get in her good books.

Immediately, I shoot up onto my feet to help her. The last thing we want is for Geraldine to fall and break a hip, today of all days. She's not exactly on board with opening the house, so that would make today a total disaster in her eyes.

As I take a step toward her, there's a strong gust of wind, and I feel my hair whip up around my face. I push it back, hitting my fascinator hat as I do. I must have dislodged it, because the next thing I know, it's somehow come loose from my hair, and caught by the wind, it flies off my head. I grasp for it, but I miss it entirely. Instead, I watch in horror as it flies straight at Geraldine and slaps her in the face.

She wobbles once more, and I decide to forget about the

hat and instead rush to her side, where I steady her with my hands on her arms.

"Are you okay?" I ask her as I glance at my hat. It's now airborne, like some little green UFO, floating away toward the pond.

"I am perfectly all right, no thanks to you," she sniffs. "Unhand me *immediately*."

I instantly loosen my grip as I hear Chris call out, "The lilypad has broken free! Don't worry, Texas. I'll go get it for you." He rushes past me toward the pond, pulling his jacket off as he goes like some kind of superhero, ready for action.

To my utter surprise, Sebastian springs into action, darting past us as he says, "Oh, no you don't! She's *my* fiancée, so I'll get the darn hat."

What the...?

Together, Geraldine and I and the rest of the garden party watch with our jaws dropping to the ground as both men chase the hat, which remains out of arm's reach as it drops into the pond with a small splash.

Kennedy appears at my side. "They're not going in after it, are they?"

"No way," I declare.

But I'm wrong.

There's a rush of people around us as the two men reach the edge of the pond and begin to strip off their shoes and jackets.

"They're going in!" someone yells behind me, and immediately people race past us to get a better view.

I look at Geraldine. Her face is a study in bewilderment. "Are you all right?" I ask her.

"I am, thank you," she sniffs.

I return my attention to the pond as first Chris and then Sebastian, stripped down to their shirts and pants, dive into the pond. There's much thrashing and splashing, and we all watch in wonder as the two men battle it out to reach my lily pad of a hat first.

I rush down to the water's edge, followed by a crush of people. I'm not sure if Geraldine has followed, and right now my mind is on the weird event unfolding in front of me.

"What are you doing?" I call out, but neither of them is listening. They're too busy trying to get to the hat first to notice me.

"I've got it!" Chris holds it up in the air in triumph, and the people around me applaud, several cheering him on.

"I'll have that, thank you," Sebastian says, swiping it from Chris's hand and turning to swim back to dry land.

"Dude! Not cool," he complains before he too swims toward us all.

Reaching the shallows, Sebastian stands up, clutching the now bedraggled hat in his fist. There's a collective intake of breath around me as he strides out of the pond, his white shirt clinging to every contour of his chest, looking like he's in a sexy calendar designed for women. The handsome, hunky guy, saving the day. Only in this case it's a limp and soggy fascinator hat that looks like a wilted lily pad for a frog.

"It's the pond scene," a voice says beside me, and I turn to see a woman about Jemima's age, a large, feathery hat atop her head, her face bright with excitement. "Oh, dear Lord have mercy."

"I guess so. He's in a pond," I reply

"No, I mean it's *the pond scene*," Yellow Hat repeats. "As in Colin Firth as Mr. Darcy in the BBC's version of *Pride and Prejudice*? Surely you know it. It's an iconic scene."

"It wasn't in the book, you know. Jane Austen would never have written a scene like that," another woman says.

"But I bet she thought about it," Yellow Hat says. "I know I would have if I were her. Thought about it, dreamt about it." She lets out a sigh.

The famous scene flashes before my eyes. Mr. Darcy dives into the pond when he's all hot and sweaty after riding his horse to Pemberley as he tries to fight his overwhelming feelings for Lizzie Bennet. Mr. Darcy exits the pond, his white shirt clinging to his chest as he walks toward the beauty of Pemberley, his feelings for Lizzie remaining unconquered as he broods.

Mom used to go all silly over it.

And Heather McCabe wanted it in her show.

It's at this moment that Chris pops up out of the water behind Sebastian. His white shirt is also clinging to his muscular frame, just as Sebastian's had, and I swear I hear at least a couple of women swoon around me.

"Oh, my. There's *two* of them," Yellow Hat says as she grips onto my arm.

"There are," I reply dumbly, pointing out the obvious.

Chris stops and poses, clearly enjoying the attention being lavished on him by the surrounding audience as people video and photograph them both.

Kennedy pushes through the crowd with, "Excuse me," and comes to a stop beside me. "And Sebastian said he didn't want to be the eye candy."

"Fail," I reply.

Sebastian reaches me, dripping wet, his hair stuck to his head, and looking just about as sexy as I've ever seen him. He holds out the fascinator hat. "I believe this is yours, Brady," he says to me with a small smile, panting lightly from exertion.

Marrying Mr. Darcy

I take it from him. "Thank you," I reply, adding with a waggle of my eyebrows, "Mr. Darcy."

The crowd around us erupts into excited applause, and Sebastian plants a wet kiss on my lips before he smiles out at them all and takes a bow.

"More! More!" Yellow Hat insists to cheers of agreement from others.

"You want me to dive back into the pond?" he asks with a laugh. "No thank you."

"I'll do it again," Chris calls out from the ponds edge, and all eyes turn to him.

"That won't be necessary," Sebastian replies like a stern father. "Now, if I could ask you all to return to your seats, we can get back to the task at hand—officially opening Martinston up to the public."

Everyone returns to their seats, some more reluctantly than others, and Sebastian and a now recovered Geraldine declare the house open to the public. We celebrate by raising our glasses and cups, marking this historic occasion in Martinston's history.

"Let's go get you dry," I say to Sebastian once he's seen Geraldine safely back to her seat. "I'll grab some towels."

"That would be great. I know I made a total spectacle of myself."

"I kinda liked you being all heroic, saving my poor hat."

He chuckles. "I'm not sure it was the most thought out decision I've ever made in my life. Chasing after my fiancée's ugly hat?" He shakes his head.

"Was it because Chris went chasing after it?" I ask.

He looks sheepish. "Would I sound ridiculous if I said yes?"

"No. I kinda liked it."

He reaches for my hand and gives it a squeeze. "You're worth it."

A man approaches us and slaps Sebastian on the back, saying, "That was quite a show you put on back there. Should the good people visiting Martinston expect that every visit, or was this a one-off?"

Sebastian laughs. "Definitely a one-off. Spencer, have you met Emma, my fiancée?"

Spencer offers me his hand. "Charmed. You've got quite the catch here with this one, haven't you?"

"I sure do. I'm gonna get that towel," I say to Sebastian.

As I make my way back through the guests, I spot Kennedy talking with Jemima and Zara. "I'm getting a towel," I say as I approach them.

"What was my brother thinking?" Zara says with a shake of her head.

"I don't know. It seemed like a very Mr. Darcy thing to do," Kennedy says.

"Oh, yes. The pond scene," Jemima says. "And all for your hat, Emma."

"Kinda embarrassing," I reply as I begin to walk away.

"Sebastian Huntington-Ross, fascinator hat rescuing hero," Kennedy teases. "That'll be a story for the grandchildren."

"I know, right? How grandpa saved the errant hat, melting every middle-aged female heart in the process."

"I'm sure I caught a couple of your friends swooning, mum," Zara says.

"Well, he's a good-looking fellow," Jemima replies. "And I can say that because I made him."

"I'll catch you all later," I say as I begin to walk away. "A wet fiancé needs a towel."

I make my way up the gentle incline that leads to the

formal gardens by the house. I smile to myself as I think of Sebastian gallantly chasing after that silly hat—and the fact that he wanted to beat Chris Hampshire to it.

I round a topiary bush only to come face to face with a now partially dried Chris. I stop in my tracks. He's holding a white towel in his hands, his shirt still clinging to him in all the right places.

Not that I'm looking.

"I think he's been working out lately. I was sure I had it in the bag." He flashes me his grin.

"I think the better man won," I reply, only half joking as I resume my walk.

"Have you thought any more about what I said?" he asks.

"I haven't given it a second thought."

"I think you have. I think you've begun to question this supposedly good guy of yours. I think you've begun to see he's not all he's meant to be."

"Enough. I won't doubt him, not now, not ever. Now, if you'll excuse me, I need to get my fiancé a towel."

And with that I turn on my heel. I refuse to entertain Chris's idea that Sebastian is anything less than I know he is. He's the man I love, and I'm one hundred percent committed to him, no matter what some guy in a pond may say.

Chapter Nineteen

"I cannot *believe* you did the pond scene without us there to capture it, Sebastian," Heather says, her hands on her hips, her eyes wild as she stands in Martinston's formal reception room. "The. *Pond*. Scene. Do you know what that would have done to *Saving Pemberley*'s ratings? Skyrocketed them, that's what. Skyrocketed them. People absolutely love a wet, sexy guy in a pond."

"Heather, it wasn't planned. I simply chased after Emma's hat after it blew off in a gust of wind, and it happened to land in the pond. I acted rashly, and I'm actually quite embarrassed about it, truth be told," Sebastian replies.

I shoot him a smile. "I thought it was romantic. A little crazy but romantic all the same."

He chuckles as he shakes his head. "It was a little crazy."

"We had it all planned," Heather continues as she comes to a stop by the one of the large windows with a view of the pond itself. "You were going to dive into your pond here." She gestures out of the reception room window.

Marrying Mr. Darcy

"We'd capture you looking all manly and brooding, just like Mr. Darcy himself, and then we'd pan to an image of the woman of your desire, a not so subtle hint at the passion that rages beneath."

Heather had turned up and banged on the front door five minutes ago, and despite the fact he'd vowed never to see her again following her treatment of me, Sebastian had let her in out of sheer politeness.

I bet he's rethinking his good manners right about now.

"Heather, it wasn't 'the pond scene,' as you call it. There was no brooding, and I was myself, *not* Mr. Darcy."

"My point is, Sebastian, that was the perfect moment to capture on film. It was a beautiful day, you were wearing exactly the right top, I hear, and there was an audience of gushing women. *Gushing women*, Sebastian."

"There certainly were gushing women," I confirm as I think of Yellow Hat and her cronies.

"And. We. Weren't. Even. There." She spells out each word as though he'd intentionally performed the pond scene without her and now deserves a good scolding.

"Of course you weren't," Sebastian replies simply.

Frank slinks into the room, announcing himself with a series of meows as he does. I lean down and pick him up, his purr drumming against my chest.

"I heard there was another man in the pond, too, and that he was wearing a white shirt and looked even better than you." She flops down on one of the vintage couches and exhales loudly, holding her hands up in surrender. "I have no words, Sebastian. No words."

I try not to scoff. *I think you've got a lot of words, actually, Heather.*

Sebastian moves forward in his seat. "Heather, I believe I've made my position clear on this *Saving Pemberley* show.

I told you I would only do it if Emma was involved. You will recall that the idea was unpalatable to you, and so we agreed to go our separate ways. Me entering my pond on my private land has nothing to do with you or your production company."

She opens her mouth to reply, but Sebastian raises his hand and continues, "Please hear me out. Unless you're here to offer us *both* the show"—he indicates the two of us—"with Emma as involved in it as I am, then my answer remains the same."

I beam at Sebastian. He's sticking to his guns—for me. *Again.* As Lizzie Bennet once said of Mr. Darcy, he is the best of men.

Heather crosses her arms, her mouth tightening as she stares Sebastian down. I bet she's cracking the whip on the hamsters in her head, making them sprint their poor little paws off as her brain ticks over.

Sebastian stands up, signaling the conversation is now over. "It was a pleasure to see you, Heather. Now, I really must ask you to leave. We have a lot to do now that the house is open to the public, and we've got a wedding to get to shortly as well."

She stays seated. "I've got an idea," she says, ignoring him.

Those hamsters have clearly been busy.

Sebastian cocks an eyebrow. "What is it?" he asks with obvious caution.

"How about we do the show with her and a bunch of the other *Dating Mr. Darcy* contestants?" she begins, talking as though I'm not even here.

Nice, Heather, real nice.

"That way she gets some airtime and we get a broader audience. We'd bring back some of the more compelling contestants, and they can all stay here, just like they did on *Dating*."

"And I look like I'm running a harem here at my family home?" Sebastian shakes his head. "No thank you."

"You'd be like Hugh Hefner surrounded by his centerfolds," I say.

I imagine Sebastian wearing a velvet smoking jacket and cravat, surrounded by the contestants in bunny costumes. It's a stark contrast with the majesty and elegance of Martinston, a real, *bona fide* mansion.

"It wouldn't be like that. We could give them jobs here at the house. The house is now open to the public, so we could have the girls as ushers or making tea for the punters, maybe clipping the hedges. That sort of thing."

He shoots her a doubtful look. "Clipping the hedges?"

She gives a wave of her hand. "You know what I mean. Doing jobs around the place to give them a purpose for being here. Otherwise you're right, it could look a little like the Playboy mansion, and we don't want that." She looks into the distance as she taps her chin. "Or do we?"

I shut her new train of thought down *pronto*. "The idea sounds good to me, Heather. With a few tweaks. Seb, having some of the contestants on the show could increase its popularity."

"See? Emma likes the idea," she says pointedly to him.

"As long as Emma is shown as my fiancée, and it's made abundantly clear the former contestants are not here to compete for me. This won't be *Dating Mr. Darcy, the Sequel*."

"Of course not. It's *Saving Pemberley*. You know, I think we may be onto a winner with this one, especially if all the contestants watch you as you do the pond scene again. This time with the cameras capturing your every sinew and muscle. Do you think we could get that other guy, too? I heard he was hot."

I answer quickly for Sebastian. He doesn't need to be reminded of Chris Hampshire right now, or at any time. "Isn't the pond scene all about Mr. Darcy? I mean, Colin Firth didn't have any friends dive into the water with him, did he? It would feel less...*authentic* if someone else were there, too."

I'm making this all up on the fly.

"You may be right," she replies.

"How do you feel about it, Seb?" I ask, knowing the idea won't be in the least appealing to him. "You'll be the one in the dripping wet shirt."

"I cannot tell you how much I love the idea of being treated as a sex symbol," he replies with enough sarcasm to fill the room.

"If it'll mean we get to do the show?" I lead.

"And you'll be in it with me," he adds, smiling at me.

I smile back at him. "Exactly."

Heather claps her hands together. "It sounds like we might have a deal."

"We'll need to have say over which contestants come back here," Sebastian warns.

"Oh, definitely," I say. "Kennedy for sure and Reggie and Phoebe, if she can fit it into her new married life."

"And Camille," Heather interjects. "She makes for great TV. Viewers love to hate her, let me tell you."

Camille? No. Freaking. Way. That woman made the characters on *Mean Girls* look like genuinely best friends.

Sebastian shakes his head. "We draw the line at Camille. And anyway, I very much doubt she'd want to be on the show, considering I rejected her publicly in the finale."

Heather's lips curl into a smile. "All the better."

Sebastian shakes his head. "No Camille."

She exhales, clearly annoyed. "All right. No Camille. What about Hayley?"

I shudder at the thought of Camille's BFF and fellow Mean Girl. "Wasn't she kicked off the show because she was married?"

"True, but she was a perfect villain. We need someone the public can love to hate."

"Do we though?" Sebastian questions. "I thought this show was meant to be about saving my family home."

"Oh, we can iron out the details," Heather says as she pulls a notepad and pen out of her purse and scribbles something on it. "For now, this is what we'll offer you to do the show." She hands the piece of paper to Sebastian, and I lean in to read the figure.

My eyes pop at the number of zeros, and my excitement begins to rise. This has got to be more than enough to save the house and then some! I nudge Sebastian in the ribs, and he shoots me a look that says "OMG!" Well, in Sebastian speak it's probably more like "Goodness me, this is a jolly lovely sum of money, eh what?" but you get the idea. This sum is way too good to pass up.

"We will discuss it and come back to you. I'll see you out," he says.

I stand. "Heather, can I ask you something?"

"Of course."

"What made you change your mind about me? You weren't my biggest fan."

"In this business, sometimes you've got to take what you can get. After seeing the footage of Sebastian in that pond, I knew I wanted him back in front of the cameras, and *Saving Pemberley* was the perfect vehicle. You come with all that."

I try not to be offended. "So, I'm collateral damage."

"Who knows? You might end up being the star of the show," she replies, avoiding answering my question.

"I'm sure she will," Sebastian says. "I'll see you out, Heather."

A moment later, Sebastian strides back into the room and collects me in a hug. "I'm so sorry about how she treats you. We don't need to do this show."

"Hello? Did you not *see* how much they're offering? I can take being collateral damage if it means Martinston is safe."

He kisses me on the lips. "It will be safe, thanks to the show. And to you. You're amazing, did you know that?"

"Keep talking, mister."

He chuckles. "My own harem here at Martinston. What the heck was she thinking?"

My giggle ends in a snort. "I don't know. You'd make a good sultan. I can see you in a kaftan with the headgear."

He pulls me in for a kiss. "Can you now?" he asks with a suggestive lilt. "Does that mean you'll dress as a belly dancer and do a little dance for me?"

"Whatever the sultan wants," I reply as I run my fingers through his hair.

We kiss, and I forget about Heather and the TV show.

"I wish we could do this all day, and more, but I really do need to get going," I say in between kisses. "And Kennedy will be waiting."

"Can't we skip it?" he asks as he runs his hands down my back.

"Skip your best friend's wedding in which you're the best man and I'm a bridesmaid?"

"Well, not when you put it that way..." He kisses me

Marrying Mr. Darcy

some more. "But don't you agree this does feel spectacularly good?"

With every ounce of self-control I can muster, I pull away from him and literally hold him at arm's length. It's the only way I can keep my head straight, what with all the kissing and touching and the sheer sexiness of the man. "I'm taking my role as Phoebe's bridesmaid very seriously, you know."

He pulls me into him once more, and I feel the tentative hold I had on my resolve only seconds ago slip away. "Just one sexy belly dance for your sultan before we have to go?" he asks.

"Ahem."

Uh-oh.

We immediately step back from one another, thoughts of belly dancing scattered in the wind. I turn to see who's interrupted us.

Of course it's Geraldine.

"Hello, Granny," Sebastian says smoothly as I rearrange my top, my cheeks flaming hot.

I know we were getting up close and personal in the reception room, but it would have been way better to have been caught by Zara, by Jemima, by *anyone* else.

"Who just drove down the driveway as though they were in some car chase movie?" she asks.

"That would be Heather McCabe from the production company."

"The *television* production company?" There's no disguising the note of revulsion in her voice, and part of me cannot blame her. Doing a reality TV show sure feels a little like selling your soul.

"That's right. We need to discuss what they're offering us, Granny."

"It's a game changer," I add.

"We've already opened up the house to vagabonds and pick pockets and goodness knows who else. Now you want us all to be on television?"

I blink at her. Vagabonds and pick pockets?

"You won't have to, Granny. Just me and Emma and some of the contestants from the *Dating Mr. Darcy* show."

"Have you totally lost your mind, Sebastian?" she asks in outrage.

Sebastian shakes his head. "Granny, we've got this wedding to get to now. Let's talk about this later, shall we?"

"You already know what I'll have to say," she sniffs.

Geraldine Huntington-Ross, ladies and gentlemen. Voted Most Likely to Be Open to Others' Ideas by the Class of '81—*1881*, that is.

"I thought you'd rejected the idea because of the slight on Emma."

"That's what changed. Heather McCabe realized that as my future wife, Emma is as much a part of Martinston as you and I. Isn't she, Granny?"

I know he's testing her. He wants to know whether she's begun to accept me.

I lift my eyes to Geraldine's. I don't even bother holding my breath as I wait for her response.

"As much a part of Martinston as you and I?" she questions. "Of course she is."

If I wasn't holding onto the back of the chair, I might have fallen to the floor.

I give her my biggest smile. "Thank you, ma'am. You saying that means a lot to me."

She returns my smile. It might not be beaming, exactly, but it's definitely a smile. Inside, I'm dancing on tables, doing high kicks, and toasting this momentous occasion.

Marrying Mr. Darcy

Geraldine Huntington-Ross thinks I'm as much a part of Martinston as she is. She approves of me. She *smiled* at me. Things are looking up and up.

"Don't you have to go?" Sebastian says to me.

I glance at my watch and get a start. "Wow, yes! I do." I plant a quick kiss on his lips and then turn to Geraldine. "I'll see you both in the church. I'll be the least pretty of the bridesmaids. Phoebe's sisters and cousins all look like her."

"I'm sure you'll look quite lovely, Emma," Geraldine says.

Two compliments? I've hit the jackpot here.

"Thanks." I kiss Sebastian once more before I skip out of the room on ballerina light feet, dash up the stairs, and ready myself to meet Phoebe and her bridesmaids.

Despite all the setbacks—and let's face it, there have been quite a few—I have finally won Geraldine's approval. I only hope it will last.

Chapter Twenty

I hold my bouquet of exquisite pale pink roses and baby's breath carefully at my waist and follow one of Phoebe's equally blonde and beautiful sisters down the flower-lined aisle of the gorgeous, old village church. There are cameras around us, recording every moment for the TV special, *Marrying Mr. Bingley,* but amidst all the color of the flowers and the guests in their hats, they're barely noticeable.

As I walk slowly to the music, I spot a couple of the contestants from the show. Hayley is next to Camille, the two Mean Girls together once more, and they both shoot me withering looks. Nothing's changed there. They were Phoebe's roommates on the show, and unlike the rest of us, she refused to believe they were anything but nice, decent human beings.

Fun fact: they weren't.

As I pass by Kennedy, she winks at me, and I waggle my eyebrows at her in response.

As I approach the altar, I smile at Sebastian standing next to an excited Johnathan as his best man. They both

Marrying Mr. Darcy

look incredibly handsome in their tuxes, and my heart expands as Sebastian throws me a grin.

Next time I venture up an aisle will be to marry him.

There are eight of us bridesmaids in total, so it takes a while to get us all to where we need to be for Phoebe's grand entrance. But the quartet ensures the music stretches out long enough for us all to find our positions and wait for the bride to follow.

As the opening bars of *Loving You* play—officially Phoebe and Johnathan's couple's song following her perfect performance of it on *Dating Mr. Darcy*—the bride begins her walk down the aisle. Although I know it's a total cliché, she is a vision in her stunning ivory dress with its full skirt and bodice, topped off with a love heart neckline. As she walks down the aisle arm in arm with her dad, you could not find a happier or more beautiful bride.

I watch the way Johnathan looks at her with such love in his eyes, and I swear I hear angels weep. These two are just perfect for one another, and they are so in love. I am honored to be a part of their special day.

The ceremony is sweet and heartfelt, just like Phoebe and Johnathan, and before long they're declared married, and we all leave the church in high spirits, ready for the reception. It's being held at Johnathan's family estate, a stunning, oversized stone house about thirty-five miles from Martinston. With its large windows and ivy-covered walls, it's the perfect backdrop to a romantic wedding for two people who could not be more perfectly suited.

After a delicious meal and funny speeches, including Sebastian's in which he shared a story about how Johnathan once tried to sail down the River Cam at Cambridge in a cardboard boat that sunk after about three seconds, the bride and groom have their romantic first dance, and then we all get to join in.

"Did you go in that boat?" I ask Sebastian as he holds me in our first dance together.

"It's a Cambridge tradition. We all did it, only Johnathan's boat was the worst of the lot."

"You'll have to take me to Cambridge one of these days."

"How about once we've finished making *Saving Pemberley*?"

"Deal."

The song changes to something more upbeat, and we dance up a storm together, laughing and simply enjoying one another's company.

Hot from the dancing, I tell Sebastian I'll meet him outside, and as he goes to the bar to get us some drinks, I make my way through the throngs of people to the Buckingham Palace-style balcony overlooking ornate, formal gardens below.

I reach the edge and let out a deep, contented sigh, the music from inside floating out to touch me, the cool evening breeze brushing against my bare skin. Being here at the Bentley's fairy-tale house on this fairy-tale day knowing how happy my sweet friend Phoebe is, feels beyond wonderful.

"It's quite a lovely outlook here, isn't it?" a familiar voice says beside me.

I turn to see Geraldine standing beside me, her hands on the stone railing as she looks out into the dark night sky.

"Of course it's nothing on Martinston, but then, nothing is," she adds.

"I've got to agree with you on that. Martinston is so special. I can barely believe I get to live the rest of my life there." I tilt my head in her direction and smile at her. Knowing she finally approves of me has whisked my usual anxiety around her away, and I feel calm and relaxed, ready to bond with my future relation.

She turns to me and appears to study my face.

"What is it? Have I got some lipstick where it shouldn't be or something?" I rub my finger around my lips, just in case. "We've been dancing."

"It's not your lipstick, dear," she says, and I can't help but feel touched that she's called me dear.

"Phew! You know how sometimes you think you look gorgeous, and then you realize you've been walking around with your eye makeup so smudged you look like you're a panda? I thought I was having one of those moments."

"Your makeup looks perfectly fine." She turns back and stares out at the view once more. "You do know no one wants you here, don't you?"

Wait, what?

"Excuse me?" I ask, wondering if I heard right. Did she just tell me no one wants me here?

"You heard me," she replies without looking at me. "Even that hideous woman from the television company wants you gone. I imagine that's the only thing we agree on." She turns her whole body to face me and squares her bony shoulders. "It's time for you to do the right thing, Emma. This charade of yours has gone on quite long enough."

I knit my brows together, my heart rate leaping as my belly sinks. "Charade? What are you talking about?"

"I'm talking about you, Emma Brady from Houston, Texas," she spits. "You have bewitched my grandson for your nefarious and selfish means, and we have all had enough. It's time for you to go back to where you're from and leave my poor grandson to find a more suitable match."

My anger flashes. "There's nothing nefarious about me." Not that I know what nefarious means, but considering the context it was delivered in, I know it's got to be something terrible. "Sebastian and I love each other. We're getting married. I...I thought we were getting along."

"Who are you? Who is your family? They're no one. You are just an American gold digger from peasant stock."

"Peasant stock?" I repeat in shock, barely believing my ears.

Is this really happening?

And how can I gold dig when there's no gold to be dug?

"Your father was a builder, of all things. Your mother? Well, goodness only knows what she does."

"Mom works in admin at an insurance office," I explain weakly.

"Do you expect me to sit around and watch my grandson throw away the family name on *you*? Some girl of no consequence, with nothing to her name, who he met on a *television show*? Sebastian must learn to value his family, his standing, his very self. If you have any feelings for him at all you will see that and leave. Either that or you will irrevocably *divide this family*."

Finally, I find my voice.

"I love Sebastian, we are getting married, and I'm not going anywhere. I'm sorry that you feel I'm dividing the family. That was never my intention. I hope you can learn to accept me. But if you don't?" I pause. What am I going to say? Screw you? I don't give a damn? Even if I think those things, I can't say them. She's an old woman, Sebastian's granny, and despite the things she's saying to me right now, she's still someone I want to win over. So instead, I finish my speech with, "I really hope you can find it in your heart to accept me."

"Accept you?" she scoffs. "You've known him all of what? Five minutes? It won't last, Emma. What you fail to appreciate is that you're not our kind. You're not one of us. You're"—she looks at me with pure venom in her eyes—"no one."

I suck in air.

Everything I've wanted, everything I've tried to do is to fit in, to show Geraldine and everyone here that I'm worthy of Sebastian's love, that I'm enough.

"I'm not no one," I say through gritted teeth as tears threaten my eyes. "I'm Sebastian's future wife."

"You obstinate, headstrong little minx," she spits at me.

I half expect her to launch into Lady Catherine de Bourgh's speech, asking whether by marrying me *are the shades of Pemberley to be thus polluted*. Which I realize with a stab of shock she is.

"How dare you pretend to be something you're not. You don't fit in now, and you never will. You mark my words."

I'd like to shove your words where the sun don't shine, lady.

We glare at one another, my tummy in knots. Before this moment Geraldine had always been civil enough, often with the odd barbed comment thrown in. Sure, I knew she didn't approve of me, but I thought we could work on that, and earlier today, I even thought she was coming around.

I feel such a fool.

"If you need any help getting yourself back to Texas, I'd be more than happy to help," she says.

"Are you offering to pay for my flight?"

"I'd buy you the plane if it meant you'd leave tonight."

"Enough!" I say loudly before I check my volume.

"Enough. You've made your point perfectly clear. But I'm here to stay, so you'd better just get used to it."

Before I say any more things to her I can't take back, I turn on my heel and stomp away. She may be a nasty old woman with venom pumping through her veins, but she is Sebastian's grandmother.

At the door leading inside, I literally smack straight into Chris Hampshire.

"Geez. Where's the fire, Texas?"

As the tears I've been holding back begin to well in my eyes, I dart a look from him back to Geraldine. She's watching me, one eyebrow arched, judging my every move.

"Pardon me," I mutter as I push past him. I search the room for Sebastian, but I can't find him. Instead, I rush around the edge of the dance floor, holding in my tears as best I can. I dash out of the ballroom and into the grand hallway.

I reach the end, far from the dancing, and slump down the wall to the floor beside a velvet curtain. As my butt hits the floor, I let the tears flow. They're tears of sadness, they're tears of anger, and they're tears of frustration. Frustration that all my efforts to get Geraldine to accept me have come to nothing.

And now she's literally offered to pay me to leave.

It's insane, like an old novel with an evil queen and a poor, peasant girl.

"I thought you could do with one of these."

It's Chris. Again. I look up through blurry eyes at him. He's smiling down at me in my crumpled position on the floor, holding a glass of champagne in each hand, one of which he holds out for me.

I wipe my face with the backs of my hands. "I'm not exactly in a celebratory mood."

Marrying Mr. Darcy

He slides down the wall and sits next to me. "I find alcohol helps, no matter what your mood."

"What are you doing here?"

His lips curve into a smile. "Saving a damsel in distress."

I scoff. "I'm no damsel, and I don't need saving. I mean, what are you doing at this wedding."

"Jilly invited me, although I was late and I only got here a while back. Just in time, by the looks of things. Here."

With a sigh I take the drink from him and take a gulp. The bubbles tickle my nose as the cool liquid slips down my throat.

He clinks his glass against mine. "Here's to dramatic exits from ballrooms."

"I'm not sure I want to drink to that."

"Just drink then. You'll feel a lot better. Champagne is magic, especially this super expensive kind."

I take a gulp. "I don't know anything about champagne."

"All you've got to know is this is the good stuff and it would be rude not to drink it."

I take another sip and begin to feel the alcohol warm my belly. I can't deny it feels good.

"She was being an old bitch, wasn't she?"

I know I shouldn't trust this guy. I know Sebastian hates him and he hurt Jilly. But he's here, and he's being kind, and I need a shoulder to cry on. "She told me I don't belong here and I should just leave."

"I think you fit in perfectly here, although between you and me, I've noticed a bunch of other girls in the same dress tonight."

I let out a sudden laugh despite myself. "Being a bridesmaid kinda requires you to look the same as each other."

"Is that what that's about? I just thought it was some weird chick thing."

I laugh, almost glad he's here. Almost.

"You didn't mean here at the wedding. You meant *here*. She told you you're not good enough for her family, didn't she?"

I give a reluctant nod. "I always knew she wasn't my biggest fan, but this was straight up vicious." To my dismay, fresh tears sting my eyes, and I wipe them away quickly.

He loops his arm around my shoulder and gives me a squeeze. It's oddly comforting. "Aw, Texas. That sucks. You knew this would happen, though."

"No, I didn't."

"Yeah, ya did. Remember what happened to me? I wasn't one of them either."

I sniff loudly, wishing I had a Kleenex. "You mean with you and Jilly?"

He nods. "It was made pretty darn clear that I wasn't good enough for her. And you know what? Screw them, because I *am* good enough. And so are you."

I lift my chin, bolstered by his words. "I know that."

"Then why are you out here crying and not in there dancing up a storm with your soon-to-be husband? Be honest with yourself. She got to you. And it sucks."

I hang my head. "You're right. She did."

"I'm sorry, Texas. You deserve more. A whole lot more." He raises his glass. "A toast. To not fitting in and not giving a damn."

I giggle and take another sip of my champagne, and I'm surprised to see I've finished off the glass. "You're right about something else, too. Champagne is a miracle worker."

"Geraldine who?" he says kindly.

I smile at him. "Thanks, Chris."

"You're welcome. Chasing after pretty girls is my specialty, you know."

I shake my head. "I bet it is."

"I like you, Texas. You're all right."

I smile at him, warmed by the camaraderie—and the champagne. And then, before I even realize what's quite happening, he cups my face in his hands and brushes his lips across mine. Immediately, I recoil from him, shocked that he would step over the line in this way, not only in taking advantage of me in my emotional, vulnerable state, but knowing I'm engaged to Sebastian.

"Chris, why—"

"What's going on here?"

I snap my attention to the location of the voice, only to see Sebastian, his hands on his hips, scowling at us, with Jilly lurking behind. His anger is almost visible in jagged edges around him.

"Sebastian," I say breathlessly. Immediately, I free myself from Chris's embrace and leap to my feet, my champagne flute smashing on the hardwood floor.

But I'm too late. He's already turned on his heel and stormed off, leaving me, Chris, and Jilly in the hallway.

"Emma, how could you?" she says.

"Looks like you're in the bad books with another Huntington-Ross tonight, Texas," Chris says as he looks up at me from his spot on the floor, his eyes bright.

"Well, I'm not sticking around to see you two together," Jilly sniffs before rushing after Sebastian. "Sebby, wait!" she calls.

I round on Chris and snap, "Why did you do that?"

He pushes himself up off the floor until he's standing right in front of me. He has the audacity to place his hands on my shoulders. I shrug them angrily off, and he takes a step back from me, his hands up in surrender.

"I've tried to get you out of my mind. I know you're

engaged to Sebastian. But you've got to know how I feel about you."

"How you feel about me?" I sputter. "Chris, what are you talking about?"

"I'm talking about you and me, Texas. We're the same. We're not like these people. You know you feel it, too." He reaches out to touch me once more, and I shrink away from him.

I suck in air, the shock of the last few moments beginning to dissipate as I regain my composure. I stand tall, squaring my shoulders and reply forcefully, "I'm in love with Sebastian. You've been kind to me tonight, and I appreciate that, but you're so wrong. You're not the man for me. Sebastian is, and I need to go find him and tell him that."

The look on his face morphs from smug confidence to fear.

Ha! That told him.

But it's not me that's caused the change. I turn to see Sebastian behind me, seething with anger, his eyes trained like tractor beams on Chris.

"It's time you left," he growls through gritted teeth.

"I think you'll find this isn't your house."

"I don't care. You need to leave. Now."

Chris shakes his head and forces a smile. "Dude. She's not even a good kisser."

Uh-oh.

Sebastian's features harden. "What did you say?"

"I said, she just sat there like a freaking statue, all frigid and cold."

In one fluid movement, Sebastian takes one step closer to him, and *pow!* he punches him right in the face. In a flash

Chris is hurtled against the wall, his hands flying to his nose as blood oozes down over his mouth.

Sebastian stands over him and says, "I should have done that a long time ago." As he turns to leave, his eyes meet mine briefly before he strides away down the hall, leaving me openmouthed, trying to process what's just happened.

Chapter Twenty-One

I've got to find him. I've got to find Sebastian.

I rush down the grand hall as fast as my heels will take me, leaving Chris to his broken nose and damaged ego—although knowing him as I do, I suspect one of those will heal a whole load faster than the other.

"Seb?" I call out into the first room I find. It's dark and empty, and there's no sign of life. I rush to the next, and then the next.

How many freaking rooms are there off this oversized hallway?

Then I see him.

He's rounding the corner, Jilly following close behind.

"Seb, stop! Please," I call out.

They pass through a door, and I follow them into a darkened room. I fumble for the light switch, locate it, and flick it on, the room instantly bathed in a warm glow. When my eyes adjust, I see Sebastian, his back to me, Jilly with her hand on his shoulder, trying to comfort him.

"Jilly? Can you please give us the room?"

"Are you serious? After the stunt you just pulled, Emma, I'm not inclined to give you anything," she replies.

I appeal to my fiancé. "Seb, please."

He takes a deep breath and says, "Jilly, I need to talk to Emma alone."

"I won't leave you," she sniffs.

"I'll be fine," he insists.

She presses her lips together as she looks between the two of us, seemingly deciding whether to stay or go. "All right, but I'll be out there waiting for you, Sebby."

"Thanks, Jilly," he says softly.

She shoots me a lethal look before I close the door behind her.

With his back still facing me, I notice his shoulders are tense.

I move closer to him. "Seb?"

After a beat, he turns to look at me, and the pain in his eyes has my breath catching in my throat.

"I'm so, so sorry," I gush, moving over to him. "I didn't mean for any of that to happen. I was upset, and he followed me out into the hallway. You've gotta believe me. I didn't do anything to make him think I wanted him to kiss me. That's the God's honest truth."

He presses his lips together as he casts his eyes down. He exhales heavily and then looks back up at me, his shoulders slumping. "I believe you, Brady."

Relief floods through my veins. "You do? Oh, Seb." I rush over to him and wrap my arms around him. Although he hugs me back, his body remains taut. I pull back from him and our gazes lock. "You hit him because of the kiss?"

"Partly that and partly something else," he replies evasively. "Chris Hampshire had it coming, believe me."

"Why? I get that he's a bit of a slime, and I'm pretty sure

he's never heard of the #MeToo movement, but why did he have it coming? Is it because of Jilly?"

"Let's sit. I should really tell you the whole thing."

We pull a couple of padded wooden chairs out from the large dining table and sit down facing one another. I take his hand in mine and wait for him to begin.

"Chris Hampshire has done more damage to my family than any living person."

I pull my brows together in confusion. "To your *family*? I don't get it."

"Years ago, when we met at Cambridge, I genuinely enjoyed his company. I brought him home to Martinston to stay, and we spent a lot of time together. He even spent Christmas with us one year when he didn't go home to Boston. Then, of course, he was dating Jilly. Everything seemed great for a while, that is until I discovered his true character."

"What did he do?"

"Unbeknownst to me, he had Jilly paying for everything, from his rent to their summers in the South of France and ski trips to the Alps."

"That's not a crime, though. She's from a super wealthy family, and he's not. They're kinda us in reverse, in some ways."

"Believe me when I say, Brady, you are nothing like Chris Hampshire. Over time, it became clear to me that he was taking advantage of her, so much so that when he asked her to marry him, he stipulated in their prenup that he would get half of her wealth should they separate within two years. More if they remained together for three."

"She signed something like that?"

"Of course she did. She was besotted with him."

"She didn't mention that."

Marrying Mr. Darcy

"It was a hard time for her. What made it harder was when I caught him with my girlfriend in a, shall we say *compromising* position."

My eyes get wide. "Seriously?"

"Seriously. When I challenged him, he practically admitted he was using Jilly for her money. That's when I stepped in. I didn't feel I had any choice. This guy was using my good friend and sleeping with my girlfriend. Not exactly the type of guy you want in your life."

"You saved Jilly," I say, my voice heavy with emotion. "No wonder you punched the guy."

"I wouldn't go that far, but I certainly tried to act in her best interests. But the problem was, he'd seduced someone else at the time, too. Someone very close to me. Someone I loved."

"Not Zara?" I say in a gasp.

He shakes his head. "Thank God, no. It was my father." He looks down at his hands as his words sink in.

"Your *father*?"

"He wormed his way into my father's good books. They became great friends. Chris introduced him to another world."

My breath catches in my throat. "Gambling."

He nods, his features grim. "I knew they would go to the races together. Heck, I went with them sometimes. But it wasn't until right before my father's death that the full picture of Chris's influence over him emerged. Father told me he took him to casinos in Monaco for high stakes gambling and that he financed Chris into the games, believing his stories that he was a proficient gambler. He told my father he could help him make enough money to ensure we never lost the house and would live comfortably for the rest of our lives."

"How do you know all this?"

"Father told me one day when I found him sobbing in his study. It was...a difficult conversation."

I position myself on his lap and pull him into me for a long hug. "Oh, Seb. That must have been so hard for you."

His gaze locks with mine, and I see the pain as clear as day lurking in his eyes. "Losing the family wealth was hard, but not as hard as knowing Chris Hampshire was closer to my father than I would ever be."

"I'm so sorry, Seb. No wonder you hate him. And then you saw him kiss me."

"That wasn't my favorite moment," he replies, the edges of his mouth lifting a fraction.

"Why didn't you tell me all this before when you told me about him and Jilly?

"I was ashamed. I brought Chris into our lives, into Jilly's life. My father knew him because of me. *I* caused my father's downfall."

"No, you did not. That's crazy talk! How could you have known what would happen?"

"Without me, no one would have even known Christopher Hampshire."

"That's why you did *Dating Mr. Darcy*. Because you felt responsible."

He gives a grim nod. "All they know is Father lost our money and put the house in jeopardy. They don't know about Chris's involvement or even the extent of our debts."

"Seb, no one would blame you for your dad's decisions."

He gives me a sardonic smile. "Have you met my granny?"

"Good point. She, ah, she was the reason Chris was comforting me just now."

"Oh?"

Marrying Mr. Darcy

"She told me I would never be good enough for you or your family."

His face turns to thunder. "I see."

I hang my head, the numbing effect of the champagne wearing off as the hurt returns. "All the effort I've been putting into making her like me was a waste of time, Seb."

A beeping sound comes from his pocket.

"Is that your phone?" I ask.

"It can wait."

"But it's almost midnight. Maybe it's something important?"

He pulls the phone out of his pocket and reads the screen. "It's from your mum."

I take the phone from him.

Hi Sebastian. I'm trying to get a hold of my girl. Can you get her to call me when you get the chance? Thanks.

Worry hits me between the eyes.

"What do you think it's about?" he asks me.

"I don't know. Do you mind if I call her? She knows the time difference, so something must be wrong."

"Of course."

I pause before I hit the *call* button. "Seb, I think you need to tell your family about what Chris did and about the extent of your dad's gambling. You can't carry all this weight on your shoulders. It's too much."

He exhales. "I know you're right. It's been so hard." He offers me a weak smile before he instructs, "Now, call your mum."

I press *call*, and immediately it begins to ring.

"Hi, Sebastian," Mom says. "Thanks for calling me back so fast."

"Mom, it's me."

"Oh, hi, honey. How are you?"

"Is everything okay? Your message got me worried."

"Of course it is," she replies breezily and then adds, "Well, mostly."

"What does that mean? Stella didn't eat all your arugula again, did she?" I ask, trying to make light of the heaviness settling in my belly. Stella is Mom's Jack Russell, and she's got some interesting taste in food. That dog will eat anything. Literally. Once when I was visiting with Mom, she had to scoop a rusty razorblade from her mouth. Another time, it was a rock. Who knows what the doggy thought process was behind eating either of those, but it's a good thing neither managed to get down her throat.

"Oh, no, Stella's fine. Don't you go worrying about her. How are *you*, anyway?"

"I'm good," I reply as I hear muffled sounds and a distinctly female voice down the line. "Mom? Are you with someone?"

"Your Aunt Judy's here. She popped in to say hi," Mom replies.

There's more muffled sounds.

"Say hi from me."

"Emma? It's your Aunt Judy," my mom's older sister says unnecessarily.

"What's going on, Aunt Judy?"

"Your mom has some news, honey, but the problem is, she needs to grow a pair of ovaries and tell her only daughter."

"Ok*aaa*y."

So not a good image.

"I'm gonna hand you back to your mama, and she's gonna tell you. Aren't you, Charlene? Charlene!"

"All right. You don't have to get so pushy with me.

Marrying Mr. Darcy

Geez. You're only twenty-one months older," I hear Mom say in the background. "Hey, honey. It's me again."

"What's your news, Mom? And why's Aunt Judy bossing you around? Forget that—she always bosses you around."

"Oh, my sister is the queen of bossy, honey. We all know it."

"Get on with it!" Bossy Aunt Judy yells.

"Okay, okay. I'm on it. Don't lose your false teeth over it."

"I don't have false teeth, and you know it, Charlene."

These two are like a comedy duo right now.

"Mom?"

"Look, Emma," she begins, and instantly my hackles are up. She never calls me Emma."

Not unless there's something wrong.

"Quit messing around and tell me what's going on, Mom."

"It's, ah, well, I've got some news. A while back, I found a lump, and I went to the doctor. She ran some tests and, well—" I can hear her take an audible gulp of air, "Honey, I've got cancer."

My hand flies to my mouth as I take in a sharp breath. "You've got cancer?" I say, my voice suddenly breathless, like the air's been sucked right out of me.

Sebastian pings out of his chair and is at my side almost before I finish my sentence.

With the mention of the word, my world comes to a crunching halt. Sebastian's revelations about Chris, my failure to fit in in Geraldine's eyes, Heather and her *Saving Pemberley* plans, Timothy's distinct lack of British success. All of it falls into silence, and I'm left with that one word in my brain, the word that changed my life when my dad was diagnosed.

Cancer.

"Honey?" she questions when I don't reply. "Are you okay?"

"You said a lump. Is that a breast lump?"

Sebastian's face creases in concern.

"What type of cancer is it? When did you get it? Can they fix it?"

She laughs. She *laughs*.

One of us is clearly taking this better than the other.

"I can't give you answers on all those questions. All I can tell you is that I found a breast lump a couple months back and—"

"*A couple months?* And you're only telling me *now*? Mom!"

Her voice is quiet when she replies, "I'm sorry, honey. I wanted to be sure before I said anything to you. You know, what with your dad and all."

At the mention of my dad, my tears begin to well, and a lump tightens my throat. Dad died of his cancer. Does that mean Mom will, too?

"Women find lumps every day, and they amount to nothing, you know. Modern medicine is a miracle. I didn't want to disturb you over there with Sebastian. You've got a wedding to plan, a new life to build. You've got enough on your plate."

I try to keep my voice from cracking when I reply, "But, Mom, it's cancer. This is serious."

"I know, honey," she says quietly, and the softness of her voice causes my tears to overflow, running down my cheeks, my tightened throat heating up. "It took me a while to wrap my head around it, too."

Marrying Mr. Darcy

I slump down in the closest chair, the energy draining out of me, like air from a punctured balloon. "Tell me everything."

And she does. She tells me how she went to see her doctor just as soon as she found the lump, how her doctor sent her for tests, how she nervously waited for the results, how she's now got a treatment plan in place and is forging ahead with it. All the while I'm listening intently, I clutch onto my phone, tight.

I've lost one parent to cancer. I don't want to lose another.

"I'm coming home," I announce once she's done.

Sebastian squeezes my hand. "Whatever you need."

I nod at him as tears prick my eyes.

"No, honey. Stay where you are. Your aunt may be the bossiest older sister on the planet, but she's here for me. I'm in good hands here, and I've got total trust in my doctors."

"But—"

"But nothing. Now, tell me all about Phoebe's wedding. Is it as *Downton Abbey* as I imagine it to be?"

"Mom."

"Please, honey. I need to think about something else for a while."

"Sure."

Sebastian holds me as I tell her about Phoebe walking down the aisle, about how everyone was dressed, about Sebastian's best man speech, about the other contestants from the show. I try to remain positive. I try not to fear the worst. But literally thousands of miles from her, I feel utterly helpless.

I've never felt so far away from home.

Chapter Twenty-Two

Blindsided. That's what I am. Although Mom had been contacting me more than I'd expected she would since I've been here, I'd put it down to her missing me.

Not cancer.

Last night, after the initial shock, Sebastian and I went back home and talked through my next steps. He encouraged me to go back to Houston to be with my mom, telling me he'll be here, waiting for me when I get back. Although I knew I'd miss him terribly, I also knew it was what I needed to do.

And now we're locked in an embrace, saying goodbye on Martinston's front steps. My head is filled with worry for Mom, and my heart is sitting heavily at having to leave.

"You're doing the right thing, Brady. Your mum needs you right now."

"I know," I reply with a super unsexy sniff, the result of hours of tears. "It's just so hard to leave you after...after what happened last night."

I don't mention Chris's name. I don't have to.

"There's nothing to worry about. We'll get through this."

"We will," I reply with certainty. Because I am certain. I love Sebastian, and I know he loves me. Sure, we've had more than our fair share of curve balls thrown our way in the last few months—everything from Geraldine to Chris to the media's dislike of me—but we're solid.

More than solid.

Frank's face appears around the front door, and I crouch down and rub my fingers together, and he comes running over to me with a loud meow. I collect him in my arms and nuzzle his warm fur. "You look after Seb for me, okay, Frank?"

"It might be the other way 'round," Sebastian replies with a smile. "I'll be sure to keep him stocked up on tasty treats and catnip."

I place Frank on the ground, and he rubs up against my legs. "Thanks." The emotion wells up inside me once more. I'm leaving both my guys, Sebastian and Frank, and it feels pretty darn crappy.

"I'll be over to visit soon," Sebastian says. "You just concentrate on being strong for your mum."

I give him a watery smile. "I will."

Kennedy walks down the steps and pulls me into a hug. "I'm so sorry about your mom. Are you doing okay?"

"As good as I can, I guess," I reply.

"I'm gonna miss you."

"You can stay as long as you like, Kennedy," Sebastian says.

She smiles at him. "Thanks. I might stay a couple more days then hit London and Paris. Maybe take in Rome."

"On your own? Is that safe?"

"I'll be fine. Who knows? I may meet the man of my dreams on my travels."

The taxi crunches across the gravel of the driveway and comes to a stop beside us.

Kennedy gives me another quick hug, saying, "I love you so hard, Em. Take good care of your mom and take super good care of you."

"I will," I croak, my voice heavy with emotion as tears roll down my cheeks.

Who knew you could cry this much? I sure didn't. I must be in serious fear of dehydration by now.

Sebastian opens the door to the taxi for me as the driver puts my luggage in the trunk.

"I wish you'd let me drive you to the airport, Brady," he says.

"Just look at me." I point at my face, which I know is super *not* attractive right now. I'm no Hollywood crier. I'm full-on ugly, from my red and puffy eyes to my bulbous nose. "This would get even worse if I'm forced to walk away from you at Heathrow."

He smiles down at me as he brushes an errant clump of hair that had gotten stuck to my cheek. See? Not a pretty crier. "Brady Bunch." His voice is soft and full of love, bringing on a fresh wave of sadness.

"I love you," I manage, before I choke right up, halting any further words I might try to utter in their tracks.

He kisses me and replies, "I love you, too."

I get into the taxi and paste on a brave smile. Leaving Sebastian for an unknown amount of time to be with Mom as she goes through her treatment is one of the hardest things I've had to do. Almost as hard as saying goodbye to my dad.

"I'll call you."

Marrying Mr. Darcy

I nod, not trusting myself to speak. I glance up at the house, and my eyes land on one of the large windows on the second floor. I see a someone staring down at me, a self-satisfied look on her face. Geraldine must be beyond delirious that I'm leaving, no doubt hoping I'll never be back. I give her a brief wave, and she raises her hand in response, her features hard.

"Go," I instruct the driver, because there's no way I could manage a full sentence right now. As he drives off, I look back at my fiancé standing in front of his huge house, watching me leave.

* * *

Mom is at George Bush Intercontinental to meet me, a huge smile on her pretty face, my Aunt Judy at her side. I drop my bags and collect her in a hug, holding onto her tight as I try to stem the tears that threaten to burst from me. I need to stay strong for Mom. She's the one with cancer. She's the one going through treatment. I'm only here to support her.

"My baby girl," she coos softly in my ear. "It's so good to have you back home, although I'm so sorry you had to leave Sebastian back in England."

"How are you feeling?" I ask as I release her and greet Aunt Judy.

The two sisters look like two peas in a pod, dressed in slacks and cute blouses, both of them with a bobbed hairstyle.

"I'm doing great, honey. You tell her, Judy."

"Your mom is an all-star, Emma, but I'm sure she's real happy her only baby is back home."

"I'm happy to be home, too. I bought you a gift, Mom." I reach into my bag and pull out a green double-decker bus toy with the word *Harrods* written on it and hand it to her. "I got it at Heathrow. I know how much you want to visit London, so I thought I'd bring a little piece of it to Texas for you until you can get there yourself."

"Oh, sweetie. Thank you," she says with a smile. "We'll go to Harrods together, you and me, when I come over for your wedding."

"It's a plan."

With my luggage collected, we get into Aunt Judy's old Toyota, and she drives us back to Mom's home, the house I grew up in and the place I'll be living while she has her treatment. As she drives, Mom asks me about life at Martinston, and I share some of the highlights, avoiding the aspects that are, shall we say, less than optimal. Mom doesn't need my worries right now, and she sure as heck doesn't need to know Geraldine thinks I'm not good enough for her grandson.

By the time we pull up outside the house, she's convinced I live a fairy-tale life akin to *Downton Abbey*'s Lady Mary—not that her life was exactly a fairy tale, but if that's the way Mom wants to think of it, then Lady Mary I am. I figure Mom needs some escape, and I'm happy to provide her with it.

Once out of the car, I regard the home I grew up in with fresh eyes. It was always going to pale in comparison with Martinston—what house wouldn't? Martinston is a freaking manor house—but Mom looks after it well, from the little garden out front to the faux window shutters and the brightly painted, glossy red front door. As I step out of the car, the humidity and heat hits me like a hairdryer on full, and for a moment, I think I actually miss the cool English rain.

An hour later, I've unpacked in my childhood bedroom,

Marrying Mr. Darcy

and we're sitting in the small living room with its 80's pastel walls and lampshades as Mom talks me through her treatment plan and Stella sniffs my legs with her tail wagging at full speed.

"My surgery is all set for Tuesday. You're gonna love Dr. Michaels, honey. He is so nice, isn't he, Judy?"

"What your mom is saying is that he's handsome," she teases.

"I can't help that I like a man with dimples," she protests. "Just like your dad's," she says to me. "He had the cutest dimples, that man."

And that does it for me. All my plans to be stoic and strong fly out the window and into the thick Houston air as I crumple with tears.

"Oh, honey." Mom comes to sit next to me on the couch and wraps me up in one of her world-famous hugs as my tears flow, and Aunt Judy busies herself in the kitchen making me some iced tea.

Eventually, the flow of tears stemmed, I blow my nose. "I'm sorry. I wanted to be strong for you."

"I know, sweetie." She strokes my back, just like she used to when I was sick or upset as a kid. "I should never have mentioned your dad. Not when you're tired out from a long trip."

"No. Mom, it's fine. We need to be able to talk about Dad."

"Even his dimples?" she asks with a wry smile.

"They were pretty good dimples."

"Oh, yes, they were. I always told him if it wasn't for those dimples of his, I would never have taken a second look at him in high school." She smiles at the memory, before her features grow more serious. "I get it. I know what you're feeling. We lost your dad to cancer, and now you're worried you're going to lose me. But, honey, that's not going to happen. I promise you. We caught this early, and Dr. Michaels says I've got a real good chance here. So, don't you go worrying about your old mom."

I give her a watery smile. "I always worry about my *old* mom." I nudge her lightly with my elbow.

She shakes her head as she laughs. "Less of the old, thank you."

Aunt Judy enters the room with a tray with a jug of iced tea, tall glasses, and a stack of chocolate chip cookies. "I baked some of your favorite cookies, Emma, to welcome you back home."

With a better grip on my emotions, I reply, "You're the best, Aunt Judy," and we spend the next hour eating and drinking and talking about anything but my Mom's impending surgery and the radiation that follows. Although I already miss Sebastian like the desert misses the rain, it feels good to be home, home in my family's unconditional love. Home where I can be myself and don't even have to try.

I hear my phone's ringtone coming from my bedroom down the hall, and I excuse myself to go answer it, hoping it's Sebastian. After the long flight, I'm feeling a little woozy, like I'm not quite in the room, and I'd love nothing more than to hear Sebastian's voice. And then sleep.

Definitely sleep.

I pick up my phone and see it's not Sebastian calling. It's Jilly. Although the last time I saw her wasn't exactly the greatest moment—Kissgate with Chris Hampshire in the great hall—I'm pleased she's calling me. It must mean she's had a chance to cool down and remember we're friends.

"Hey, Jilly. It's so nice to hear from you."

"Is that all you've got to say for yourself? It's nice to hear from me? Really, Emma, I would have thought you'd have had a script all organized and ready to go by now."

"A script?" I ask, pulling my brows together. She's clearly still pretty angry. "Look, Jilly, I know you're probably still upset with me about the thing with Chris last night. Was it last night? I'm so out of it right now, I barely know which way is up."

"I bet you don't, juggling two men the way you have been. You must barely get any time to sleep at all."

"I'm not juggling two men, Jilly," I say in exasperation. "He kissed me, and I definitely never did anything to encourage him."

"I'm not talking about you kissing him. I'm talking about the affair you two have been having behind everyone's backs."

"Oh, come on, Jilly! That's insane. I'm not having an affair." I rub my eyes, tiredness, jetlag, and the stress of the last twenty-four hours hitting me. "I've been on a flight forever, I've only just got to my Mom's house, and I'm totally shattered. Can we talk another time? Like when my brain's working right?"

And you've calmed the heck down?

"How could you do it, Emma? How could you do it to Sebby? Oh, what am I talking about? Of course, Jilly. Silly me. I know how you could do it. He's catnip. He's impossible to resist."

She might not be over Kissgate, but I am definitely over this conversation.

"I'm gonna go now, Jilly."

"So, you've got nothing to say? No comment on all those photos?"

Alarm forces it through the quagmire of my brain. "What photos?"

"Don't play innocent with me, missy."

Missy?

"Jilly, I don't know about any photos."

"I've just sent you a link."

I open her message and click on the link. It takes me to a site that screams in bold letters, *Mr. Darcy's Emma is a love rat!*

What the…?

I scroll down and see a series of images of me with Chris that day I bumped into him at Mia's Café. There's one of us sitting at the café together, looking happy. There's of us one outside on the sidewalk, with his hand on my arm, smiling at me.

I blink at the screen. Who would have taken photos of us together, let alone then sent them to a news outlet? I may have been a failed contestant on *Dating Mr. Darcy*, but I'm hardly paparazzi fodder. Who could possibly want to slander me like this?

"Who would have taken those? And more importantly, why? It doesn't make sense."

"Because you're Elizabeth Bennet playing around with someone else behind the much loved Mr. Darcy's back, that's why," she replies with a snide tone that gets my back right up.

"But I'm not," I insist forcefully. "And I didn't even win that show in the first place."

Which feels super irrelevant right now, but I still feel the need to make the point.

"Look, I get it. The heart wants what the heart wants. I only wish you'd not hurt Sebby in the process."

"Jilly, I'm going to say this one more time: I am not having an affair with Chris Hampshire!"

She harrumphs, clearly not convinced.

"I love Seb. He's my world."

"Well, it certainly *looks* like you're having an affair."

"I'm not," I say firmly, sensing her conviction slipping.

She exhales loudly. "Emma, can I say something to you?"

"I should go call Seb. I need to clear this mess up with him."

"You know how much I value our friendship and how much I love you. Truly, truly love you."

"Sure," I say dismissively.

"I'm not saying this lightly in the least."

Frustrated, I reply, "Can you please just spit it out, Jilly?"

"There have been so many obstacles in your relationship with Sebby, haven't there? There's the negative press. Your little social *faux pas*, of which there were several. Need I remind you of the Rasmus toilet debacle? Not to mention Geraldine's obvious contempt for you and the fact the production company didn't want you on the show."

"Are you trying to make me feel bad on top of accusing me of having an affair with Chris Hampshire? Because you're definitely heading in that direction right now."

"I'm saying this as a friend, Emma, and I really want you to hear it."

I refrain from scoffing. Accusing me of cheating on Seb isn't exactly top of the list of things friends do in my books.

"At what point do you decide enough is enough? At what point do you throw in the towel? The universe has been screaming at you, Emma, telling you that you and Seb are not meant to be."

"What? No, it hasn't."

"Emma, *please* be honest with yourself. You must know it. Everything is pointing to the fact that you're simply Not.

Meant. To. Be. Together." She enunciates each word in staccato to make her point.

"That's crazy talk."

"Poor Sebby is suffering, Emma. Please. Do what's right for him. Let him go."

I let out an exasperated—and frankly deeply insulted—puff of air, say a stern "Good-bye, Jilly," and hang up.

What is she talking about? The universe hasn't been screaming anything at me, let alone the idea that Seb and I aren't meant to be. That's ridiculous. We are meant to be, and right now, I need to get ahold of him to make sure he knows it.

Chapter Twenty-Three

As soon as I've hung up from speaking with Jilly, I call Sebastian. It rings and rings until it goes to voicemail. When I hear his voice asking me to leave a message, a flood of emotion washes over me. Love, happiness, anxiety, dread.

I hang up and immediately tap out a message.

Call me! This is insane! I love you xoxo

I press send and scroll through my messages. I've had a couple missed calls from him as well as a message asking me to call him.

No kisses. No hugs.

Fear twists inside. What if he believes I'm having an affair with Chris Hampshire? He did walk in on us in the hallway at Johnathan's house. Not that I consented to that kiss, of course. Sure, he believed me at the time, and he opened up and shared Chris's involvement in his dad's gambling habit. But what if he now thinks I lied to him? That I don't love him? That I've been stringing him along as I play away?

He can't. Surely he has faith in me?

I look back to the photos Jilly sent me. I can't help myself. To someone who didn't know, you would think we were together. We're happily laughing at the café, looking every inch like a couple out for a coffee together. And the photo of his hand on my arm outside looks super intimate, even though I know it's not.

I bring up Sebastian's contact details and call him again. This time, it goes straight to voicemail. I check the time. It's got to be eleven thirty at night in England. Maybe he's gone to sleep?

"Honey? Aunt Judy's leaving," Mom calls from the other room.

"Coming!" I slip my phone into the back pocket of my jeans and say a silent prayer Sebastian still has faith in me and that he'll call me back and put me out of this misery.

That night, after a meal of mac and cheese with Mom, during which I try not to let my anxiety over the photos come out, I slip between the crisp, cool sheets of my childhood bed, physically, emotionally, and mentally exhausted. There are no messages from Seb, which I tell myself makes perfect sense. It's got to be two in the morning over there by now. He's not likely to call me at that time. He'll be asleep, dreaming good thoughts about me, trusting in my love for him.

I lie in my childhood bed and stare at the ceiling of my old room, willing sleep to come. Although I'm beyond exhausted, jet-lagged, and a total emotional wreck, sleep evades me.

I count the glow-in-the-dark stars Mom stuck up on the ceiling when I was seven and wanted to be an astronaut following a school visit to NASA. Sleep doesn't come.

I'm too amped. I've got too many things competing for thinking space in my brain.

Sebastian.

Those darn photos.

Mom.

Thoughts click over and over in the dense forest of my mind as I try to find a wooden bench on which to rest.

Jilly's words roll through my head. The universe has spoken. Seb and I are not meant to be. I begin to wonder whether she's right. All the things that have gone wrong for us—and the list is long—point to it.

Perhaps I'm no good for him?

Perhaps he'd be better off without me?

My belly in knots, I roll over and pull my knees up to my chest.

I love Seb. I love him with all my heart. There's no denying it.

When I went on *Dating Mr. Darcy*, I never in a million years thought I would end up falling in love with him. I figured there was something wrong with a guy who wanted to pose on TV as one of the most adored romantic heroes of all time. He was either a publicity-hungry narcissist or totally deluded into thinking he could find love on a reality show.

He was neither.

He was a guy who was desperate to save his family home, who felt responsible for their loss of fortune, who put himself on the line to protect his family. He was noble, he was strong, and I fell for him.

Oh, how I fell for him.

Now? Now here I am, back where I started, only things have changed irrevocably. My heart, once untouched, is now his. Fully and completely. And I know deep down inside, that will not change. My love for him will not fade. He is the best man I've ever known, and I know he loves me.

It's as certain as I know the sun will rise tomorrow.

But…is that enough?

Jilly took things too far, saying we're not meant to be, but she's right about one thing: I've brought stress and challenges into his life. I've divided his family, caused him embarrassment, and the production company was clearly against me.

My phone vibrates on the nightstand, causing my heart to leap into my mouth. I check the screen.

It's Sebastian.

"Hey," I say as my pulse threatens to burst out of my chest.

"I'm sorry to call you so late. Are you okay?"

"Have you seen the photos?" I ask breathlessly.

"I have."

"Seb, it was all totally innocent. I'm not having an affair with Chris Hampshire or with anyone else for that matter. You've gotta believe me."

"Of course I believe you."

Tears prick my eyes, my throat tightening. "You do?"

"Brady, photos of you and Chris at a café aren't going to dent my trust in you. I love you."

"Oh, thank God," I say in a rush. "I love you, too. So much. This is all so horrible."

"Someone is trying to stir the pot with those photos. I don't know who, but we're not going to let it get to us. Not now, not ever."

Tears roll down my face, my heart contracting in my chest. "You're incredible. You know that? You see photos of me with your arch nemesis, the guy who caused your dad's downfall, and you call me to say you love me."

"You're going to be my wife, Brady. I absolutely trust you."

A sense of euphoria settles over me. "Thank you, Seb. I was twisting myself up in knots after Jilly called to tell me about them."

"Jilly called you?"

"Yeah. She was all 'let Sebby go' and stuff, telling me she thinks the universe is telling us not to be together."

"Did she now? I'm not sure when she found the time to do that, exactly, since she was here until late last night with Granny while I dealt with Heather."

My euphoria evaporates in a flash. "What did Heather have to say?"

"A few things. The upshot was she's adamant she won't have you on the show now."

"I figured that might happen. Who can blame her? Photos of me with another man turn up when she didn't even really want me on the show in the first place. You can do it without me. It's fine. I'm over here looking after Mom for a while, anyway." I prop up my pillow and lean back against it. "It'll keep you off the streets," I joke.

"Brady, I've turned the offer down," he says quietly.

"No, Seb. Don't do that. It's too much money to pass up."

"You're too important to me. I won't compromise on this. On *you*."

I'm doing some serious swooning over how noble my fiancé is right now. He's turning down a lucrative TV show to defend my honor. This guy is perfect.

He's also acting like an idiot.

I take a deep breath, my tummy knotted so tight I doubt it'll ever unravel. I have to speak my mind. I have to tell him what's been plaguing my thoughts. Even if I know it's going to hurt like hell.

"Seb, don't you see? Jilly's right. Everything is against us. *Everything.*"

"It's not. It just feels a little like that right now, that's all."

I count off on my fingers. "Heather won't have me on the show because it looks like I'm cheating on you. Those photos proved her initial decision."

"Brady—"

"Seb," I say. "Let me finish. I need to get this out."

"Okay."

I exhale before I press on. "I can't get Timothy off the ground in the UK. No one returns my phone calls, and Denise is the only person to show even a tiny iota of interest in the label. Then there's your granny." An image of Geraldine, her eyes filled with hatred, her lips pulled into a thin, angry line the night she came clean about what she thinks of me pops into my head. "Seb, she has made it abundantly clear that I am not right for you. No matter what I say or do, I will never be good enough for you in her eyes. She told me if I married you, I would divide your family. Seb, I can't do that to you."

"Don't listen to her. I love my grandmother, but she's a bitter old goat."

"But she's family. How can I live in a house with her when I know she hates me? When I know she sees me as the axe that will split your family in two?"

"I don't care about all of that. I care about you."

"And I care about you. I love you. I love you more than I ever thought possible." My breath is ragged, my heart pounding in my ears. "And that means I need to do what's best for you."

Marrying Mr. Darcy

"What's best for me is you."

"Seb, I-I need to let you go."

There's a long pause before he asks, "Are you...ending this?"

Am I? Is that what I'm doing? Am I ending my relationship with Sebastian?

I take a long, deep breath and try to clear my head. So much has happened in the last forty-eight hours, I'm jet-lagged, and I'm sleep deprived. But there's one thing I know for absolute certain—I love Sebastian and I want the best for him. No matter what that looks like. No matter how much it hurts.

I scrunch my eyes shut, my fist balled at my side. "I'm sorry." I try to swallow down the lump in my throat as a brick settles in my chest. "I can't wreck your life like this. I just can't. I care too much for you to put you through anything else."

"No, Emma. I won't allow you to do this. You're worked up because you're stressed about your mum being sick and all the things that have been challenging for us. That's all. I have never loved anyone the way I love you. I *cannot* lose you."

Tears stream down my face, my voice soft as I reply, "I can't stand by and watch you lose your home. I can't divide your family. You mean too much to me to do that."

"Brady," he says, and the pain in his voice slices through me like a freshly sharpened sword.

"I'm sorry, Seb. I'm so sorry. I've-I've got to do what's right." With choking tears streaming down my face I click *end*.

Dropping my phone, I'm thrown back into the silence of my childhood bedroom. I bury my head in my pillow and let it all out, my body wracked with heart wrenching sobs. The pain, the sadness, the terrible, deep sense of loss. The loss of the man I love.

I know I've done the right thing for Sebastian. Me no longer being in his life is the only choice for him.

I had to set him free.

But dammit if the pain isn't tearing me in two.

Chapter Twenty-Four

I sit in the olive vinyl chair I've been in for hours, and I hold my mom's hand, watching her as she sleeps. She looks so peaceful, her dark lashes against her pale skin as she breathes evenly.

It's been a big day, and she's come through the surgery like the fighter she is. It's late in the afternoon now, and she's already been awake and seen the surgeon, who told her that she'd removed the lump and all was looking good.

Both Aunt Judy and Penny have been amazing. Between the two of them, they've sat with me, brought me snacks and coffee, always with a positive message and a smile on their faces. Aunt Judy told me stories I'd not heard about when she and Mom were young. My mom, it would seem, was a little wild in her youth. Now that I'm enlightened, I fully intend to revisit some of the groundings she gave me for lesser teenage crimes once she's back to full health.

Penny's had to go back to work now, so I sit on my own with Mom until Aunt Judy returns with coffee.

"How's your mom doing?" Aunt Judy asks quietly as

she places a steaming hot cup of coffee on the side table next to me.

"She's been sleeping for a while now. The nurse said that'd happen, and that it's good for her to rest."

She sits down on the other chair in the room, and the vinyl makes a weird squeaking sounds as she settles. "Tell me about this fiancé of yours. I can't believe you're engaged to be married and I've never met the man."

"Oh, Sebastian? He's great," I say as I paste on my most convincing smile.

"I'm sure he is, but your aunt needs details, honey. Lots and lots of details."

"Err, well, he's super tall, and he's real handsome, and err, he's got a really nice sister." I pause my terrible description of the man I'm meant to be marrying when I notice the look on Aunt Judy's face.

"You okay, honey?" she asks. "You're all tearing up and stuff."

I let go of Mom's hand and touch my face. Sure enough, it's wet with tears. I wipe them away hurriedly. "I'm fine," I lie as the tightness I'm now familiar with grows in my throat.

"You know, when your mom and me were growing up, Emma, she had this terrible poker face. Still does, now that I think about it. I could always tell what she was thinking, even when she didn't want me to know. You're just like her."

"Am I?"

She nods her head. "Horrible poker face. Wanna tell me what's going on with you? I'd be more than happy to lend an ear."

I open my mouth to respond then clamp it shut. I could tell her I'm upset about Mom, and that would be a completely legitimate thing to say because I *am* upset about Mom. But I'm devastated about Sebastian, and I've kept it from Mom and Aunt Judy. I didn't want them to worry about me.

Not at a time like this.

"It's your fiancé, isn't it?" she asks softly.

I look down at my hands and nod.

"Did you have a fight?"

"No, I, ah, I broke up with him."

"Oh, Emma."

I feel a warm hand on my back, and I've got to work hard at not losing it, sitting here on this awful olive vinyl seat.

"What happened?"

"I tried and tried, but I couldn't fit into his world. The media over there said they wanted him to marry one of the other contestants, and there's this show, *Saving Pemberley*. They don't want me on it." I wring my hands and look up through watery eyes at my aunt's kindly face. "I kept on messing up, Aunt Judy, and his granny told me I wasn't good enough for him, that I'd never be 'one of them.' That I would never be good enough."

"She did?" Her eyes bulge. "Sweetie, I may not be from some fancy aristocratic family in England, but I do know you are a fine woman. Your mom is so proud of you, and you have achieved so much in your life so far. You *are* good enough. Don't let anyone tell you otherwise."

"Not for Geraldine Huntington-Ross I'm not."

"Well, Geraldine Whatever can go take a flying leap for all I care. Any man would be lucky to have you."

I perk up a little at her words. "Thanks, Aunt Judy. There's more."

"Oh?"

I tell her about the photos, and I tell her about how no one seems to want to stock Timothy, no matter how hard I try. "I figured I was hurting Sebastian and his family by staying with him. Dividing his family was the last thing I wanted to do. I love him so much, but I knew I was hurting him, just by being with him." I drop my head as tears sting my eyes. "I had to make the decision to leave, Aunt Judy. I had no choice."

"You always have a choice, honey," a croaky voice says, and I snap my attention to the bed where my Mom is lying. Her eyes are open and clear, and she's gazing at me, a small smile on her face.

"I'm so sorry that we woke you, Mom." I collect her hand in mine once more and give it a squeeze.

"It's fine, honey," she replies, and the softness of her voice has a lump growing in my throat as fresh tears well in my eyes.

You see, I've been doing a lot of crying lately. Like, *a lot*. It's fair to say it's been a pretty turbulent time in my life. Watching my mom battle the disease that stole my dad from us has been incredibly hard, and I've got a newfound respect for Mom as I've seen her handle everything so well—and so much better than me.

Then there's Sebastian. It's been a week since I told him it was over. A week since I broke not only his heart, but my own heart as well. I will not lie. It's been incredibly hard, and I've almost called him at least once a day. Okay, more like once every hour. But every time I hold that phone in my hand, ready to press that button, I remember the reasons why I broke up with him in the first place, and I switch my phone off, my heart breaking afresh once again.

Breakups suck.

Marrying Mr. Darcy

Especially when you're still hopelessly in love with the guy.

Sebastian, on the other hand, has not given up. I've had beautiful fresh-cut flowers with heartfelt messages of love every day, and he's called and left messages many times. I listened to the first voicemail, but it was so hard to hear the pain and longing in his voice that I gave up after that. There's only so much mascara a girl wants running down her face in a day, you know.

"How are you feeling?" I ask Mom as I shift closer to her bed.

"Groggy and a little tired but otherwise good," she replies. "Did I hear right? You've ended things with Sebastian?"

"Mom, now's not the time to—" I begin, but Aunt Judy cuts me off.

"Your daughter is being a fool, Charlene," she says with surprising force. "She thinks she's being noble by throwing away the best thing that ever happened to her."

I cock an eyebrow at her as I try to make light. "I think Mom's beef brisket is the best thing that ever happened to me. Not some guy in an old house on the other side of the Atlantic with a mean granny."

"But you don't think that. Do you, honey?" Mom says softly.

I look into her eyes and a surge of emotion threatens to overtake me. I don't trust myself to speak. Instead, I simply shake my head as I fight back the tears.

"Come here." She extends her arms, and I give her a tentative hug, extremely mindful of the fact she's only been out of surgery for half a day.

"She's awake!"

We look up to see Penny at the door, a large bunch of

flowers in one hand and a grin on her face. "How are you doing, Charlene?"

"I'm great, Penny," Mom replies as I pull away from her and wipe away my tears before Penny notices.

Man, I've got to get a grip! I cry more than a toddler in a tantrum. Only with less screaming and throwing of fists as I lie on the floor.

"The flowers are beautiful, thank you, Penny," Mom coos as Penny places them on the windowsill.

"You're welcome." She smiles at Mom, and then her eyes find mine. She pulls her brows together in question, and I shake my head, warning her to leave it alone.

"Charlene? I forgot to bring my phone. I left it in my car, and in today's heat it'll be melted in ten minutes. I'm gonna go get it."

"Sure, Penny," Mom replies.

"Emma, I sure could use your help," Penny says.

I shoot her a questioning look. She needs help to retrieve her phone from her car? Before I have the chance to respond, she takes me by the hand and leads me out of the room and down along the hospital corridor until we're out of hearing distance.

"What is it? Bad news? Has your mom gone downhill since I was here earlier?"

I shake my head. "Mom's doing great. The doctor said the lump was about an inch in diameter, which isn't too large."

"That's good news. When does she start radiation?"

"Not for a month."

"So you've got some breathing space, huh? Timothy needs you back, baby."

I smile at her. "You got it."

"How are you holding up?"

"Oh, you know," I reply with a shrug that's convincing no one. "The doctor is optimistic, so I've gotta be, too."

"I meant about you and Seb."

The mention of his name shoots pain through my chest. "Oh."

"I wish it didn't have to be like this for you guys. You're so in love."

"I wish a lot of things, Penn, but wishing isn't going to change anything. He's better off without me."

"But are you better off without him, Em?"

Of course I'm not. I'm bereft without him. But I'm not going to tell Penny that. I've cried enough on her shoulder over the last week. So instead, I reply, "I'm working on it, Penn. My priority right now is my mom. It's got to be. Then, well, then I'll try to get myself happy again."

"Oh, Em." She wraps her arms around me and holds me tight. "I wish I could fix this for you."

"It'll get easier. I just need to give it some time."

As the words leave my lips, I know they're not true. My love for Sebastian is so deeply embedded within me, it's become a part of who I am.

I know I'll never get over Mr. Darcy.

Chapter Twenty-Five

It's just over a week later, and you'd think Mom had never even had surgery, she's so full of energy. She's got me helping her reorganize the kitchen cabinets, out walking with her through Memorial Park, and visiting our favorite market to get treats like cheese and jalapeño cornbread, cherry pie, and of course, the best chocolate chip cookies in the state.

Sebastian's gifts and messages haven't stopped. With enough flowers to decorate a church, Mom's living room looks more like a greenhouse than an actual room. The messages are always the same, and every time I read those three little words, I kick myself for opening the cards.

I know I need to respond, but I keep putting it off. At the very least I need to arrange to have the rest of my stuff sent over, and I need to get Frank back. I miss his furry face.

"Mom?" I call out as I walk from my room down the corridor.

"In here, honey," she says from the kitchen. She's sitting at the table, reading her phone with her glasses balanced on the end of her nose.

Marrying Mr. Darcy

"I'm gonna head out, if that's okay with you. I thought I might go to Central Market and pick up one of those platters we had last week.

"Oh, that was delicious."

I grab the keys to Mom's Hyundai from the kitchen counter. It's a stark contrast to Sebastian's classic Aston Martin, but at least the steering wheel is on the correct side of the car. "Be back soon."

"Honey?" She removes her glasses and looks up at me. "I know you don't want to talk about you and Seb, and I get that. But it's been playing on my mind these past few days, ever since I heard you talk to Aunt Judy about him and you, and I cannot rest until I say my piece."

"Mom, I don't want to bother with this. That's why I didn't tell you about us breaking up."

"I don't think Sebastian wants to be broken up." She eyes the latest beautiful bouquet to be delivered, this one a selection of red roses and yellow lilies.

She pats the seat next to her. "Come, sit."

I slump down in the chair.

"I want to tell you a story. I was in my junior year in high school, and I met this man in his senior year. Well, he was just becoming a man at the time, but he looked pretty darn good to me. And oh, how I fell for him."

I smile. "Dad."

"That's right. Timothy Brady was the best thing to ever happen to me. But it wasn't easy, not to start with anyway. His mom took a disliking to me, you see."

"Grandma Jane?"

She nods. "She thought I was trailer trash, that I wasn't good enough for your dad. Although she was right in that I did grow up in a trailer, I never saw myself as trash, and I never let her opinion of me dent my love for your dad. Not even when she refused to come for Thanksgiving and Christmas, telling anyone who would listen what a low-class woman I was and how I'd dragged her son down to my level."

"That must have been so hard."

"No, honey, it wasn't hard. You know why? He did not let her come between us. Your dad stood by me, just like Sebastian has stood by you. She softened over the years, and you coming along sure helped with that, but she never thought I was good enough for your dad. She still doesn't to this day."

"How did I not know any of this?"

"We decided early on that we would not let her come between us. She could try to poison us all she liked, but we were going to stick together, this little family of three. Telling you how she treated me would only cause a rift in the family, and we did not want her to have that power over us." She reaches across the table and takes one of my hands in hers. "Honey, I know you feel like you're doing the right thing by stepping back. You think you're doing what's right by the man you love."

My throat tightens as a brick settles in my belly. "I do, Mom. There are too many things against us."

"So you're just going to give up? That doesn't sound like the daughter of Timothy Brady to me. What was that expression of his? The one he said described the two of you to a *T*?"

"Never give up until the thing is done or dead."

"Honey, tell me if I got this wrong, but you're not done with Sebastian. Are you?"

My throat tightens. I shake my head. "I don't know if I ever will be."

"Then what are you doing here in my kitchen?"

"Mom—"

"I've read the cards on the flowers he sends every day, honey. That man loves you. He *loves* you. Do you know how rare it is to find a love like that in this world?"

"But the show and the media and his granny," I protest.

"They're all just noise, honey. None of them mean a jot when you find your big love."

I hang my head as tears spill from my eyes.

"Love is enough, honey."

I exhale as I look up into her soft eyes full of warmth and love for me. "Is it?"

Slowly, she nods her head, her pretty face lighting up as her lips curve into a smile. "Love is everything."

I chew on my lip, thoughts rolling around my head like marbles in a tin. Love. Sebastian. Geraldine. *Saving Pemberley*. Chris Hampshire.

And then it all becomes clear. None of it matters. All that matters is the fact that I'm in love with a man, a *good* man, a man I want to spend the rest of my life with.

I stand bolt upright, my chair scraping across the tiled floor. "I've got to go," I say.

"To the market?" she questions.

I can't stop a grin bursting across my face as I reply, "Change of plans, Mom. Change of plans."

She beams back at me, her hand over her heart. "Go get your man, honey."

Here's the thing, when the guy you broke up with lives in another country and you want to go find him and tell him you made a huge mistake and beg him to come back to you. You need a passport. You need a change of clothes. And most important of all, you need a flight.

I race around organizing them all with Mom's help. She finds me the next available flight to London and books me a ticket. It costs me a small fortune, but I figured it was for a worthy cause—to go get my man.

Once I've got everything, she sees me to the door and pulls me in for a hug. "Never give up, honey. You got this."

"Oh, I so do." I give her a kiss on her cheek and race out the door and into the waiting Uber, which gets me to George Bush Intercontinental in record time.

Once inside the terminal, I gaze up at the departures screen. In all my excitement to get to the airport, I'd not considered the fact that the flight doesn't actually leave for hours and hours. With check-in not even open, I find a place to sit, and plunk myself down. I pull out my phone and begin to scroll through social media, liking friend's posts and commenting on a few baby pictures and selfies.

My phone rings, the name *Kennedy Bennet* flashing up on my screen.

I make my tone upbeat when I answer with, "Kennedy Bennet, intrepid traveler. Where are you, and how are you?"

"I'm back in England after my trip to Florence. It's a-mazing. You have got to go, girl. The buildings, the food, the gelato. And the men. Oh my, the men."

I giggle. "I'm happy for you."

"Hey, Em, I wanted to call to let you know something, and I'm a not a hundred percent sure how you're gonna feel about it."

The tone of her voice has changed, and immediately my hackles are up.

I brace myself and ask, "What is it?"

"Phoebe called just now to tell me that Sebastian is coming to Houston."

"He's what?"

"He asked Phoebe and Johnathan to look after the place

because he didn't know how long he'd be gone. Apparently, he told them he wasn't ready to let you go."

Love swells in my heart. "Did he?" I ask, suddenly breathless.

"I know you ended things with him, so I thought I'd better call and let you know so you can be ready."

"But...but I'm already at the airport. I was going to come find him."

"You were? Oh, how romantic. You're both totally in sync with one another."

"We are. Do you know when he left? What time his flight was? Anything?"

"Call Phoebe, babe. She'll know."

"Okay. Gotta go." With shaking fingers, I hang up from Kennedy and immediately find Phoebe's details.

She answers on the third ring. "Emma. How wonderful to hear from you. How's your mom?"

"She's good. Kennedy said Seb is on his way here to Houston. Do you know his flight details because I'm at the airport myself, waiting to check in to a flight to come to England, can you believe, and so I need to know where he is, like, now," I blurt out.

"You're at the airport?"

"Yes!"

"Is that to come back to Sebastian?"

"It is, but now he's on his way here, and I need to find him. Can you help me?"

"Oh, Emma. I love this for you two. Let me find out what I can, and I'll get right back to you, okay?"

"Thank you, Phoebe. Thank you so much," I gush.

"Emma? I'm so happy for you. Sebastian has been lost without you."

Guilt twists inside. "Has he?"

"He knows it's been hard for you, but he loves you. It's as simple as that."

"And love is enough," I say, repeating Mom's words.

"Love *is* enough. It's more than enough."

I smile to myself. "I know that now."

"Oh, I am so excited for you! I'll get back to you ASAP."

I spend an anxious ten minutes pacing up and down inside the terminal, willing Phoebe to send me Sebastian's flight info. I've been staring at my phone so long that when she texts me with his flight number, I can barely believe it. I read the screen. The ETA is at six twenty-five. I glance at the time on my phone. That was thirty-seven minutes ago!

I need to get to Arrivals, and I need to get there *now*.

I grab my bag by its handle, and I run. I dash around people, excusing myself as I go, my bag spinning off its wheels more than once. As I run, I calculate how long it would take for him to collect his luggage and to clear customs and immigration, all the while hoping against all things holy I haven't missed him.

I reach Arrivals and search the screen, panting from my exertion. I find his flight number and see it landed sixteen minutes early. *Gah!*

With sweaty palms, I locate the area he should exit from, and I stand and wait, my eyes trained on that exit, my pulse drumming in my ears.

"Going somewhere?" a familiar sexy English voice says behind me.

Startled, I turn and gaze up at him.

Sebastian.

His jawline is stubbled, his hair tousled, and there's tiredness around his eyes. But it's him. It's *him*.

Boom. Mic drop.

"I'm-I'm booked on a flight to London," I reply, amazed

I actually have the power of speech as I gaze at this man in front of me. "I-I was coming to see...you."

"Well, great minds must think alike, because I came here to see *you*."

My heart dances as the edges of his mouth lift into a smile, his eyes soft and full of love. For me.

"Brady Bunch," he says, and as happiness bubbles up inside of me, I drop the handle of my bag and leap into his arms, pressing my lips to his as my love for him overflows. He kisses me back, holding me close to him as I wrap my legs around him.

As tears of joy spring to my eyes, I say, "I'm so sorry, Seb. I love you so much, and I made a huge, huge mistake."

He brushes hair back from my face and looks at me with such love in his eyes it sucks the air from my lungs. "You showed me that you would sacrifice your own happiness for me. That is the most incredible thing anyone has ever done for me, Brady. I didn't think it were possible to love you any more than I did, but I do. Oh, how I do."

I pepper his face with kisses, and after a while he places me back on my feet. "I love you so much," I gush.

He pulls me into him and claims my lips with his once more. "I know you do, and you've made me the happiest man on Earth."

Epilogue

We stand together hand in hand, facing one another, our gazes locked.

This is it.

This is the moment.

Sebastian looks more handsome than I've ever seen him —which I did not think was possible. This guy looks good in sweats, he looks good first thing in the morning, and he even looks good when he's got a cold.

Not that I'm complaining.

Today, he's wearing the black tux with a crisp white shirt he was wearing the day we met, and he's added a buttoned-up waistcoat to the look—his little nod to Mr. Darcy.

He's my dashing gentleman, and I'm his blushing bride.

Okay, not *blushing* exactly, more unbelievable ecstatically deliriously happy bride.

As I stand beside the man I love, I feel absolutely beautiful in my dress. After Jilly's terrible advice that women of the British aristocracy choose to look like the Stay-Puft Marshmallow Man on their wedding day, I called Susan at the village wedding shop to save me the very first dress I tried on. The dress I fell in love with. The Empire dress with the deep V-neckline and pretty chiffon layers that made me think of Lizzie Bennet.

Which is one hundred percent appropriate, considering who I'm marrying today.

Jilly, it turns out, wasn't exactly my friend. Far from it, in fact. She had been trying to break us up from the moment Sebastian declared his love for me in the final episode of *Dating Mr. Darcy*.

Nice, right?

When I met Chris at the opera last summer, Jilly saw an opportunity to drive a wedge between Sebastian and me. Knowing what Geraldine thought of me, Jilly approached her with a plan: photograph me in a compromising position with Chris Hampshire, send those photos to news outlets at the right time, and let Sebastian see what a lowlife I truly was. Jilly would then swoop in to comfort Sebastian, he would realize she had been the woman for him all along, and I would be well and truly forgotten.

Chris had happily gone along with the plan. Not because he had any real interest in me, but because he had a real interest in getting back at Sebastian for him wrecking his plans to steal Jilly's money.

As Kennedy said when I divulged the whole sorry tale to her, Chris would make a very good George Wickham. But then I reminded her this is my life and not a Jane Austen novel.

Jilly had broken down when Sebastian questioned her about why she told me to let him go, and she came clean about the whole sordid plan. Although I would never in a million years stoop that low to get the man I loved, I get why she did it. Sebastian is a truly special guy, and I'm the lucky girl who gets to keep him for the rest of my life.

Geraldine, rightfully ashamed by her actions, apologized to us both for her involvement. She claimed she was stressed over the fact we were facing losing the house, and I've chosen to accept it. Not that I believe it, of course. I didn't come down in the last English rain shower, you know. But I have chosen to accept her apology because she's my soon-to-be grandmother-in-law. And now, almost a year on from all the drama, as much as I know she still disapproves of me, I'm not going to bend over backwards for her anymore.

No way.

In my efforts to fit into Sebastian's world, in my vain attempts to make Geraldine accept me, I'd lost something incredibly important.

I'd lost me.

And I'm not going to let that happen again. I'm not going to change myself for anyone. Emma Brady is an okay chick, a "top bird" some might say, and you know what? I kinda like me.

I'm me. Take it or leave it, people.

In the beautiful sunlight, filtering through the stained-glass windows, Sebastian's face lights up in a gorgeous smile, and my heart flutters. This man is about to become my husband.

My Lord Martinston.

My Mr. Darcy.

"I now pronounce you husband and wife," the priest says with a smile. "You may kiss the bride."

With a huge grin on his face, Sebastian takes a step closer to me and loops his hands around the back of my head. He leans down and kisses me, and everything that has gone before, all our challenges, all our hurdles are rendered completely irrelevant.

I'm his, and he's mine.

I wrap my arms around him and pull him close, kissing him back as the congregation erupts into applause around us.

Suddenly sheepish, I turn to face them all. "We're married," I say, barely able to process it myself.

"Yeah, you are, girl!" Kennedy calls out to whoops and more applause.

As the Bruno Mars song *Just the Way You Are* begins to play, I can't resist a glance at Geraldine. She's seated in the front row, between a grinning Jemima and Zara, looking severe and formal in a navy Chanel suit and her habitual strings of pearls. I remember she insisted we have nothing but organ music play at our wedding and certainly didn't want anything from the last century. But disapprove as she might, we like this song, and that's why we're playing it.

Ladies and gentlemen, the new Emma Brady. Make that Emma Huntington-Ross, the very new *Lady Martinston*.

My mouth goes dry.

Wow, I'm still not sure I'm ever gonna get used to that.

"Shall we?" Sebastian says as he takes my hand in his.

I grin at him. "Let's do this."

We walk down the aisle together, hand in hand, all our friends and family grinning at us as we pass them by. We step out of the little chapel and into the heat. I look up at the building, gleaming white in the hot Texan sun.

"This was the perfect place to get married, Brady," Sebastian says.

"It was, wasn't it?"

As our friends and family spill outside and surround us,

they offer us their congratulations with hugs and kisses and handshakes.

"You make such a beautiful couple," Zara says as she gives me a hug. "I am so glad you're my new sister."

"I'm so glad you're my new sister, too."

"I feel so pretty. Thank you for choosing a bridesmaid dress that actually makes me look sexy."

"You, Phoebe, Kennedy, and Penny look incredible today," I reply as the rest of my bridesmaids surround me. They're all in slinky, charcoal gray halter-neck dresses from Susan's bridal store. Zara came in with me when I went to claim my dress, and she was smitten the moment she tried one on.

"We do not look as incredible as you, babe," Kennedy says to me. "Maybe you'll start wearing dresses and ditch the activewear a little more often now?"

"Not now that we've got Timothy into a UK store she won't," Penny replies with a laugh.

I grin at her, thinking about how amazing it is that we finally look set to make some headway into Britain, thanks to me and my bra fitting skills with the elderly. "Denise's store may be small, but it's been a great start."

My bridesmaids fall into silence with the arrival of Geraldine. She attempts a smile when she says, "Congratulations on your nuptials, Emma."

I raise my chin. "Thank you. That's very kind of you to say."

"Yes. Well. We will expect an heir before too long, you know. That is your role in the family now."

Seriously, this woman lives in a freaking Dickens novel. I'm sure of it.

"We'll get working on that just as soon as we can," I reply, and Kennedy stifles a giggle beside me. "What?" I say

Marrying Mr. Darcy

to her under my breath. "I didn't mean right this minute." I smile at Geraldine and she looks at me as though I've just announced that I'm the leader of a Satanic cult and Sebastian is my latest recruit.

But you know what? I do not care. I will always try my best to be civil and inclusive of her, but gone are the days when I tried to impress her—and inevitably failed. As Mom said to me the day that lightbulb lit up in my brain and I went to go get my love, I will never let her opinion of me dent my love for Sebastian.

And anyway, if she wants to be a miserable old woman, then I'm gonna let her be just that.

"Emma, darling. Welcome to the family!" Jemima pulls me into a warm hug, and I breathe in her scent. "You make such a beautiful bride. Doesn't she, Mummy?"

"She does," Geraldine sniffs.

"Hello, Emma," a voice says from behind me.

I turn from Jemima and Geraldine to see Jilly standing before me, looking as nervous as a mouse in a garden of cats. I smile at her and bring her into a hug. "I'm so glad you came, Jilly."

"I'm glad I did, too. I know I've said it before, Emma, but I truly am sorry for everything I did. I-I should never have tried to steal Sebby from you. It was wrong of me. I can see now how much he loves you."

"Jilly, you've apologized about a gazillion times, so quit it, okay?"

She gives me a shaky smile. "I'll try."

"Good. Who knows? You might meet one of those cute Texan cowboys while you're here."

Her face lights up, and I see a hint of the Jilly I once knew. "Called Maverick or Gunner?"

"Sure. Why not, now?" I reply with a good-natured shrug.

I collect her in a hug, I know the heart wants what the heart wants, and her heart had wanted "Sebby" for years. Now, I just hope it moves on quick so Sebastian and I can get on with the important business of being happy.

"Did you like the climbing frame for Frank?" she asks me.

I think of the ridiculously huge cat jungle gym Jilly delivered to Martinston the day we left for Houston to get married. All I can say is it's a good thing the ceilings are so high. The thing is massive.

"He loves it. Thanks, Jilly."

"I thought it would be fun for the production company to film him climbing in and out of the tunnels when they start *Saving Pemberley* soon."

"Oh, he'll totally steal the show, I'm sure of it."

I feel a sudden flutter of nerves.

After Sebastian insisted Jilly go to Heather McCabe with her tail firmly between her legs and tell her that she'd made it look like Chris and I were having an affair, Heather did some quick damage control with some new photos of Jilly lip-locked with Chris and a stream of loved-up images of Sebastian and me. One of the accompanying articles was about how I'd been lending an ear to poor Chris that day at the café. According to the article, he suffers from social awkwardness and finds it hard to understand women. I'm sure he was more than ecstatic to read that particular gem.

I may or may not have had something to do with writing that article, but my lips are sealed.

"But I brought Chris Hampshire back into Sebby's life. I can never forgive myself for that."

"Jilly, as I've said before, you didn't know what Chris had done to Seb's dad."

That's one good thing to come out of the whole mess. Sebastian opened up to his family and told them about his father's relationship with Chris and how he had felt responsible for their loss of fortune. Everyone was shocked and told him he wasn't to blame. Even Geraldine. But then, Sebastian is her favorite grandchild, so it makes sense.

"Let's just enjoy today, okay?" I say to her hopefully.

She nods, attempting a smile. "Okay."

"Can we please get out of this heat?" Geraldine says, looking uncharacteristically pink. "It is absolutely insufferable. I don't know how Texans cope."

"Of course," I reply.

As our guests begin to make their way to the reception, I find my new husband. I take him by the hand and kiss him on the lips. "Thank you."

"For what?"

"For taking me back. For agreeing to marry me here in my hometown. And most of all, for loving me."

"What can I say, Brady Brunch? This sassy, confident Texan with a dress stuck to her hair fell out of a limo and into my heart. And now, I get to be her husband."

I exhale, my grin threatening to reach my ears. "I love you, my Mr. Darcy."

"And I love you, my Mrs. Darcy."

THE END

Acknowledgments

As I sat down to write this, the second title in my *Love Manor Romantic Comedy* series, COVID-19 still had its firm grip on the world, New Zealand's borders were shut to all but returning citizens, and I began to wonder when I would see my American and Australian family again. As I write these acknowledgements, it's November 2020, and sadly nothing has changed. There is no denying that this is an unprecedented, strange, and scary time for us all. For me, writing a light-hearted rom com with a happily ever after provided exactly the escape I needed, and I've come to adore Emma and Sebastian and their world of Martinston and its surrounds. It's my happy place, and wow, do we all need one of those right now.

As always, no Acknowledgments section would be complete without thanking my husband and son for their love and support of me and my writing. You are my rock, and I thank you from the bottom of my heart for being there for me.

My critique partner, Jackie Rutherford, is a talented writer and good friend. She pulls my work apart and helps me rebuild it and is so incredibly positive and helpful to me. Without Jackie, I don't think I'd be the writer I am today. She's that good.

Wendi Baker is back editing for me, and I am so happy! Wendi never fails to make me really think and dig deeper with my characters and plot, and this book is definitely better for her input. Thank you, Wendi.

Another blast from my writing past is Julie Crengle, who proofread some of my earlier works. Her nickname in law school was "Eagle Eye," which is very fitting for someone who not only catches typos and misuse of words but remembers *everything*. And I mean everything. Julie, I'm so happy to have you back on my team.

Sue Traynor created another gorgeous cover for me for this book, as she always does. Thanks, Sue. Thanks also to the authors in Chick Lit Think Tank and Chick Lit Chat Head Quarters. The members of these groups are so giving and supportive, and there's never a dumb question to be asked. Before I entered this literary world, I didn't know authors would be as supportive as they are, and it feels great to be a part of it all.

And finally, as always, a HUGE thank you to you, my readers. I love to write, and you make that possible for me. I hope to keep on writing fun, feel-good books for you!

About the Author

Kate O'Keeffe is a *USA TODAY* bestselling and award-winning author who writes exactly what she loves to read: laugh-out-loud romantic comedies with swoon-worthy heroes and gorgeous feel-good happily ever afters. She lives and loves in beautiful Hawke's Bay, New Zealand with her family and two scruffy but loveable dogs.

When she's not penning her latest story, Kate can be found hiking up hills (slowly), traveling to different countries around the globe, and eating chocolate. A lot of it.

- facebook.com/kateokeeffeauthor
- instagram.com/kateokeeffewriter
- bookbub.com/authors/kate-o-keeffe
- amazon.com/Kate-OKeeffe/e/B00KIZGG1O

Made in the USA
Middletown, DE
25 March 2023